PICTURE IMPERFECT

THE LEAFY HOLLOW MYSTERIES, BOOK 7

RICKIE BLAIR

BARKLEY
B O O K S

PICTURE IMPERFECT
Copyright © 2019 by Rickie Blair.
Published in Canada in 2019 by Barkley Books.

ISBN-13: 978-1-988881-12-6

To receive information about new releases and special offers, please sign up for my mailing list at www.rickieblair.com.

Cover art by: www.coverkicks.com

PICTURE IMPERFECT

TAPPING A SHARPENED garden knife against her thigh, Rosie Parker scowled at her crushed flowers. Judging from the tire tread that chewed through the earth, her neighbor's Hyundai sedan had mounted Rosie's charming bricked curb and then lurched off, scattering bricks, before coming to rest in the middle of their shared drive—after knocking over Rosie's recycling bin. As she glared at the strewn cans and bottles, her fingers twitched on the knife's handle.

She had been trying for weeks to discuss the parking situation with Dakota, her young neighbor. Yesterday, she'd spotted the girl in a flimsy nightgown—no bra, as usual—rushing out with an overflowing bin to catch a garbage truck rumbling down the street. Rosie had barreled outside, hair wild and housecoat flapping, to try to catch her. Dakota eluded her, leaving Rosie to lift a finger to the wolf-whistling garbagemen.

This morning, she had been standing over the crushed

foliage, tapping her knife and looking aggrieved, for at least ten minutes. Any normal person, Rosie believed, would have come out onto their front stoop by now to ask if something was wrong. But not Dakota.

Seconds ago, a curtain on the second floor had twitched, almost as if the girl didn't want to be seen. Yet her grandmother's old Hyundai was parked plumb in the middle of the driveway. The granddaughter must be in the house.

Still tapping her knife, Rosie realized she'd been too friendly. She should have made the rules clear right from the beginning. Like the fact—obvious to civilized human beings—that you can't monopolize a shared driveway.

Instead, she had welcomed the young woman to the neighborhood. With Barb, her neighbor of twenty years, confined to the locked ward of a nursing home, Rosie had been glad to make the acquaintance of Barb's granddaughter, newly arrived from out east.

Newfoundland, the girl had said.

Although, that was odd. Barb had always called Canada's easternmost province—that foggy, windswept island in the northern Atlantic—The Rock. But that was when she still made sense, Rosie realized.

Pursing her lips, she stalked past two neighboring houses, pivoted, then stalked back, giving her neighbor's windows another glance through narrowed eyes.

Parking spaces were hard to come by in this neighborhood of two-story houses with dented aluminum awnings in the southern Ontario city of Strathcona. If her driveway was blocked, Rosie had to circle the block to find a spot. At the moment, she couldn't even do that, because her car was trapped behind the Hyundai.

Resolutely, she marched up the cracked sidewalk to Dakota's front door. To her surprise, it was ajar.

"Anybody home?" she called, pushing the door open by several inches and sticking in her head. "Dakota?"

No answer. Rosie walked in, closing the door behind her while letting her gaze sweep around the narrow front hall. Grime caked the corners of the worn wooden steps leading to the second floor. As Rosie ran a disapproving finger along the dusty banister, a *thump* on the floor above drew her attention. It was followed by a shuffling sound, almost as if—

She grimaced. Dakota must be moving furniture.

Rosie hesitated, wondering whether to quietly back out. The last thing she wanted was to be roped into hauling a heavy armoire or bed around the place.

That was when she noticed a lighter rectangle in the wall paint in the exact shape of Barb's grandfather clock. Frowning, she tiptoed over to the living room entrance. The Victorian parlor table and Tiffany stained-glass lamp were also missing. Dakota must be selling off her inheritance one piece at a time, she thought.

Before her grandmother was actually dead.

Rosie stood with her hands on her hips, studying the shiny oval on the floorboards where an Aubusson rug had once lain. No wonder Dakota had never invited her inside— she must have realized her grandmother's neighbor would notice the gaps in the furnishings.

Not only that, but Rosie was convinced that Barb would have wanted some of these items to go to her long-time neighbor—like, say, the Italian silver cow creamer displayed on the mantelpiece. With a furtive glance over her shoulder, Rosie tucked it into the front pocket of her canvas gardening apron—after *tsk*ing at the dust that coated it.

A brightly colored brochure stood out among the objects on the mantel. She picked it up to read the cover.

HEMSWORTH'S FINE ART AND COLLECTIBLES
LEAFY HOLLOW, ONTARIO

Replacing the brochure on the mantel, Rosie glanced around with displeasure. Barb was past caring what her granddaughter was up to. But that didn't make it right.

Satisfaction soon washed away her indignation. If Dakota was selling her grandmother's possessions, the house itself would soon be on the auction block. Then she'd be rid of her troublesome young neighbor for good. And when the new neighbors moved in, she'd make the parking rules understood from day one.

Meanwhile, her car was still trapped.

With determination, she mounted the stairs to the second floor.

"Dakota? Are you here?" She paced down the hall and into the back bedroom. It was empty. A few steps farther, and she was in the master bedroom.

Rosie stepped back, puzzled.

Her neighbor lay on her stomach, on the floor beside the wrought iron bed, with one arm outstretched. At first, Rosie assumed Dakota had dropped something and was looking for it under the bed.

"Hello there," she said.

The girl did not move.

Dropping her garden knife on the mattress, Rosie bent to shake the young woman's shoulder. "Dakota?"

No answer.

She felt the girl's wrist. No pulse.

Then she noticed the blood matted in Dakota's hair.

Feeling sick, she rose, holding on to the bedpost for support. *Get help*, she thought, twisting toward the door.

Her chest convulsed with an agonizing thump that forced her back a step.

Rosie looked down to see the handle of her garden knife sticking out of her chest.

Puzzled, she lifted a finger to touch it. But before she could reach it, she pitched forward into darkness.

CHAPTER TWO

TWO WEEKS LATER...

When the calls first started, I was delighted. *Coming Up Roses Landscaping* had never been so popular. If there were still such a thing as a hook, my phone would have been ringing right off it and landing, exhausted, on the floor. Leafy Hollow residents were clamoring for me to administer TLC to their troubled lawns and gardens. I even practiced a bashful wave that I could use to acknowledge their gratitude while tackling their overgrown flora.

At least, that's what I imagined. Until the trickle of calls turned into a flood, far more than I could handle. And I realized they were coming from clients of *Fields Landscaping*, my main competitor. The tall, blond, and perpetually cheerful owner had always been the favorite choice of the village's lawn-obsessed homeowners. What possibly could have turned them against him?

My name is Verity Hawkes—full-time gardener, part-time sleuth, and fairly recent resident of Leafy Hollow, a picturesque village nestled at the foot of the Niagara Escarpment in southern Ontario. After arriving as a twenty-eight-year-old widow a year earlier, it had taken me months to gain the villagers' trust and rebuild the business I had acquired from my secretive aunt.

I couldn't blame the residents. My occasional brushes with the law—and a handful of inexplicably dead bodies—may have had something to do with their reluctance. People can be so petty.

But Ryker Fields had been generous and welcoming, sending clients my way, doling out advice, even loaning me equipment. To be honest, I was flattered by the attentions of the six-foot-two blond Adonis with impressive pecs, even though I knew he flexed those pecs at every female within winking distance.

I certainly didn't intend to thank him by poaching all his clients. So, I put in a call of my own to Ryker.

No answer.

By the third unanswered call, I started to worry. It wasn't like Ryker to take a vacation without letting his clients know. What if he'd finally purchased that lakeside cottage he was always talking about, only to drown during a weekend visit?

With a shudder, I dismissed that thought. If Ryker had toppled into a lake, it could only have been while displaying his washboard abs and sexy grin from atop a racing speedboat. A spectacular crash like that would have made the news.

Stop jumping to conclusions, I told myself. *What you need are facts.*

So, when the next client to jump the Fields speedship called to enlist my services, I insisted on knowing the reason.

She was surprised. "I thought you knew. Ryker stopped showing up. My lawn hasn't been cut for weeks and neither has my neighbor's." She paused, then added, "They're going to call you, too."

"Did Ryker explain why he fell behind?"

"He doesn't answer his phone. I've left messages, but he never gets back to me. I only knew to call you because it's on his voice mail. *Call Verity Hawkes.*"

"Is he ill?"

"I don't know. Are you available or not? Our grass is so long Winston got lost in the backyard the other day."

Since Winston was a Bernese Mountain Dog, I was fairly certain this was an exaggeration. "I'll see what I can do."

"Please hurry. The dandelions are out of control."

Sighing, I ended the call. It was my fourth promise that morning to take on additional work. My landscaping assistant, Lorne Lewins, was not going to be happy.

A sharp rap on Rose Cottage's front door, accompanied by a flurry of barks, announced Lorne's arrival. Usually, he texted me from the driveway. No point in getting the dog involved. But today, he must have gotten tired of waiting.

Arf-arf-arf. Arf-arf-arf. Arf-arf-arf.

Wincing, I headed for the door.

Boomer, the hyperactive terrier-cross I had inherited from one of those dead bodies, took advantage of every opportunity to prove his guard-dog credentials. Unlike those amateurish Bernese, Boomer would never allow long grass to get the upper paw. If necessary, he'd pummel it into submission with every fiber of his fourteen-pound body.

"I'll be right there," I called over the din.

In the tiny foyer, Boomer was bouncing up and down like a spring.

Arf-arf-arf. Arf-arf-arf. Arf-arf-arf.

I nudged him aside with my foot while opening the door. "Stop!" I demanded.

Boomer skidded to a halt, eying me with surprise.

I was even more surprised. That had never worked before.

Lorne grinned, bending to pat the terrier's head while pulling a biscuit from his pocket. "Hiya, Boo-boo."

Boomer snatched up the biscuit, managing to crunch furiously while simultaneously watching Lorne's pocket for a possible top-up.

"Truck's loaded," Lorne said, straightening.

I glanced at my pickup parked in the driveway. Its Pepto-Bismol-pink doors were painted with clusters of oversized red roses. It always made me grin. My industrial-sized lawnmower was on board.

"Thanks for doing that," I said, shooing Boomer back inside then locking the door. "Sorry I'm running late. I got four more calls from Ryker Fields' clients this morning."

"How many does that make?"

"I've lost count. Several dozen, though."

Frowning, Lorne brushed a lock of tousled brown hair off his forehead. "Ryker should be careful. It's cheaper to retain an existing client than gain a new one."

I smiled at this truism from Lorne's business-college studies. "Let's take a detour past Ryker's house. I'd like to check with him in person before snatching all his customers."

We climbed into the truck and headed for the road that zig-zagged down the three-hundred-foot-high Escarpment hill and into the village. Dappled sunlight danced on the truck's pink hood, filtered through the overhanging branches of chestnuts and maples. I rolled down the window to draw a deep breath of early-morning air. We still faced the hottest months of the summer with their parched gardens, but for now everything was green and fresh and lush. A pair of eastern bluebirds flitted across the road in front of us.

Ryker's own truck was parked in the driveway of his suburban split-level home. The four-door shiny black pickup —with *Fields Landscaping* etched in green and gold on its doors—was normally polished to a mirror finish. Even his industrial mowers and the trailer he towed behind the truck were always spotless.

Not today. Someone had finger-painted *Wash Me* in the grime coating the truck's back end. Not only that—one tire was flat. A sense of unease twisted my stomach. After a shared glance with Lorne, I headed for Ryker's front door.

As I walked up the path to the house, a young woman stepped out, shutting the door behind her. Streaked blonde hair tumbled over her shoulders, her trendy blue jeans were torn in strips across the thighs, and her bow lips formed a pout. Most of the residents of Leafy Hollow were familiar to me, but I'd never seen this woman.

"Can I help you?" she asked.

"Verity Hawkes." I extended a hand. "I was hoping to speak to Ryker. Is he home?"

"Oh," she said, looking pained. Clasping her arms across her chest, she added, "I'm afraid Ryker's not seeing anybody at the moment."

I lowered my hand. "What do you mean, not seeing—"

"He's not well," she added hastily.

"I'm sorry to hear that. Has he seen a doctor?"

"It's not that." Biting her lip, she tossed a glance over her shoulder before leaning in, lowering her voice. "He's...depressed."

I was taken aback. I'd never known Ryker to be depressed. Puzzled, I shook my head. "I have to talk to him about his customers. Nothing personal. It would only take a moment."

"I'm afraid that's not possible." Her expression was sorrowful, like a lion who had polished off the last of the leftover gazelle minutes before the arrival of a visiting, and hungry, pride.

I made to leave. Then the vertical blinds in Ryker's front window twitched. A face flashed, then the blinds fell back.

"He's right there." I pointed to the window while surging forward. "I only need to talk to him for a minute."

She gripped my arm to stop me. "I'll give Ryker your message. Is there a number he can reach you at?"

"He knows my number. I told you, I'm Verity Hawkes. His clients are calling me. I'd like to know why." Twisting my arm out of her grasp, I narrowed my eyes. "Who are you, by the way? If I'm allowed to ask."

That was a bit snarky, but she deserved it.

"Didn't I say? I'm Shelby—Ryker's sister."

I stared at her, dumbfounded. On the many occasions

Ryker and I had lifted a beer together at the Tipsy Jay, the subject of a sister never came up. In fact, he said he was an only child, like me.

"Ryker doesn't have a sister," I said.

"Half-sister, if we're splitting hairs." She stepped back, holding up both hands. "Turns out our father"—she flexed her eyebrows—"got around."

"Are you saying—"

"That he had other children? That's exactly what I'm saying."

"Ryker didn't know?"

"None of us knew."

"Then how—"

"It's a long story," she said with a shrug.

"I've got time." Crossing my arms, I gave her what I hoped was a look that meant I wouldn't back down. *Amaze me,* I thought.

And she did.

"You've heard of DNA testing?"

"Molecular biology? Naturally." I lobbed glares at her while keeping one eye on the window blinds, hoping for another twitch.

"It's always been a particular interest of mine. A while back, I paid for one of those online DNA tests. The company sent back my results along with an updated family tree. All Ryker's relatives are on it. Including ones he never knew about. Like me."

"You said relatives, plural. You and who else?"

"A cousin, right here in Leafy Hollow." She spread her arms. "It's exciting."

Narrowing my eyes at her, I wondered why—if it was that exciting—Ryker was so depressed he couldn't leave his house. As an only child, I'd always wished for a sister. Why would that discovery upset him?

"Then you're not a Fields?"

"Oh, no. I'm a Wynne. Shelby Wynne."

I assessed her appearance. Her eyes were deep blue, like Ryker's, and there was a definite resemblance around the nose and mouth. "Are you here to...catch up?"

"Well..." She shrugged before pivoting to stand beside me, shoulder to shoulder, to join my scrutiny of the window blinds. "Of course, I'd be lying if I didn't say the inheritance was also of interest."

I gave her a sharp look. "What inheritance?"

She swiveled her head to face me, her eyebrows lifting in surprise. "*Spirit of the North?* Lawren Harris?"

At my blank look, she added, "Group of Seven?"

My earlier confusion was nothing compared to the fugue I found myself in now. "I have no idea what you're talking about."

"Our cousin? Perry Otis?"

"Still not—"

"Perry Otis was an old man who lived in the village. He was Ryker's—excuse me, *our*—cousin. He died of a heart attack and left Ryker the painting. It's quite famous, I understand."

"Perry... Perry..." I puzzled it out. "Wait—did he live on Tulip Crescent? In that old brick farmhouse that was remodeled? The one you can't see from the road because it's set so far back?"

She nodded. "That's the one."

Now it made sense. I remembered Ryker grumbling about an elderly cousin who always expected his lawn cut and flower beds weeded without any money changing hands. But come to think of it, he did say this cousin had some painting he promised would be Ryker's one day. I got the impression Ryker didn't care about it much. Or know its value.

Unlike his half-sister.

"It's worth a lot of money," she confided. "High six figures, according to Nigel Hemsworth."

My eyebrows lifted in astonishment. Nigel Hemsworth was the village's art dealer. I'd often seen him behind the counter of *Hemsworth's Fine Art and Collectibles* during the slow winter months, using artist's chalk to color in mass-produced pen-and-ink drawings of local landmarks. His *Village Scenes in Winter* series—framed and signed—was particularly popular with tourists. Whenever he sold "the last one," he'd pop another up in the shop's window minutes after the buyer departed. Villagers turned a blind eye.

Nigel did have a keen eye for real art, though. His gallery was filled with pricy offerings that drew patrons from Strathcona and even farther, according to Emy Dionne.

Emy was my best friend—and Lorne's beloved. She owned the *5X Bakery* on Main Street, a few doors down from *Hemsworth's*. Once, while munching on one of her prize-winning lavender-lemon scones, I had watched Nigel stroll along the sidewalk holding a large rectangle wrapped in brown paper. "Where does he get them all from?" I asked her.

"Estate sales, mostly," she had replied. "That's what I heard."

But Ryker had never mentioned Nigel Hemsworth to me. I didn't know they were even acquainted.

After a last glance at Ryker's front window and its motionless blinds, I turned away. "I have to get going."

"So long." Shelby stayed at her post. "I'll give Ryker your message."

"One thing, though, if you don't mind?"

She inclined her head, her pout even more pronounced.

I took that as permission to go ahead. "If Perry Otis has been dead for weeks, why hasn't Ryker claimed that painting yet?"

She straightened her head, looking annoyed.

I met her gaze, wondering vaguely if a Krav Maga elbow strike would loosen her tongue. *Probably not a good idea*, I decided. *Defensive purposes only*, I heard my aunt warn.

"Everything's stalled in probate," Shelby said finally. "And now that there's a new heir"—she scraped back her streaked blonde hair with one hand—"the lawyers have to start the process all over again."

Nodding to show I understood—though I most definitely did not—I strolled back to my truck. Lorne was leaning against the cab, long legs crossed, humming softly under his breath. "Well?" he asked as I opened the driver's door.

"You're never going to believe this," I muttered. While we drove away, I passed on Shelby's story.

Lorne was suitably impressed. "Whoa. That's intense."

"It certainly is." I was silent the rest of the way to our first appointment of the day, because I was busily mulling over Shelby's parting words. *Now that there's a new heir...*

If Perry left the painting to Ryker, why would Shelby think she was entitled to a share? There must be something unusual about Perry's will. I was determined to find out what that strange feature might be. And whether it had anything to do with Ryker's depression.

It was none of my business, of course. But when had that ever stopped me?

CHAPTER THREE

"VERITY—ARE YOU LISTENING?"

"Huh?" I swiveled my head to face Lorne in the front seat. "Did you say something?"

Shaking his head, he shot me a grin. "The same thing I've been saying for the past two miles. If you take on any more of Ryker's clients, we're going to need help."

I returned my attention to the gravel road we were bumping over. "Sorry. My mind was elsewhere. You're right. Let's put our heads together later to think of someone."

My worries about how I'd manage extra clients had been knocked right out of my head by Shelby's news. Mulling it over while driving to our first job of the day, I recalled that Thérèse Dionne—the village's formidable chief librarian and Emy's mother—had mentioned the demise of Perry Otis a few weeks earlier.

At the time, I was devouring my usual mid-morning

scone and coffee at the 5X. The update on Perry Otis was part of Thérèse's comprehensive weekly rundown of deaths in the village. If I didn't know her, I might have found that a macabre interest. But Thérèse prided herself on keeping up with local events, and Emy liked to humor her. Normally, I paid no attention. The only reason I'd even paused in my appreciation of the Scone of the Day—a delectable bacon-toffee—was because I recognized, not Perry's name, but the street address of his property—Tulip Crescent.

It's one of the pitfalls of mowing lawns for a living. We tend to identify clients as "the two-acre with the pond," or "that blasted hawthorn hedge," or, in one lamentable instance, "Crabgrass Central."

So, I had looked up with interest to ask, "Huge perennial borders, old pear orchard, empty paddock that formerly housed goats?"

Thérèse had eyed me curiously, then nodded before resuming her news bulletin.

I had filed it away for future reference. I'd often admired Perry's hobby farm—as much of it as you could see from the road, at least—while mentally adding up the fees I could charge to maintain it. If Ryker ever got tired of doing it for free, that is.

So, when the road sign for Tulip Crescent appeared ahead, I couldn't resist.

"Time for another detour," I told Lorne, swerving the *Coming Up Roses* truck onto Tulip Crescent with a spray of gravel. Lorne braced himself with a hand on the dashboard but said nothing. After months of working with me, he'd learned to zig when I zagged.

We followed Perry Otis's curving driveway past rows of gnarled pear trees, a dilapidated wooden fence surrounding a deserted paddock, and up over a hill. Tulip Crescent had dropped out of sight behind us before we saw the house.

It was worth waiting for.

I halted the truck to take in the scene. "Ryker said his cousin remodeled an old farmhouse, but I never envisioned this."

"Whoa," Lorne said with his usual loquaciousness.

The three-story brick-and-limestone farmhouse had been lovingly restored, with new windows, cedar shake roof, and wraparound wooden porch. It would have been impressive all by itself.

But off to the right, a glass-walled addition added fifty feet to the frontage, with a massive stone fireplace and chimney at the far end. The addition was only one story but soared to a cathedral ceiling twenty feet high. Through its glass walls, we saw a huge harvest table inside, as well as a magnificent view of the rolling fields beyond.

The renovation didn't end there. On the left side of the farmhouse, at the back corner, rose a blindingly white four-story octagonal structure that visually balanced the other addition. The architect must have intended it as an echo of an old-style grain silo—a tribute to an earlier era. Architects were fond of making statements like that. I doubted anything as mundane as corn had ever passed its threshold, though.

I pointed it out to Lorne. "What did Perry keep in there?"

"Dunno. He must have had a lot of cash to build this, though. Maybe there's a vault inside."

"What did he do for a living?"

19

Lorne shrugged. "He was really old, that's all I know."

"Speaking of old"—I executed a flawless three-point turn, then headed back to the road—"we'd better get going or Molly will wonder what happened to us."

At the end of Perry's driveway, I paused to read the FOR SALE sign I'd whooshed past without stopping on our way in. With surprise, I noted the realtor's name.

NIGEL HEMSWORTH, the village art dealer.

Retired schoolteacher Molly Maxwell was standing outside her aluminum-sided bungalow when we pulled up. No surprise there. In the fine weather, her shock of white hair was usually bent over one of the perennial borders, her arthritic hands ripping out any weeds that had the nerve to take root. As far as Molly was concerned, "taking it easy" was for other folks.

Unfortunately, her eyesight was so bad that she often pulled out the wrong plants. Her Coke-bottle glasses were the thickest I'd ever seen, but they didn't seem to help much.

Today, her arthritic hands were planted on the hips of khaki pants that hung baggily on her rail-thin frame, and she was scowling down at the front flower bed.

"Uh-oh," I said, turning off the engine and giving Lorne a quick glance.

While he unloaded the mower from the back of the truck, I trotted across the lawn, dreading what I'd find. Had Molly dug up the hydrangeas again?

She looked up, squinting through her glasses, as I approached. "Oh, Verity. It's you." She pointed to the flower bed. "Damn vandals. Look what they've done now."

My heart sank as I followed her gnarled finger. The hydrangeas were fine. But the dozens of vincas and geraniums I'd planted so carefully a few days earlier had been yanked out of the ground and left to shrivel in the sun.

I bent to pick up a geranium and examine its dried roots. "Maybe we can save a few," I said, straightening with the plant trailing from my hand. "How long have they been like this?"

Her lips twisted. "I don't know. I was visiting my sister in Strathcona, and I haven't been home for days. I found them this morning." She hoisted a tattered plant onto the toe of her elastic-laced running shoe then held it out. It hung limply over her foot. "I think they're goners, don't you?"

I had to admit, it didn't look good. I dropped the ruined geranium onto the grass. It was beyond me why anyone would vandalize an elderly woman's garden. What really rankled was the fact they'd done it twice. It was only a week since the last time Molly's flowers had been destroyed.

By someone other than her, that is.

"Why would anyone do this?" she asked, rocking on her running shoes while folding her arms and glaring at the damage. "Smart-arses."

Lorne, who had come up silently on the grass behind me, snickered at this outburst. I whacked him with an elbow, and he stifled it.

"Are we replacing these?" he asked in an earnest tone.

"Is there any point?" Molly asked. Furiously, she unfurled her arms then inclined her head to the side yard. "That's not all. Take a look at this."

I followed her around the corner of the house, where a metal pipe rose from the ground to connect with the gas meter. My eyes widened.

Orange paint was sprayed over the meter and across the wall's aluminum siding.

"Did this happen at the same time?"

"I guess."

"What did your daughter and son-in-law say?"

"I haven't told them." Molly thinned her lips. "I can't."

Molly's bungalow was on the outskirts of the village, where building lots were large. The nearest property line was a hundred feet away. Someone could easily skulk around in the middle of the night without being seen.

Molly had once confided to me over coffee in her kitchen that her children wanted her to move into the main village. "'You could buy one of those nice condos, Mom,'" she had mimicked in a sing-song voice—followed by a healthy snort. "Nice, my arse. Those condos have no garden, no view, no nothing. And what about Marmalade?" She had pointed to the overweight orange tom splayed out on her kitchen floor, his tail languidly swishing as he kept his half-closed eyes fixed on the refrigerator door. "He's so athletic. He'd never adjust to an indoor life."

I was sure Marmalade would adjust just fine as long as Molly kept up a steady stream of his favorite home-cooked chicken snacks, but I had known better than to point that out.

Now, studying the orange paint, I said, "Maybe your kids are right, Molly. Maybe it's time to move."

She heaved a sigh. "The other day some busybody left a note in my mailbox, trying to convince me to list this old house." Plunging her hand into the pocket of her fleece vest, she pulled out a business card and squinted at it through her glasses, brow furrowed, before handing it to me. "Do me a favor, Verity. Find out if they're on the level? The amount they mentioned in the note seems too good to be true."

Before thrusting it into my pocket, I scrutinized the gold printing on the heavy white card. GRACE ANDERSON. It wasn't a name I recognized.

"I'll see what I can find out. Meanwhile, Molly"—I pointed to the graffiti—"this is getting out of hand. You need to call the police."

"No." Her tone was adamant. "Please, just replace these plants before the weekend. Bridget's bringing the grandkids to visit on Saturday. I don't want them to see this."

"What about the paint? Won't they see that?"

"They won't come back here. Besides, those kids hardly ever look up from their phones."

"I don't feel right about this. There must be something—"

Lorne shook my arm. "Verity."

I could tell he was itching to propose a course of action. I don't know what I expected in the way of suggestions. A motion-activated floodlight? New locks? In hindsight, I should have known better. Instead, I walked right into it.

"Do you have an idea?" I asked.

"We can't leave Molly on her own without knowing who's responsible for this," he said.

"Well, sure. But I don't see how—"

"We need to stake out the property overnight to see who turns up."

I'd known Lorne long enough to realize his solemn expression hid a more frivolous motive—the man simply loved to do surveillance. According to Emy, Lorne had watched *The Guns of Navarone* so many times he knew the dialogue by heart. It took only the slightest suggestion of a reconnaissance mission for him to break out the balaclavas, eye black, and synchronized watches. Most of the time, it was a fairly harmless hobby.

Except when I got dragged into it.

"Is that really—"

"Oh, could you?" Molly clasped her hands in front of her chest. "I would appreciate it so much."

How can you say no to an eighty-something woman sporting braces on both knees? But someone had to be the adult. I took a deep breath to summon my reserves. "I really don't think—"

Molly clasped Lorne's arm. "I'll make sandwiches for your stakeout."

He patted her hand. "Thanks."

"Ham and cheese or egg salad?"

"Well—"

"Stop," I said.

They turned to look at me.

"We can't—"

"Verity," Lorne said, puffing out his chest. "You don't have to come. I can do this alone."

Molly shot him a beatific smile while patting his arm. "Thanks, Lorne."

I heaved a sigh. *I know when I'm beat.*

"Okay. I'll replace the damaged flowers. Then..." I lifted my hands with a shrug and a sigh. "We'll stake out the place."

Later, while tossing dead vincas into a wheelbarrow, I berated Lorne. "What have you gotten us into this time? I don't want to spend hours cramped and uncomfortable in Emy's Fiat, wearing night goggles, waiting for plant rustlers to show up."

Lorne glanced thoughtfully at our surroundings, a limp geranium trailing from his gloved hand. "Oh, we can't use the Fiat."

"What do you mean? My truck is too conspicuous."

He swept an arm at the road. "There's nowhere to hide a vehicle." Narrowing his eyes, he assessed the scene. "There. That clump of bushes by the rhododendrons. That will be perfect."

With dread, I recalled another outdoor reconnaissance mission of ours that had gone painfully wrong—for me. "You've got to be kidding."

He shook his head, looking surprised. "No." Pulling his cell phone from his pocket, he keyed in a text. "Emy will love this." Noting my sour expression, he added, "Come on. It'll be fun. The three of us haven't done anything like this in ages."

For good reason, I thought, recalling a rock-climbing quest that had resulted in a highly embarrassing rescue by local firefighters. I still winced whenever I passed the fire hall.

Peeling off my gardening gloves, I studied Molly's trim bungalow and its extra-wide property frontage. Local developers lusted after large lots with small World War II-era bungalows like hers. Within minutes of buying this place, they'd call in the construction crews. A monster home would be erected—and on the market—within months.

But if someone like that was after Molly's home, tracking a midnight marauder through her property might not be fun. It might be dangerous.

Shaking my head to dispel that cynical notion, I tossed my gloves into the back of the truck before climbing into the cab. Molly's vandals were likely high school kids rampaging through the neighborhood on a dare, leaving uprooted flowers in their wake. And what high school bad boy didn't have a can of spray paint in his backpack?

The most dangerous opponents we'd face were likely to be killer mosquitoes. "Bring plenty of bug repellent to this stakeout," I said morosely while turning the key in the ignition.

Lorne's cell phone rang loudly. "Will do," he replied absently while reaching for the ringing phone. He raised it to his ear. "Hi, babe. What's up?" His expression changed. "Emy? What's wrong? What is it?"

Put it on speaker, I mouthed.

Lorne complied, pumping up the volume. "Verity's listening in. Tell us what's wrong."

"Hi, Verity." Emy's voice was strained. "Have you heard?"

"Heard what? What's happened? It's not your mom, is

it?" With one hand on the wheel, I pulled the truck over to the side of the road and slipped the gear into park.

"No, she's fine. It's not that," Emy said. "You'll never believe this—"

"What?" Lorne and I cried in unison.

"Ryker's been arrested. For murder."

CHAPTER FOUR

LORNE and I shared shocked glances.

"That's not possible," I said. "It must be a mistake."

"No mistake," Emy said. "They marched Ryker out of his house this morning and took him to the station. It's all over the village."

Traffic whooshed past the truck, muffling her voice. I motioned to Lorne to hand me the phone, then switched off the speaker and held it to my ear. "Why did they do that?"

"The bodies of two women were found in a house in Strathcona."

"And the police think it's murder?"

"Yes." At an impatient gesture from Lorne, I held up two fingers and mouthed *two*.

"Who were these women?"

"I don't know. But there's a story in the local paper online, with photos. One of the women was young, in her twenties. The other was a neighbor."

"Strathcona's a two-hour drive from here. Why is Ryker a suspect?"

"He was dating one of the women, according to the paper."

The twist in my stomach that had begun with Emy's first words tightened into a regular Gordian knot. Ryker dated a lot of women. Feeling ill, I passed the phone to Lorne.

"Hi, babe," he said. "Do you want me to come down to the bakery?"

While they talked, I stared out the window, absently running my hand along the steering wheel. Ryker was a long-time friend of Emy's. She'd known him for years. Since high school, in fact. At one time, she even suggested Ryker and I might... My mind whirled. *Could I have ended up a murder victim?*

Stop it, I told myself.

Then I sat bolt upright, gripping the wheel with both hands. "It's not possible."

Lorne gave me a curious glance. "Hang on, babe. Verity's gone all white." He lowered the phone to peer at my face. "Are you okay?"

I slapped the heel of my hand on the wheel. "Ryker couldn't possibly have murdered those two women in Strathcona."

"What's Verity saying?" Emy's tinny voice issued from the cellphone. "What? Let me talk to her."

Lorne handed over the phone.

"Emy?" I asked. "The bodies were found today, right?"

"That's right."

"I saw Ryker this morning. He hasn't been out of his

29

house for weeks. He couldn't have been in Strathcona—and he couldn't have killed anybody."

Technically, I couldn't swear I saw Ryker, unless the twitch of a window blind counted. I suspected it might not. But there was no reason to think his sister was lying. Shelby could vouch for him.

"I agree that Ryker would never kill anybody," Emy said, her voice subdued. "But the timing doesn't help. Those women had been dead for two weeks."

My stomach re-clenched. "How do you know?"

"I told you—it's on the news."

Grimacing, I imagined the state of a body that had been lying around for weeks. At least the bodies I'd found had been fresh. Except for the skeleton, but that one doesn't really count.

"How could no one notice?"

"Their bodies were in the basement. Locked door. I guess it had to get really bad before the neighbors..." Her voice trailed away.

My teeth clenched at the thought. "Thanks. I get the idea."

"What will happen to Ryker now?"

"Are you positive he's been charged?"

"That's the gossip."

"That seems like fast work. Check to see if there are any updates."

Tapping my fingers on the wheel, I waited anxiously until Emy returned.

"The latest story says he's been taken in for questioning.

There's no mention of an actual charge." Her tone brightened. "That's good, right?"

"Yes. The police probably only want details about Ryker's relationship so they can rule him out as a suspect."

I was trying to be optimistic, but I couldn't help thinking that Ryker's behavior in recent weeks was far from normal. *Had guilt kept him indoors?* Immediately, I felt a twinge of guilt myself—for even thinking that even-tempered and sunny Ryker Fields might be a killer.

"Emy, call me if you hear anything else. I'll drop off Lorne at our next job, then go to the police station to find out what's happening." I tossed the phone back to Lorne.

Then I roared up the road with a swish of gravel and a cloud of dust.

I was out of breath by the time I parked the car at the station, raced across the parking lot, up the front steps, through the double doors, and skidded to a halt at the reception desk.

"Hi, Verity," said the duty sergeant, barely looking up. He waved a laconic hand to his left. "Jeff's in the back."

"Thanks," I gasped, then sprinted down the hall.

The current love of my life, the darkly handsome Jeff Katsuro, was sitting behind a table, studying a laptop screen. He looked up in surprise when I darted through the door. "Hi, sweetheart. Why are you—"

"What's happened to Ryker?" I blurted. "Is he in a cell?"

For several seconds, Jeff merely stared.

I raised my eyebrows as high as they'd go without causing a facial tic.

"Close the door and sit down," he said.

I slumped into a wheeled armchair and swiveled to face the table, tapping my fingers on the chair's arms.

Jeff closed the laptop, pushing it to one side. "Nothing's happened to Ryker. He left here over an hour ago." He leaned in for a thoughtful scrutiny of my face. "Are you all right? You look a little...anxious."

This, I knew, was a reference to the anxiety attacks I'd suffered in the past. I appreciated Jeff's concern, but he didn't have to bring it up every single time I got a little edgy. Where was this concern on Trivia Night, for instance, when Emy and I were skunked by the grocer's team? It was a championship round, too—free lunches for a week, donated by our host, the Tipsy Jay's fabulous chef, Katia Oldani. We lost. All because we didn't know the year of the latest NFL expansion, which Jeff—who arrived too late to help—would have known in his sleep.

"I'm fine," I said, twisting my fingers in my lap to halt their tapping. "But I heard Ryker was arrested."

"No." Jeff shook his head. "He wasn't."

"Is it true two women were murdered in Strathcona and he's a suspect?"

"Two women were killed, yes. Their bodies were found this morning. As for the rest of it, I can't comment."

"How were they..." Clenching my teeth, I made a throat-slashing motion.

Jeff frowned. Before he could launch into his standard

can't-talk-about-it routine, I jumped in with, "It's all over the news. You might as well tell me."

He heaved a sigh. "One was bludgeoned. The other was stabbed with a gardening tool."

"A gardening tool?" I hesitated while digesting this. "I don't think you should jump to conclusions. Ryker's not the only person with gardening gadgets. I own quite a few."

Jeff tilted his head, regarding me with a cool professional gaze. "Should I ask forensics to take a look at your toolbox?"

His expression was deadly serious. Only the slightest tremor of his lips gave him away. If I were a criminal facing Detective Katsuro in an interrogation room, I'd confess to anything. Then Jeff tapped his lips thoughtfully, which drove it all from my mind as I recalled the previous evening when he'd—

Uh-oh, I thought. *Losing focus, Verity.*

I made a face. "I'm only saying—that's not much to go on."

"Thank you for your insight. I'll pass it along to the detective in charge."

"If Ryker hasn't been arrested, does that mean he's been cleared?"

"I didn't say that."

"Wait—you said *the detective in charge*. Aren't you investigating the case?"

"No. It's not our jurisdiction."

"You're in the loop though, right?"

He leaned back in his chair, heaving a sigh. "Why are you so interested in this?"

"Why wouldn't I be? Ryker's a friend."

The phone by his elbow rang. Jeff—still fixing me with an odd stare—picked it up. "Katsuro." Pause. "Who?" Then he covered the mouthpiece to whisper, "Why is your father here, asking for me?"

My eyebrows flexed in astonishment. Until recently, *your father is here* was a phrase I hadn't heard for twenty years. Frank Thorne left my mother and me and bolted for Australia when I was eight. As a teenager, I changed my last name to my mother's maiden name in protest. After my mother died when I was eighteen, I vowed I'd never forgive Frank for abandoning us.

Until he suddenly showed up in Leafy Hollow on "a matter of life and death," embroiling us all in a twenty-year-old mystery. It turned out my father's absence had a more complex explanation than any of us had suspected.

And now, well... Even Aunt Adeline, my mother's sister, had forgiven him. Something I had thought was impossible.

Still, I wasn't quite used to being a family again. And I had no idea why Frank would visit a police station. Voluntarily, that is. So, I merely shook my head.

Jeff uncovered the mouthpiece. "Send him in."

I sat back, fiddling with the arms of my chair, unwilling to renew my questions about Ryker in front of Frank. That made it one more on the list of topics I wasn't comfortable discussing in front of my dad—like the fact I actually *had* a dad, after twenty years of doing without. I'd welcomed Frank back into my life, but it hadn't been easy on either of us. For one thing, he still saw me as a defenseless eight-year-old who needed protection from the bad guys. After months of Krav Maga remedial classes with Aunt Adeline, I was confident I could look after myself. Besides, Jeff would hammer anyone who gave me so much as a dirty look.

After a sharp rap on the door, Frank opened it and stuck his head in. "Jeff, I was wondering if—" His gaze fell on me. "Verity? What are you doing here?"

"Visiting my honey."

Jeff cast a bemused glance at me. I thought his lips twitched, but it could have been a trick of the overhead lighting.

Frank walked in, closing the door behind him. "Then you're not here to ask Jeff about Ryker Fields' problem?"

"Why would I... Hang on. How did you hear about it?"

"The whole village is talking about it. Plus, I was at Emy's bakery this morning."

That figured. Emy had a soft spot for my dad's breezy charm and vivid blue eyes. I assumed she'd doled out a free coffee and butter tart while filling him in on the latest news.

"She seemed upset," Frank continued. "She said you were both friends with Ryker."

"Why are you using the past tense? I *am* friends with Ryker, who's done nothing wrong."

Jeff and Frank exchanged a quick glance.

"What?" I blurted. "What aren't you telling me?"

Frank looked down at his feet. "Nothing."

"Why are you here, then?"

"Just checking in."

At this, I straightened in my chair to look directly at Jeff. "Is this a regular occurrence?"

Before he could reply, my dad broke in. "So. How are you two doing?"

Jeff's smile appeared forced to me. "We're doing fine, Frank."

"Really? Then why is my daughter still single?"

I gaped at my paternal unit.

"Not that it's any of my business..." Frank swiveled his gaze to the ceiling. "Only...people are asking—"

"They are not. You made that up." Crossing my arms, I added huffily, "Besides, I'm not single. Technically, I'm a widow." I slumped into my chair and swiveled to face the wall, watching the two of them out of the corner of my eye.

"Exactly." Frank nodded sagely while looking at Jeff. "And what's up with that?"

"Don't blame me," Jeff said, holding up his hands. "I asked her. She's *thinking* about it." He rolled his eyes in mock annoyance, then gave me a soft smile—the one that usually melted me into a puddle. I steeled myself against its effects.

"What do you mean, you asked her? How did you put it?"

"I think I've said enough already."

"I'm her father. I'm concerned. You must have said something that—"

"I'm right here," I insisted. "Also, this topic is not up for discussion."

My dad pivoted toward me. "Is it true you turned Jeff down?"

"Well... It's more complicated than that."

He pivoted back to face Jeff. "You must have done something—"

"Let's change the subject," I said brightly.

The men glared at each other. If I had to step in, there

was no doubt whose side I'd take—Jeff's. *Always.* If anything happened to him, I wasn't sure I could go on living.

I was happy my father and I had been reunited. But it was a fragile thing, our reconciliation. I still harbored doubts. Jeff was always courteous to Frank. They even shared a weekend fishing trip—cut short by the fact "nothing was biting," which I assumed did not apply to their conversation. Jeff was not convinced my father had atoned sufficiently for past wrongs. Frank would have to behave himself for a long time before Jeff would relax his vigilance.

Which, oddly, I didn't mind at all.

To be fair, Frank had tried to fit in. Since Aunt Adeline had put in a word for him at a local garage, he had worked diligently, becoming one of their most popular mechanics.

"Don't they need you back at the garage?" I asked, arching my overworked eyebrows.

Perhaps realizing he'd gone too far, my father flashed a brilliant smile. "We can talk later." He gave Jeff a brisk nod before walking out.

Once the door had closed behind him, Jeff contemplated the door's worn blue paint with great interest while deliberating ignoring my gaze. "You didn't answer me," he said. "Why are you so concerned about Ryker?"

"He's a friend."

"He's more than a friend."

"What are you talking about?"

"Have you forgotten how he used to follow you around?"

"Ryker never—" My brow knit. "Oh, you meant that time when a killer was stalking me. But he was protecting me." I had a flashback of opening my eyes to find Ryker slumped in a chair, too exhausted to stand, keeping vigil by my hospital bed.

"Is that what it was? Because it seemed to me he was the one doing the stalking." Jeff turned his dark eyes to search mine.

I hesitated under his soulful gaze, momentarily unable to speak. Even after months of living together, it still had that effect on me. I recovered quickly, however, since I felt duty-bound to protest this unfair assessment of Ryker. "Much as I'd like to believe I'm irresistible, you know that's not true."

"Which part? That he stalked you, or that you're irresistible?"

"Both." I hesitated. "Wait. Is that a trick question?"

He tossed me another spine-melting smile.

I resisted it. "I tried to talk to Ryker this morning. He wouldn't even come to the door. He's hiding something."

Jeff's expression darkened. "Probably."

"What do the police have on him?"

Pulling the laptop in front of him, he flipped it open. "You know I can't tell you that." He studied the screen, brow furrowed.

"Hypothetically, then."

He swiveled his eyes to meet my gaze. "You're not going to let this go."

"No."

"All right. Hypothetically. Let's see—phone records, emails, texts, fingerprints, and other physical evidence at the home of the deceased."

"What does Ryker say?"

"I have no idea."

"Come on, Jeff. Can't you tell me *something*?"

"No. Not only because it would be wrong, but because I don't know anything. I'm not involved. It's Strathcona's case. And since I know the suspect personally, I have to steer clear."

I sat back, momentarily stumped. *Time to try wheedling.*

Lowering my voice, I leaned in. "Seriously, Jeff. What's Ryker's explanation—his alibi? He must have one, right?"

Jeff frowned. "You're awfully interested in this." His tone was surprisingly sharp.

"Ryker's a friend of mine. He's your friend, too. You played in his pickup hockey league for years. You know darn well he's innocent. You should be trying to prove it."

"I'm confident the Strathcona force can handle it."

"Really? The same people who suspected me of murder? Have you forgotten?"

Looking uncomfortable, Jeff shifted in his chair. "That was different."

"Different—how?"

"You were innocent."

I reared back. "You know something you're not telling me."

"I told you, I'm not involved in the investigation."

"I don't care, Jeff." My voice rose despite my efforts to hold it steady. "Ryker's been a good friend to me. If I can help him—"

"I didn't realize the two of you were that close."

I sucked in a quick breath. "That was uncalled for." My tone had become sharp, as well. I didn't care. "If you know something, you better tell me."

Jeff slammed the laptop closed with such vigor I feared for its hinges. "What did you say?"

Hesitating, I bit my lip. *What had come over me?*

His lips thinned. "I hope you realize Ryker Fields has had more women than Bluebeard. Your presence on that list barely rates a mention."

My eyes widened. "Surely you don't believe Ryker and I ever—"

He waved a casual hand. "It's in the past. I have work to do. I'll see you later at home." He rose to wrench open the door.

I followed him into the reception area. "Jeff, listen to me. Ryker is a friend. That's all. I could never... This is crazy."

He pivoted to face me. "You're having second thoughts, aren't you?"

My breath caught in my throat as I realized we weren't talking about Ryker anymore. "No," I protested. Placing a hand on his arm, I drew closer. "Jeff—"

He shook my hand loose before striding through the lobby and out the front door. I reached the parking lot in time to hear a car door slam. As he drove away, my stomach twisted. We'd had disagreements before, but this one felt serious.

CHAPTER FIVE

LORNE WAS WAITING by the side of the road when I arrived at our job site. He'd already finished the mowing, trimming, and blowing. He made quick work of loading the mower into the back of the truck while I stayed in the driver's seat, full of remorse.

"So?" he asked, climbing in beside me and pulling the door shut. "What's up with Ryker?"

After easing the truck into gear and driving off, I filled him in.

He nodded thoughtfully. "But that's good news. Why do you look disappointed?"

I stared through the windshield at the road ahead. "I'm not," I said dully.

"Then"—Lorne tapped out a drumroll on the dash with his fingers—"time for lunch. Emy's making sausage rolls today."

As always, I hoped that news didn't get back to the clients

of Emy's vegan takeout, *Eco Edibles*, which shared the building with her 5X Bakery. "Your favorite," I said.

"You bet. We should hurry, because sometimes she runs out."

Tapping the accelerator, I headed for Main Street. I wasn't interested in meat-filled pastries, even though Emy's were excellent. Instead, I desperately wanted to chew over the latest developments with my best friend. And not just the news about Ryker.

When I pulled into a parking spot a few doors down from the bakery, Lorne bolted out of the truck and headed for the sausage rolls. After feeding change into the meter, I strolled along the sidewalk, pausing for a brief glance in the window of HEMSWORTH'S FINE ART AND COLLECTIBLES. The shop looked deserted. The painting on display—a mottled brown landscape with three oddly shaped cows—showed signs of dust on its frame.

A few doors farther on, I came to the 5X BAKERY logo etched in gold paint on Emy's plate glass window. I pushed open the front door. The bell tinkled overhead as I walked in. With one hand on the door handle, I closed my eyes, the better to appreciate the heady aromas of lemon, lavender, and chocolate wafting my way. No matter how bad my day, it always improved after a visit to the 5X.

Lorne was sitting at the bakery's lone table, tossing back the first of what I knew would be a half-dozen flaky pastry rolls. Emy was behind the counter, arranging blueberry-lemon scones on a display platter, her dark head bent in concentration.

She lifted her face as the door eased shut behind me with

42

a whoosh of air. Her heart-shaped face crinkled into her usual brilliant smile. "Hi, Verity."

I propped myself up on the glass counter with a sigh. "Did Lorne tell you the latest news about Ryker?"

"Between bites." Emy tilted her head at Lorne, who was starting his second sausage roll.

Swiveling my gaze, I joined in her awe of Lorne's formidable appetite.

My five-foot-ten frame and strenuous job let me absorb quite a few calories without worry. But Lorne left me in the dust. Yet he was never anything other than lean and trim. In fact, I'd heard Emy's mother, Thérèse Dionne, say more than once that her daughter should "fatten him up a bit."

Emy was doing her best.

Lorne stuffed in the last of that roll then reached for a third while gulping coffee with his other hand.

I turned back to face Emy over the counter. "I need advice," I said in a voice low enough that it wouldn't attract Lorne's notice—if anything could at that point, short of an emergency recon mission.

Emy narrowed her eyes. "About Jeff's proposal?"

"How did you know?"

"Everybody knows."

"They do not. You're exaggerating."

"Well, the people who care about you know. What possessed you to turn him down?"

"I didn't—" Realizing my voice was rising, I leaned in to whisper. "I didn't turn him down. Not exactly. I needed time to...think it over."

Emy nodded thoughtfully, then bent to slide the filled

platter onto a shelf. Shutting the glass door, she straightened up to her full five-foot-one, wiping her hands on the front of her long white apron. "You know I'd tell you if I thought you were making a mistake."

"Then what's your opinion?"

"That you and Jeff belong together and this is just nerves. Tea?"

I nodded. "Thanks."

Emy picked up the kettle then stepped over to the sink to turn on the tap. "Who are you waiting for? Prince William is taken."

I made a face. "I'm not waiting for anybody."

"Huh." She wrinkled her nose before placing the filled kettle on the burner and switching it on. "Jeff won't lack female companionship for long, you know. If you reject him, I predict he'll be single for no more than ten minutes. Katia will be taking bets on it at the Tipsy Jay."

"I don't want to reject Jeff," I protested. "Nothing could be further from my mind. It's just..." As my voice trailed off miserably, my mind filled with the series of images I'd tried for three years to forget. The reel always ended the same way —with Matthew's funeral. The man who had been the first— and I had expected the only—love of my life.

Emy plonked a china plate on the counter, added a blue-berry scone, then pushed it toward me. "You think you're tempting fate."

"Is that what I think?" Morosely, I pushed the scone around on the plate with my finger.

The kettle boiled, and Emy made my favorite Assam tea in a mug. "Milk?"

I nodded.

She set the mug in front of me. After a glance at Lorne, she leaned over the counter and lowered her voice. "It's understandable. Jeff lost his wife in a tragic accident, and you lost Matthew to a devastating illness. You're afraid it will happen again."

I pushed the scone around some more. *Was that it? Was I expecting fate to sneak up behind me with a pipe wrench?*

"It's not only that, Emy," I said. "My parents' marriage was...troubled."

She puffed air out her lips, looking pensive. "That's not relevant. Those were special circumstances that will never occur again." She tapped a fingernail on the counter. "Maybe it's not fate that worries you. Maybe it's the other F word —fear."

I scoffed loudly. "I'm not afraid." Then I winced. "I don't think." I contemplated my crumbling scone before deciding on a sip of tea instead. Caffeine was never a bad idea.

"Then it's guilt. You feel guilty about being happy when Matthew's dead."

I put my mug down with a groan. "When I asked for your advice, I didn't expect it to be so depressing."

Emy reached over the counter to pat me briskly on the back. "It's not depressing. Not even a little. It's a big life decision, and you have every right to think it over. But if you give Jeff the heave-ho, I swear I'll never talk to you again."

She gave my shoulder a final pat—more of a slap, really—before strolling to the kitchen at the back of the shop. "Lorne, call me if anybody comes in?"

"Sure, babe." He reached for another sausage roll.

I remained slumped on the counter. *Give Jeff the heave-ho? Never.* But what if he gave up on me? What if he moved out of Rose Cottage? What if that slide-out sock drawer in our new wardrobe was empty when I got home? I pictured its little cubicles with only specks of lint to fill them. The thought gave me the shakes.

I had to talk to Jeff and straighten this out.

Yet I had to help Ryker, too. At the moment, his need was greater than mine.

Picking up my mug, I followed Emy—after placing my plate with the uneaten scone in front of Lorne.

"Hey, thanks," he said, without looking up.

In the kitchen, I leaned against the doorjamb to watch Emy chop candied ginger. "You didn't mean that, did you?"

"Stop right there." She pointed with her knife. "You need a hairnet to come in here."

"Sorry. Forgot." I lifted a fresh hairnet from the dispenser by the door then slipped it on before proceeding into the room, eyes averted from the huge commercial refrigerator. I'd learned to turn my head away when sidling past its shiny doors. You never wanted to see your reflection while wearing one of Emy's hairnets.

"Did I mean what?" She glanced up briefly.

"That you'd never talk to me again if I—you know." I shrugged, staying well away from the fridge, which was looming over me. Leering, almost.

Emy resumed cutting the crystallized ginger. "Of course not. You're my best friend." Then she waved the knife at me again. "But you'd be making a big mistake. And I wouldn't keep quiet about it."

I raised my hands in surrender before dropping onto a metal stool. "Noted. Meanwhile, we have to do something about Ryker."

Emy winced, holding the knife in midair. "I know. I keep hoping it's all some horrible mistake." She attacked the ginger with renewed vigor, then pushed it aside to start on a pile of shelled walnuts. "The police need a motive, don't they?"

"Yes, but what could it be?" Puffing air through my lips, I regretted my encounter with Shelby. "I should have questioned his sister more."

"Whose sister?" Emy swept the chopped walnuts from the cutting board into a metal bowl.

"Ryker's."

Holding the bowl in one hand, she shot me a puzzled look. "Ryker doesn't have a sister."

"He does now." I sighed. "I forgot to tell you." Briefly, I relayed Shelby's story. "Weird, eh?"

"It's not the first time I've heard of DNA tests flushing out unknown relatives." Emy covered the bowl of walnuts with plastic wrap. "But it's interesting she mentioned the inheritance. Did the police question her about it?"

"No idea."

"You have to get her alone somewhere and grill her." Emy rested the heels of her hands on the countertop, rocking while she thought about it. She jerked her head around. "I know—how about the Tipsy Jay? I could call her, welcome her to the village, then invite her out for trivia night. Once we get a few beers into her, she might be more talkative."

I mulled this over. "It's a good idea. Maybe we could do it tonight."

Emy pushed the bowls of chopped ginger and walnuts to the back of the counter. "Not tonight. I've got a better idea. We should check out the Lawren Harris painting. The one Perry Otis left to Ryker."

A timer beeped loudly. Emy pulled on a pair of silicone mitts, then opened the nearest oven to remove a steaming tray of chocolate cookies.

I drew the air toward me with both hands, savoring the aroma. "Those smell good."

"Dark chocolate-chili." Emy slid the cookies from the baking sheet onto a cooling rack, then took off her mitts to place them alongside. "Too hot to eat at the moment, though."

"I can wait," I said, feeling surprisingly chipper, which I attributed it to the intoxicating chocolate fumes. "Now, how do we check out the painting?"

She grinned. "I happen to know that Nigel Hemsworth is holding an open house tonight at Perry's place on Tulip Crescent."

"Ooh—that's news we can use. Come to think of it, I did see his name on the for-sale sign. When did Nigel become a realtor?"

"He moonlights. I wouldn't say he's serious about it. But Perry was a friend of his, and that's why Nigel has the listing, according to Mom. She knew them both quite well at one time, but that was years ago. Nigel was fun back then, she said, but Perry was quieter. He was a well-known art collector, though." Emy tilted her head. "Guess what the centerpiece of his collection was?"

"The Lawren Harris painting? *Spirit of the North?*"

"Bingo. I've never been in Perry's house, but I'm willing to bet that painting will be hanging on the wall tonight in a place of honor." She rolled her lips. "Under a ceiling spot, probably, flanked by exotic flowers."

"What do Lawren Harris paintings go for these days?" I asked, eying the cookies. They looked cooled to me.

"You're kidding."

"No, I'm serious."

"Google it on your phone." Emy waited, watching me, until she saw my eyes widen.

"Eleven million?" I asked. *Eleven million?*

She chuckled. "That's the record, and of course Perry's isn't worth anywhere close to that, but still..." She smirked. "Interested in seeing it?"

"You bet." I recalled the impressive renovations Lorne and I admired from Perry's driveway. "Besides, I'd love to see the inside of that house. How does this help Ryker, though?"

"Don't you think Shelby will take the opportunity to check out this fabled inheritance for herself? She's obviously curious, and the house has been locked up since Perry died. This might be her only chance before the lawyers weigh in."

"Ah," I said, realization dawning. "You're a genius, Emy. We can corner her at the open house then escort her to the Tipsy Jay for our friendly chat."

"Yes. And if I know Nigel, there will be oodles of wine at this thing. She'll already be half-sloshed by the time we strike."

We shared a high-five.

CHAPTER SIX

THERE'S no way to sugarcoat it. Nigel Hemsworth, Leafy Hollow's long-time art dealer, had enormous ears. I'm not saying they were Dumbo-sized, but he could have given Prince Charles a run for his money. His attempt to disguise those flaps with tufts of graying hair only made it worse, especially up close. In fact, when Nigel casually squeezed my hand after Emy introduced us, I found it difficult to look at anything else.

I forced myself to focus on his nose instead. It wasn't much of an improvement. I couldn't help wondering if he surrounded himself with beautiful objects in order to take his mind off the unfortunate mess Nature had made of his face.

We were standing in the octagonal addition of Perry Otis's house, only a few yards from *Spirit of the North*, among a throng of stylish gawkers munching on canapés and holding champagne flutes.

"Pleased to meet you, Nigel," I said. "I've been meaning

to stop by your shop for ages." I leaned in, lowering my voice, hoping to give the impression of a shared confidence. "Until recently, my budget did not extend to works by well-known artists."

That was a wildly inaccurate statement. The ongoing restoration of mid-nineteenth-century Rose Cottage left me broke at the end of every month. Jeff repeatedly offered me money, but I couldn't bring myself to take it. He still had a mortgage on his empty condo in Strathcona—a condo I'd encouraged him not to sell. I didn't feel right charging him rent.

Still, Nigel didn't know any of that. So, I added *until recently* hoping that if he saw me as an enthusiastic new buyer he would divulge details about the coveted painting. Like the price, for starters.

Nigel took a step back, with one hand under his elbow and two fingers resting against his cheek. I preened a bit under his scrutiny. I'd taken care with my outfit—black jeans, black sequined top, and a black handbag borrowed from Emy. When I'd admired it in the mirror at home, it gave off a distinctly artistic vibe. I also thought its monochromatic scheme made it look expensive.

I might as well have worn a flour sack.

Nigel pursed his lips while appraising my outfit. "Well... Good art doesn't have to be costly. I'm sure I could find something that would fit into your budget." He lowered his critical fingers to make a magnanimous sweep of Perry Otis's artwork-studded walls. "Mr. Otis started out small, yet look at his collection today. Magnificent. Now, consider this one..." He walked away, still talking.

Emy and I followed, nodding appreciatively, trying not to look bored. We'd been at the open house for half an hour and learned nothing that would help Ryker. Not only that, but his half-sister Shelby was nowhere to be seen.

Earlier, when we'd emerged from Emy's neon-yellow Fiat 500 to join the crowd surging toward the house, we had been funneled toward THE SILO by a signboard in the foyer. It directed the guests to walk through the great room of the main house then into the circular addition.

Once over its threshold, Emy and I halted to exchange awed glances. "The Silo" was a strange name for such an elegant space. The ceiling soared four stories to a skylight, with a white spiral staircase clinging to the rounded white walls, allowing a closer look at the art on the upper levels.

On the ground level, *Spirit of the North* hung on a partial wall set in the middle of the room, sheltered from the skylight's rays by an overhanging canvas shade. As Emy had predicted, it occupied the place of honor.

It was lit by angled overhead spots and flanked by orchids on wooden plinths. A velvet rope strung between metal stanchions prevented the riffraff from getting too close—or, heaven forbid, actually breathing on this masterpiece.

I stood outside the rope, studying the painting. It was smaller than I expected. No more than a foot and a half across. It depicted a brown, gray, and blue streetscape of semi-detached three-story houses. It didn't move me like the Lawren Harris paintings I'd seen in museums, with their crystal lakes and soaring mountains. I found it a bit disappointing.

Nigel waved at someone across the room. Before he could

abandon us budget shoppers in favor of more well-heeled candidates, I drew his attention with a flap of my hand. "This is the Group of Seven painting I've heard so much about, isn't it?" I asked, inclining my head toward *Spirit*.

He nodded, smiling. "It is indeed. One of Harris's early works. A Toronto street scene, painted around 1910."

"Is it for sale, like the house?"

His expression momentarily darkened. "Oh, no. Mr. Otis had specific plans for that piece. Although, to be honest—" He smiled. "To be honest—" Then, without warning, Nigel brushed me out of the way, raising his voice to a near-bellow. "Mayor Mullins—I'm so pleased you could join us."

Nigel strode across the room, holding out a hand to Leafy Hollow Councilor Wilfred Mullins. Since Wilf was not quite four feet tall, Nigel had to stoop.

Wilf uttered his usual guffaw as he clasped Nigel's hand. "I'm not the mayor yet, you rascal."

"Surely, the vote is only a formality," Nigel purred.

Chuckling, Wilf slapped Nigel's arm—since he couldn't reach his back—then shot him a wink.

Emy and I exchanged bemused smiles. Wilf was my lawyer, as well as my aunt's. Most of the villagers were under the spell of his exuberant personality. He'd been promising for years to run for mayor, and he was finally taking his shot.

Wilf's long-suffering executive assistant, the dignified, gray-haired Harriet, hovered behind him, clutching his royal-blue booster cushion. Should Wilf decide to stop election-eering and sit for a moment, which was unlikely, she would be ready. Harriet barely cracked a smile at Nigel's fawning. As always, I admired her professional restraint.

Wilf turned his head to speak to Harriet. She deftly tucked the cushion under one arm, then pulled an appointment diary and pen from her bag. With the pen poised, she tilted her head at Nigel, who spoke in a low tone. Harriet made an entry, then returned the diary to her bag in time to hurry after Wilf, who'd resumed working the room. By the time she caught up, he was deep in conversation with a middle-aged couple wearing a blue suit and little black dress.

I swiveled my attention back to Nigel. He stood with his hands clasped behind his back, beaming at Wilf.

Elbowing Emy, I whispered, "What do you think Nigel was going to say about the painting before Wilf came in?"

"I bet he wants to buy it," she whispered back. "I wouldn't put it past him to swoop in with a low-ball offer before anyone else has a chance. Ryker doesn't know anything about art, and now, with the murder case, Nigel probably sees him as an easy mark."

"That seems cold-blooded."

"Look!" She prodded my arm. "There's Shelby."

I swiveled my head to the entrance, where Shelby Wynne was stepping hesitantly across the threshold. Her torn jeans had been replaced by a yellow print sundress and flats. When a white-shirted waiter approached her with a tray of filled wine glasses, she took one of white.

After a quick glance around the room, Shelby turned on her heels to walk back out into the great room.

That's weird, I thought. *She only just got here.*

"Wait here," I told Emy, then followed Shelby through the house, taking care to stay behind her by several yards. She wandered through the ground-floor rooms of the main building, sipping her wine. Several times, she paused to pull a cell phone from her purse and snap a picture. But not of the paintings. Shelby was interested in the windows. A devotee of natural light, I assumed. Always important in a real estate purchase.

Or—was she assessing her share of Ryker's inheritance?

After she disappeared into the kitchen on the other side of the house, I headed back to the Silo. At the entrance, Nigel brushed past me, his lips set. Turning, I saw him enter the kitchen. Intrigued, I retraced my steps to move closer. Close enough to hear raised voices.

Then Shelby came back through the door, closely followed by Nigel, who had a hand on her shoulder. With a shrug and a pout, she slipped free. He watched her, eyes narrowed, as she walked through the great room in the direction of the foyer. Nigel continued on into the Silo.

I eyed the kitchen door, wondering what Shelby had been doing in there that aroused Nigel's wrath enough to ask her to leave.

Emy walked up behind me, sipping her wine. "Whatcha looking at?"

"The kitchen. Care to take a closer look?" I asked, eyebrows raised.

We crossed the great room and entered the sweeping space. Once over the threshold, Emy ran an appraising hand along a polished wooden countertop, exclaiming over the kitchen's professional appliances, multiple knife racks, and trio of stainless-steel dishwashers.

"Why would anybody need all this?" I asked, gesturing at a huge marble island with hardwood insets. I swear my voice echoed off the gleaming white walls, despite the presence of two aproned chefs who were refilling canapé platters then handing them off to the servers. A third chef was flipping tiny skewers of meat over an indoor grill. No one looked at us.

"It's not for the homeowners," Emy said. "It's for the caterers. Dinner parties, special events, stuff like that. Look—the appliances are all connected to the Internet."

"Of course they are," I said, musing on what kind of dinner parties required a hotel-sized prep area and appliances with their own Facebook pages. *The kind I'd never been invited to, obviously.* My gaze traveled around the room, landing on a row of casement windows between the far counter and the upper cabinets. One of the windows was open. The air conditioning was so chilly I regretted not adding a black cardigan to my outfit, yet the hired staff was allowing that cold air to billow out an open window.

I nudged Emy with my elbow. "This kitchen looks great, but there must be something wrong with the ventilation if they have to open a window just to make miniature shish kebabs." Rubbing my bare arms to warm them up, I added, "The electricity bill will be huge."

"Nigel won't pay it. It'll come out of the estate," Emy said, eying the caterers with professional curiosity. I half expected her to whip out a pad to take notes.

"Will the estate pay for the catering, too?"

"Of course." Emy held out an arm to halt a white-shirted waiter who was hustling by with a filled tray. Smiling, she lifted a morsel from the platter. While the waiter continued on his way, Emy gave the tidbit a thorough examination before popping it into her mouth. "Lobster crostini with dill sauce," she said after a moment's chewing. "Not bad. Not exactly innovative, though. I wonder why Nigel didn't ask me to do the catering?"

"Come on. This isn't getting us anywhere." I took her arm to lead her back to the Silo. On our way past the signboard in the foyer, I caught sight of a stack of business cards on a hall table and stopped to take a look. The heavy white stock and gold engraving looked familiar. I picked one up to read it.

GRACE ANDERSON

Below that, a phone number, also in gold.

I rummaged through my black handbag to find the card Molly Maxwell had given me when we discussed her ruined flowers, then held it next to the new one. They were identical.

"Hang on to this," I said, handing the second card to Emy. "Grace Anderson must be here somewhere. We need to find her."

Puzzled, Emy read the name. "I've never heard of her. Is she involved with Ryker somehow?"

"No, but I suspect she knows something about the vandalism at Molly's."

"Is that the surveillance target Lorne roped us into?"

"That's the one." I uttered a sigh. "Thanks for doing it, by the way. I know it's a nuisance."

Emy brightened, tucking the card into her bag. "I'm looking forward to it. Lorne and I have been researching camouflage options."

I shook my head, but couldn't help smiling. "You two were made for each other."

"I know," she enthused. "Isn't it great?"

We returned to the Silo. Wondering what to do next, I swept my gaze around the room, taking in the suited men and fancy-dressed women who were exchanging earnest comments on the artwork while sipping wine and munching hors d'oeuvres.

Which one was Grace Anderson?

CHAPTER SEVEN

THE OPEN HOUSE was in full swing when a woman with long platinum hair entered the Silo and strolled over to the velvet rope guarding *Spirit of the North*. One arm was raised to her shoulder, fingers coiled around the handles of a massive white handbag tossed over the back of her silk floral shift. She had a glass of red wine in her other hand, and her red-soled shoes sported four-inch spike heels.

I prodded Emy with my elbow. "Who's that?"

Emy followed my eyes. "Don't know. I don't think she's from the village." She drew in a quick breath. "Look at those shoes—Louboutin. Cost at least a grand, I bet."

"Each? Or for the pair?"

Emy ignored my jibe. "She's really interested in that painting, isn't she?"

We watched the blonde lean over the red velvet rope with her wine glass. From across the room, I saw Nigel also watching her—no doubt imagining how much *Spirit*'s value would be diminished by a vivid splash of burgundy. Fixing a smile on his face, he headed in her direction.

"Nigel's on the move," I whispered. "This should be good."

He reached her just as she swung the purse off her shoulder to unhook the rope.

"Excuse me," Nigel said with thinned lips, reaching for the hook. He tugged it out of her grip, then reattached it firmly to the stanchion—which had the effect of herding the platinum blonde back to the riffraff side.

Emy and I side-stepped closer while pretending to admire the abstract swirls of a nearby canvas. Soon we were in prime position to overhear their conversation.

"I only wanted a closer look. It's so intriguing."

"Yes, it is."

"Is it for sale?"

Nigel chuckled. "I doubt you could afford it, ma'am."

"Ma'am?" She stepped nearer—so near that her substantial chest nearly brushed against the front of his tailored suit. "I don't look like a *ma'am*, do I?"

His eyes widened. He stepped back. "No, of course not. I only meant—"

"As for being able to pay for it"—she smiled—"I assure you I can cover the cost of anything in this room. Hold this," she commanded, handing him her wine glass.

Nigel complied, looking confused.

She opened her handbag to extract a business card, then swapped it for her glass. "I'm sure we can come to an arrangement."

Despite straightening to my full five-ten, and even adding

tiptoes, I couldn't read the card. Nigel had turned his back to us, and the card was safely hidden by his bulk.

I ducked my head to one side in time to see him try to give it back. "I'm sorry, but this particular work is not for sale," he said.

She shrugged. "Something else, then?" She slid nearer, until her faultlessly manicured fingers were caressing Nigel's lapel. "I've heard about your shop, and I'm simply not willing to leave empty-handed."

"How did you—"

"Oh, I have a lot of contacts in the business. They let me know when something interesting comes up. Although..." She stepped back to study his face. "Perhaps you think I'm not trustworthy. I'm willing to conduct a preliminary transaction to prove how serious I am."

Nigel puffed out a breath, still holding her card. "Well... there might be something." He glanced rather helplessly around the room. "I might be willing to part with a few pieces of my own, but they aren't here."

"When can I see them?"

"Well..."

The blonde plucked her business card from his fingers, then tucked it into the breast pocket of Nigel's jacket. Giving the pocket a pat, she said, "Call me with the details. We'll work something out."

As she walked away, he seemed unable to take his eyes off her rear.

I had to admit it was impressive.

"I'm going to follow her," I said. You run interference

with Nigel. I have to talk to that woman. She could be Grace Anderson."

Squaring her shoulders, Emy walked briskly up to Nigel then bestowed her most brilliant smile—the one that always melted male resistance.

He was no exception.

"Nigel, I hope you didn't overpay for those canapés. I would have offered you a very competitive price." Emy grasped his elbow, steering him toward the buffet table. "Let's take a look."

At five-foot-one, Emy was tiny, but determined.

I turned my attention to the blonde, who was making a leisurely circuit of the room. Then she placed her wine glass on a table and continued into the main house. By the time I caught up with her, she was frowning at a small landscape. Cows again.

"It's nice, isn't it?" I asked, sidling up beside her.

"It's crap." She turned to face me. "Who are you?"

"Verity Hawkes. A local landscaper. And you are?"

"A landscaper? Meaning you know nothing about art."

"I wouldn't say that," I bristled, recalling the hardbound edition of *Modern Art for the Time-Challenged* in my book-case at home. Not to mention *Masterpieces of Decoupage* and *Ten Ways to Fold a Dinner Napkin*.

She waved a hand while renewing her scrutiny of the oil. "Leave me alone."

"Are you Grace Anderson?"

"No," she replied without looking at me.

"Then how do you know Nigel Hemsworth?"

Her eyebrows rose as she swiveled her head toward me. "Excuse me?"

"Well, I couldn't help overhearing you negotiating a purchase. And since this is basically a real estate open house that has nothing to do with art, I naturally wondered how—"

"What did you say your name was?"

"Verity Hawkes."

"Thanks. I'll keep it in mind for the civil suit."

"What civil suit?"

"The one I'm going to bring asking for an injunction if you don't stay at least fifty feet away from me from now on."

I gaped at her. "You're joking, right?"

Pulling a rose-gold phone from her purse, she held it up. "Should I call my lawyer?"

"I was just leaving."

She nodded, then resumed her examination of the artwork.

Back in the Silo, I found Emy alone at the buffet table, dropping canapés into a folded napkin.

"Is the 5X out of food?" I whispered in her ear.

She clapped a hand to her chest. "*Cheesit.* Don't sneak up on me like that."

"Sorry. But what are you doing?"

"Checking out the competition. Did you get anywhere with dragon lady?"

"No. That's an apt metaphor, by the way. She threatened to have me arrested. Sort of."

Emy tucked another morsel into her napkin while scanning the rest of the platters. "Good thing you're used to that."

I made a face. "Thanks for the support. Did Nigel tell you anything interesting?"

"Nothing. But he's nervous about something."

"Maybe the way the open house is going?"

"It's not that. He's held open houses and art show openings before. He's usually pretty cool. But today..." She twisted the top of the napkin shut, then opened her purse to drop it in. "He seems distracted."

"Did you ask him about Ryker?"

"I didn't get the chance."

"Speaking of open houses, isn't this a little upscale for a *check-out-the-closets* function? Why are all these people here?"

"To see the art," Emy said. "Perry always kept it under wraps. The villagers are curious."

Out of the corner of my eye, I saw Nigel scanning the crowd. "But Nigel told dragon lady that none of this was available."

"Hmm. I bet he's negotiating a bulk purchase from Ryker. Then he can resell the paintings at a profit."

Meanwhile, Nigel had found his target—a tall, tanned man in his early sixties, wearing a blue linen jacket with a wrapped cigar tucked into the breast pocket. His movie-star physique contrasted painfully with Nigel's puffy middle.

They spoke only briefly before Nigel became agitated. He gripped the man's sleeve, his voice rising. "That's not the deal we agreed on."

"That deal died with Perry," the other said in an equally loud voice, shaking his arm free. Pivoting on the heel of his Italian loafers, he walked off.

Nigel glared after him. With a sour expression, he turned to the nearest observers, who hurriedly looked away. "Having fun?" he asked through clenched teeth before seeking out the nearest waiter, grabbing a wine glass, and downing it.

Behind me, Emy sucked in a breath.

"Do you know that man in the blue linen jacket?" I asked.

"That's Isaac Damien. He hasn't been back to Leafy Hollow for years. Not since the court case."

My attention was instantly awakened. "What court case?"

"Ask me later. Look—she's back."

I turned my head. Shelby stood in the doorway, her gaze fixed on *Spirit* while she wolfed down a lobster crostini. We weren't the only ones to notice her. From the other side of the room, Nigel jerked his head up, pinning Shelby with a murderous look.

"Come on," I said. "Let's talk to her before Nigel throws her out."

Shelby had shoved a second crostini into her mouth and was busy chewing when we approached.

"Shelby, hello—just the person I wanted to see," I said cheerily.

"*Mmmffffph*," she replied, holding two fingers over her mouth.

"I'd like to introduce my friend, Emy Dionne. Emy owns that wonderful bakery on Main Street."

Emy held out a hand. "Pleased to meet you. Ryker and I have been friends since high school. I'm delighted about the addition to his family. He must be thrilled."

Emy's hand quivered in midair while Shelby stared at her. I knew that Emy's gymnast physique allowed her to hold out that hand forever, if necessary.

Eventually, Shelby surrendered. Shifting her wine glass to her left hand, she clasped Emy's. "I'm afraid Ryker hasn't mentioned your name," she said coolly.

"Well—" Emy notched up her smile a beam or two. "He's been occupied." She shook Shelby's hand with a sympathetic look. "It must be hard for you, finding a long-lost brother and having to face...well, you know." She shrugged sadly. "Verity and I were hoping to take you for a drink. The Tipsy Jay, on Main Street, is one of Ryker's favorites. And it's trivia night." She smiled again. "Please say you'll come. It'll take your mind off things."

Shelby stared.

After a moment's silence, Emy added, with a rather desperate air, "Our treat."

Shelby shook her head. "I can't leave Ryker alone that long."

"He could come, too," I blurted. "Ryker's terrific with sports trivia. That's always been our weakest area. We could use his help."

With a forced smile, Shelby swept past us.

"Our weakest area?" Emy hissed in my ear. "What were you thinking?"

"Sorry," I replied dejectedly. "We didn't exactly hit it off, did we?"

She waved a dismissive hand. "Let's check out trivia night anyway. We could use the distraction. Why don't you text Jeff to see if he's available?"

"He's working tonight." I sighed, remembering our last conversation.

"Never mind." Emy squeezed my arm. "Everything will work out for the best."

As we headed for the door, I glanced over my shoulder at Shelby, who was standing in front of the Lawren Harris painting. She sipped her wine without taking her eyes from the canvas. She appeared to be mesmerized by it.

CHAPTER EIGHT

SHELBY WYNNE FROZE as an owl hooted overhead. The branches above her swayed as the raptor swooped out of the spruce trees, silhouetted against the full moon. Something unseen chattered in response. A chill slithered down her back. How could a village this close to the highway shelter so much wildlife?

With a shiver, she renewed her scrutiny—of Perry Otis's farmhouse in general, and the open casement window above the kitchen counter in particular. Hours earlier, during the evening's event, that window had been open. She had hoped no one would think to close it. They hadn't. Even from across the lawn, she saw moonlight glinting off the open pane of glass.

While roaming through the house, she had noticed something else about that window. It was not hooked up to the electronic security system, possibly because it was so small. Which made it ideal.

The guests had left hours earlier, followed by the caterers. Nigel Hemsworth had been the last to leave the farmhouse, shutting off the lights before he drove away in his Mercedes convertible.

Since then, she'd been arguing with herself. *Perhaps this was a bad plan.* But the alternative—waiting months for a bevy of high-priced lawyers to decide if she was entitled to a share of Ryker's estate—was even less appealing. What if they said *no*?

Whereas, if she took the painting now and squirreled it away—and she had the perfect hiding spot for it—Ryker would merely file an insurance claim. Which she would also share. Really, it was a win-win.

And tonight was perfect for what she had in mind.

So many people in and out of the house in the past twenty-four hours.

So many suspects.

So much blame to go around.

It was a small window, true—but she was slim. She could manage it. She stepped out from under the spruce trees then walked across the lawn, her running shoes silent on the grass, until she was right under the window.

There she paused, brow furrowed, reevaluating her goal.

The window was eight feet above the ground. She'd forgotten to allow for the basement portion of the wall. Cursing under her breath, she cast about for something to stand on, then spotted a rain barrel under a downspout at the corner.

It was half full. She grunted as she pushed it over, watching water course across the lawn. Once the barrel was empty, she dragged it back to the window, tipped it so that the base faced up, then positioned it directly under the window.

Once that was done, she scrambled onto the top, balancing carefully to prevent the empty barrel from tipping, and reached for the window. She pulled the casement all the way open.

It was more difficult than she'd expected to slide through on her belly. The edges of the window frame scraped gashes on her arms and legs, despite her yoga pants and hoodie. Worse, her thrashing legs tipped the barrel over halfway through the maneuver, leaving her bottom half hanging in midair.

Twisting her head in a pointless attempt to see the toppled barrel, she cursed again.

Too late to turn back. Inching forward, she squeezed through. Then, with a twist, she jackknifed her legs and swung them around.

Sitting on the counter, she glanced through the double kitchen doors into the main portion of the house.

She sucked in a breath. There it was—visible through the entrance to the Silo on the other side of the great room—the painting she'd come to claim. The spotlights were off now, but enough moonlight came through the skylight that she could pick out its gilt frame.

Pride surged in her chest. *Why shouldn't she have the painting?* It was all in the family.

Turning her head, she evaluated the alarm keypad by the back door. It was flashing green, meaning she'd correctly assessed the setup. The open window she'd wiggled through was not part of the security system. *No one knew she was here.*

She did not notice a blinking red light on the massive refrigerator across the room.

That was her first mistake.

Smiling, Shelby fingered the folded box cutter in her pocket. It was sharp—sharp enough to cut through canvas. Then she jumped off the counter, landing nimbly on both feet.

That was her second.

Searing, stabbing pain shot up her legs.

For an instant, she froze, her breath caught in her throat. Then her shrieks echoed off the walls of the empty kitchen.

After a few moments, Shelby realized she might have overreacted. She stopped screaming.

She wiggled her left foot and gasped in pain. But this time, she realized the discomfort was not localized. Instead, it was spread across the soles of both feet. She tried to lift one foot off the floor.

Nothing happened. It was stuck to the tiles.

She tried the other foot. Same thing.

The curses that echoed off the marble island and the slate backsplashes did not ease her pain, but they were creative. She had learned them from four foster brothers whose practical jokes made her childhood a misery. Like the plastic wrap stretched over the toilet in the middle of the night. The fake tarantula on her pillow. The candles with a firecracker inside. She could still hear their peals of laughter. It was her own fault, they said, because she was a sucker. A pushover. A *dupe*.

Therefore, she knew what had just happened to her in Perry Otis's kitchen.

As a child, she'd been unable to combat cruel tricks. But she was older now. *And nobody's dupe.*

Gingerly, she pulled a penlight from her pocket, then directed the beam to the floor at her feet. A portion of tile about three feet square was darker than the rest.

Hanging on to the counter with one hand, she slowly sank to the ground and reached out her other hand. The floor was spread with something so sticky that her fingers came away with a sucking noise—leaving a sliver of skin behind. Without thinking, she raised her traumatized fingers to her mouth to suck on them. Which left them stuck to her lips.

She tugged her fingers from her mouth, tears springing to her eyes.

Bloody hell. Somebody would pay for this.

Rising, Shelby pulled up one foot as hard as she could, until her running shoe cleared the floor with a rebound that sent her hurtling backward, causing spasms of pain as her other foot yanked free.

She lay on the ground, the penlight gripped in her hand, not moving for several moments. Then she turned the beam on the patch of floor she'd escaped. There was something else on the tiles—roofing nails, stuck in the glue with their sharp tips sticking upright.

The floor under the counter window was covered with them—except for two size-six sections. Those missing tacks were stuck into the rubber soles of her running shoes.

It took fifteen minutes to pry each tack loose with the blade of her boxcutter and drop them on the floor. Even though each wound was tiny, her feet were on fire. It was lucky she'd kept her shoes on. In stocking feet, she would have been in agony.

Shelby stood, filling her lungs with determination, then limped through the kitchen door toward her objective. It would take more than dirty tricks to deter her from her goal.

Whrrrrr.

At the sound of a siren outside, her head jerked around and her stomach turned over.

Whrrrrr.

It was getting louder.

Coming closer.

It shut off, directly outside the farmhouse.

Wildly, she glanced around, the penlight's beam bouncing off the cabinets as she dashed for the counter, hopping from foot to foot.

Ow, ow, ow, ow, ow.

Flashing blue lights beamed through the foyer's sidelights and reflected off the walls near the kitchen.

Car doors slammed.

Shelby leapt onto the kitchen counter and slid her head and arms, up to the shoulders, through the window.

Then she remembered the missing rain barrel.

In the driveway, another vehicle pulled up, and another door slammed.

She shimmied through the window, gasping in pain as she forced her torso through. Then, bending from the waist with her palms flat against the brick wall below her, she dove for the ground.

She landed with an *oof* of expelled breath and a sharp

pain in one elbow. Within seconds, she was on her feet. A glance over her shoulder as she hopped for the cover of the spruce trees showed a third car pulling up beside the house.

She ducked under the branches, headed for the path that led back to the village, bouncing from foot to foot, letting only her toes hit the ground.

Ow, ow, ow, ow, ow.

Shelby clenched her teeth as she traveled the spruce-needled path.

This wasn't over.

On the wraparound porch of Perry Otis's farmhouse, two policemen were discussing the nocturnal alarm with Nigel Hemsworth, whose pale blue convertible had pulled up on the street behind their cruiser.

"Thanks for your quick response. I really appreciate it," Nigel said, brandishing a jingling key chain. "I can take it from here."

"We should check the interior before we leave," said one of the officers.

"It's not necessary. The front door's closed and locked. It was a false alarm."

The cop shrugged. "Sorry. It's routine."

"Of course." Smiling, Nigel bent to the lock then opened the front door.

While one officer waited on the porch, the other followed Nigel into the foyer, pausing to look around and say, "Nice house."

"It's for sale—make us an offer," Nigel countered.

The officer only chuckled.

Nigel led him through the great room, followed by a quick circuit of the Silo. "Nothing's been disturbed," he said.

"Is this the picture everybody's making such a fuss over?" the officer asked, peering at *Spirit of the North.*

"Beautiful, isn't it?" Nigel made no move toward the light switch, which would have enabled a closer look. Instead, he gestured to the exit. "Shall we?"

On their way out, Nigel paused by the kitchen door, his bulky frame blocking the officer's view into that room. "Thanks again, officer. I'll re-arm the alarm system before I leave."

Once the police cruisers had disappeared up the driveway and over the hill, Nigel retrieved the knapsack he'd dropped in the foyer. Pulling out a bottle of solvent and a roll of painter's rags, he headed for the kitchen.

An hour later, he packed up the last of his cleaning supplies then slung the knapsack over his shoulder. Turning on the outdoor lights, he went out the kitchen's French doors onto the patio.

After replacing the rain barrel by the side of the house, Nigel pulled a flashlight from his knapsack. He followed footprints in the sodden grass that led to a clump of spruce trees on the edge of the property. He shone his light toward the path behind them.

It was deserted.

He was alone, except for an owl that hooted as it whooshed out of the branches.

At his feet, an object gleamed in the glare of the flashlight. He stooped to pick it up, then rose, balancing it on the palm of his hand.

It was a boxcutter. The folding kind. Tightly closed.

Grinning, he tossed it in the air, catching it on the way down, then stowed it in his knapsack before heading back into the house, rearming the alarm system, and leaving for home.

CHAPTER NINE

JEFF WAS asleep when I tiptoed out of Rose Cottage the next morning. He'd come home late the night before, and I didn't want to disturb him. "*Shhh*," I told Boomer as I let him out the kitchen door. "Jeff will walk you when he gets up. If you're a good boy, you might even get bacon."

Boomer's ears pricked up at the mention of his favorite treat, and he pawed excitedly at my leg. "*Later*," I said. "Not now." His ears sagged—until he caught sight of a cheeky squirrel. While he tore off in pursuit, I tugged my cardigan tighter and sucked in a deep breath of brisk morning air. In the distance, steam rose from the purple-hazed woodlands of Pine Hill Valley. At my feet, General Chang—the scruffy, one-eyed tomcat who'd insinuated himself into Rose Cottage days after my arrival—snaked around my legs, purring loudly. Thus far, it was a perfect day.

Naturally, it couldn't last.

Ethan Neuhaus, one of Ryker's employees, had asked to talk to me. He suggested the Tim Hortons donut shop on the highway, and I agreed to meet him there before my first job of the day. I had no idea what Ethan wanted, but I hoped he'd be able to shed some light on Ryker's strange behavior. Such as why he refused to provide an alibi for the Strathcona murders.

When I parked the *Coming Up Roses* truck in front of the restaurant's plate glass window, Ethan was sitting inside, nursing a coffee. He wore a baseball cap, head hung low. On my way to the entrance, I tapped on the glass. Ethan looked up then gave me a desultory wave.

The Tim Hortons outlet was on a corner where two four-lane highways intersected a mile from the village. It was nestled in a commercial setup that included rows of gas pumps, parking for long-haul trucks, a car wash, and a crowded convenience store. Tim's shared its glass-walled building with a hamburger outlet, whose industrial-sized vents blew the unmistakable smell of grease through the parking lot. Inside, brightly colored chairs were permanently attached to matching tables. They were not comfortable. The entire restaurant was designed to encourage rapid consumption and equally rapid departure. It seemed an odd choice for a first encounter—unless Ethan didn't want our meeting witnessed by villagers.

There were certainly none of those lined up at the Tim's counter. Instead, the staff hustled to serve harried parents and their ice cream-coated children, tired truckers with tanned arms, and young men and women in sturdy hiking boots.

I picked up a double-double coffee at the counter, then made my way over to Ethan and slid into a chair opposite him. Ethan was hunched over the table, his stubby, tanned fingers fiddling with an empty paper cup. There seemed to be something odd about his hands. I couldn't quite make out what, other than his nails were broken and filthy. Obviously, this was a man who worked with his hands and didn't much care what they looked like.

Or maybe it was simply a sign he was unattached. Emy would never have let Lorne's nails get to that state.

"Hi," I said.

He merely grunted.

While waiting for Ethan to get to the point, I studied his nails again, recalling Emy nagging Lorne to "drop by Zoe's and get a manicure, for heaven's sake."

"I can't go in there," he had replied. "That's for girls."

"Girls?" The inflection in her voice had been unmistakable.

"Women—I meant women," Lorne blurted, with a side-eyed glance at me.

In response, I had displayed my own, occasionally manicured fingers and blown on them to mimic nail polish drying.

"Can't I file them or something?" Lorne whined.

"On what?" Emy asked. "The sidewalk?"

Lorne had tilted his head. "Would that work?"

Ethan brought me back to the present by flipping off his baseball cap and dropping it on the table. His hair was shorn so short it was barely more than a suggestion. Scars traced his scalp. He looked like a character in a prison-break movie.

When he slapped his hand on the table, I realized what was odd—he was missing a finger.

"What happened to your finger?" I blurted.

He frowned. "Lost it when I was a kid."

"How did that—"

"Kids at school thought it was hilarious. *Stumpy,* they used to call me. And worse." He resumed fiddling with the empty coffee cup. "*Nine Finger* was one of their favorites."

At my confused look, he added, "James Bond?"

Ohh— I nodded, then my face flushed hot. "It's none of my business, really."

"Forget it." He pushed the cup away then straightened in his chair. "You must wonder why I wanted to talk to you."

"To be honest, I wanted to talk to you, too. About Ryker."

"Yeah. Figured. Thing is—with Ryker the way he is, I have no work. I can't claim unemployment insurance, because I was never on the payroll. Ryker called me in when he needed extra help." He spread his hands.

I tried not to stare at his fingers. "So, you're looking for work?"

"More or less."

I sat back, beaming. This was the perfect development. Lorne and I needed help with Ryker's clients. Ethan knew those customers and their requirements. He was the perfect hire.

At least, that's what I thought. Until he opened his mouth again.

"You shouldn't have taken those clients without talking to me first. It wasn't right." After crushing his coffee cup in one hand, he sent it sailing across the room toward the garbage can with a single, fluid motion.

The cup bounced off the top of the bin then landed on the floor. Ethan paid no notice.

"What are you talking about?"

"I should have had first pick. How did you know I wasn't going into business for myself?"

"Were you planning to do that?"

"Maybe. But I can't now, can I?"

"Why not?"

His voice rose. "Because you poached all my customers, didn't you?"

As two of the harried parents swiveled their heads toward us, my spine stiffened. *Coming Up Roses'* bright pink landscaping truck was parked only yards away. I couldn't risk becoming an object of gossip. Or an online video. When you're running a business, the last thing you want is to be pegged as a shrew. Assertive men are considered forceful, whereas assertive women are called—well, we know.

I forced a smile.

"Ethan. I understand why you thought that. But Ryker recommended my business to his customers. It wasn't my idea."

"Ryker did that?"

Since the look of astonishment on his face appeared genuine, I tried to dial back my irritation. "Perhaps he didn't know about your plans." I hesitated, wondering how to elicit the information I wanted. "Have you discussed it with Ryker since—"

"Since those two women got themselves topped in Strathcona?"

I nodded, choosing to ignore his colorful language.

He extended grubby fingers to fiddle with the sugar packets stacked by his elbow. "He won't talk to me."

"You don't know what's going on, then? With Ryker, I mean?"

Dropping the packets with a sigh, he slumped back in his chair. "No. But somethin's not right. I've never seen him the way he is now. I wouldn't be surprised if he packed it in."

A wave of unease swept over me. "You're talking about the business, right?"

"No." He shook his head. "I meant..." He drew a finger across his throat.

I shuddered. Ethan Neuhaus was quite the ray of sunshine. I couldn't imagine working with him every day. "Ryker would never do that."

"I dunno. I read somewhere that—"

"Can we not talk about this, please?"

"Suit yourself."

Sipping my coffee, I glanced around the restaurant, trying to collect my thoughts. Ethan's disclosure made me even more determined to find out what had driven Ryker to distraction. I placed my cup on the table then leaned in. "Did Ryker ever mention that woman in Strathcona? The one he was supposedly dating?"

Ethan snorted. "No *supposedly* about it. They were definitely getting it on."

"Then he did talk about her?"

He shifted uncomfortably in his chair. "Not exactly. He

never told me about her. But he was leaving work early a couple times a week, and I know that's where he went. I saw her address in the office. I knew it was her that got killed, soon as I heard the news on the radio."

"If Ryker never mentioned her, how did you see her address?"

"He sent her flowers one day and charged it to the biz. I saw the invoice."

This sounded like the Ryker I knew. He never boasted about his conquests. Despite appearances, I liked to think he was searching for someone to settle down with. For a while, I imagined it might be me.

But Jeff had been wrong. I never encouraged Ryker. Other than a few shared meals—dinner at *Anonymous*, the village's most notorious eatery, came to mind—I was oblivious to his interest. Since arriving in Leafy Hollow, I'd only ever had eyes for Jeff. Ryker knew I was a lost cause. It didn't bother him. He was an optimist.

However... What if my rejection had contributed to his depression? Tapping my fingers on the table, I dismissed that thought as ridiculous. I recalled what I told Jeff.

Much as I'd like to believe I'm irresistible, you know that can't be true. He's hiding something.

Narrowing my eyes, I regarded Ethan. "Do you think they had an argument?"

He hesitated, then leaned his elbows on the table, resting his chin on his hands. "They sure did."

I sat back, startled. "What about?"

"She dumped him, didn't she?"

"Did she? How do you know?"

"Because that's when it started—this depression thing. He came back from Strathcona one day and threw equipment around his garage, kicked the tires on the truck, swore a bit. He was pissed off."

"When was this?"

"I can't recall, exactly. It mighta been on the day of the murders."

My stomach clenching, I pushed my coffee cup away. "Did you tell the police about this?"

He shrugged. "Maybe." At the look on my face, he added, "I don't want trouble with the cops. Why shouldn't I answer their questions? I'm not the one with the criminal record."

"Oh, come on. Ryker was a juvenile. It doesn't count."

He shrugged again.

I pursed my lips, mulling this over. Jeff was fond of quoting dialogue from *The Godfather*. As Michael Corleone liked to say, *keep your friends close, and your enemies closer*.

At least, I think it was Michael Corleone. It could just as easily have been Kermit.

In any event, it was clear Ethan bore hostility toward Ryker. I suspected jealousy was the root of it. Whatever the reason, I wanted to keep an eye on Ethan Neuhaus.

Picking up my empty cup, I rose to my feet. "All that aside, Lorne and I do need help. Are you available? Usual rates."

"Sure. When do you want me to start?"

"Today would be good. Meet us at the Blakelys' place, on Concession Road." I raised a hand in caution. "But this arrangement lasts only as long as Ryker doesn't need you.

When he's ready to resume work, I'll return all his customers." I paused. "And employees."

Without waiting to check Ethan's reaction, I pivoted, heading for the exit. On my way past the recycling bins, I plucked his crumpled cup from the floor. I dumped it and my own in the receptacle before walking out the door.

CHAPTER TEN

LORNE WAS NOT surprised to hear I'd hired Ethan.

"He's a good worker," he said while unloading the mower from the back of my pickup, then bending to check the oil.

"Then you don't mind?"

He gave me a surprised look. "Why would I? We need the help, he's experienced, he knows Ryker's clients—what's to mind?"

"Ethan can be a little...moody."

"Doesn't bother me."

"That's great, then, because he'll be here shortly. Meanwhile, I'll check in with our new clients to ask about any special requirements."

Lorne swiped a rag along the dipstick before replacing it on the side of the mower. "Ask about Ryker, you mean."

"If the topic comes up," I replied stiffly. "Why not?"

Lorne only grinned.

At the sound of a noisy vehicle, we turned our heads to

see a rusty Camaro pull in beside my truck. Ethan emerged. He had to slam the driver's door twice to get it to stay closed. Then he headed in our direction.

I waved at him before turning to deliver one last instruction to Lorne. "Don't let Ethan tell you what to do. You're in charge."

Lorne shot me a quick salute before wheeling the mower toward the lawn. I climbed back into my truck. As I drove past Ethan, he looked straight at me. Neither of us was smiling.

The first house I pulled up to was a yellow brick split-level. Massive flowerpots flanking the front door were spilling over with weeds—matching the ones in the perennial border.

I paused by the pots to take a closer look at the tiny white flowers, then puffed out a breath. Garlic mustard. *Great.* An invasive plant that would take over the entire yard if left to propagate. The darn things shot up practically overnight. I glanced apprehensively at the giant maple soaring overhead. Garlic mustard was toxic to trilliums and trout lilies, two of my favorite wildflowers, but it could also affect maple tree roots.

I rapped on the door.

It was wrenched open by a flustered woman in yoga pants and T-shirt. Her fingers curled around the edge of the door—ready, I assumed, to slam it in my face. "What is it? I'm busy."

"Fern Ripley? I'm Verity Hawkes," I said quickly. "You called me about lawn and garden help?"

Her gaze swerved to the pink truck in her driveway. Then her eyes widened, her mouth forming a perfect O. She flung open the door.

"I'm so sorry, Verity. Yes, I definitely did. I didn't mean to be rude, it's just that—"

"Mom," came a plaintive cry from inside.

"In a minute," Fern yelled over her shoulder. "Verity— please come in."

With a fixed smile, I stepped gingerly over the knapsacks and running shoes scattered across the floor. Empty pizza boxes were jammed haphazardly into a blue recycling bin. Stacks of mail and flyers competed for space on the hall table with a pile of tangled keys and two opened bags of gummy candies.

Sighing, Fern tried to clear a path. "I'm afraid we're in a bit of a state today. My eight-year-old is sick, and he's cranky. I stayed home with him, but—"

Rrrrrrr. Rrrrrrrr. Rrrrrrrr.

She paused, her attention riveted by a vibrating cell phone on the cluttered hall table. "Sorry. My office keeps calling. Can't do without me, apparently."

There was a definite hint of irritation in her statement.

Fern snatched up the phone. "What is it now? Uh-huh. Can't you— All right. Leave it on my desk. I'll be in tomorrow." Clicking off the call, she slid the cell phone into her pocket before realizing her yoga pants had no pockets. "Damn," she muttered, bending to retrieve it from the floor.

"Mom," came the voice again. "Mom."

"I'll be there in a minute," she called through clenched teeth. "Verity, could you take a look at the yard by yourself? Whatever you can do to help, we'd appreciate it."

"Absolutely." If I was going to get any questions answered, I'd better ask them quickly. "Has Ryker been cutting your lawn for long?"

She wrinkled her nose while contemplating my question. "I don't recall. Couple of years, maybe? His crew usually comes by when no one's at home. They leave a monthly bill in the mailbox."

"So you don't talk to him often?"

"Now that you mention it, I don't think I've ever talked to him. Except when I hired him, and that was over the phone. Is he ill? Is that why you're filling in?"

"Sort of." Clearly, Fern Ripley was not keeping abreast of village developments.

"*Mom*." The voice was growing more petulant.

Fern shrugged apologetically. "I'm coming," she called. "Well—"

"I'll take a look around outside and be on my way."

"Thanks." Fern opened the door, and I walked through.

"Wait." She pointed to the weed-filled flowerpots. "Could you put something in those on your next visit?"

"Flowers?"

"Anything," she gushed before closing the door.

———

My next visit was marked on my list as *Mr. and Mrs. Terence Stamp*. I did a double-take. That couldn't really be the man's name, could it? I paused, trying to remember the late-night movies I'd watched as a child. How old was the real Terence Stamp?

I pressed the buzzer. While waiting, I admired the cheerful gathering of plaster gnomes on the bungalow's front porch. Their colorful knitted caps had tassel cords tied under their chins, and name tags were wired around their ample waists. I bent to read the nearest ones.

Happy.

Sleepy.

Bashful—

The frantic yipping of small dogs on the other side of the door announced the imminent arrival of the homeowner. The door opened to reveal three long-haired Chihuahuas, dancing on their hind legs and yelping boisterously. They wore knitted vests—pink, yellow, and blue—with their names blazoned in white popcorn stitch. *Bella*, *Bubbles*, and *Barney*.

They were prancing around a wizened, stooped little man with the biggest hearing aid I'd ever seen. Big enough to stream Netflix, I suspected. The dogs continued to yip while the man—Terence Stamp, I assumed—stared at me with watery eyes, his fingers quivering on the doorknob.

I extended a hand. "Hello. I'm Verity Hawkes, Coming Up Roses Landscaping." I raised my voice to be heard over the Chihuahuas. "I'm filling in for Ryker Fields."

His hand continued to quiver on the doorknob.

"Who is it, Terence?" came a reedy voice.

The door was pried out of his grip to reveal an equally small, and equally stooped, woman. She glared.

I hoped this wasn't *Grumpy*.

"Shut up, you silly animals," she snapped.

Instantly, *Bella*, *Bubbles*, and *Barney* sat, tongues lolling, staring at her with rapt attention. As a fellow dog owner, I recognized that expression. *Time for treats?*

I began my spiel again. "Hello. I'm Verity Hawkes. I'm filling in—"

"I heard you the first time." The woman—Mrs. Terence Stamp, I presumed—pointed a thumb at her husband. "He's the one with the hearing aid." Turning, she trudged indoors.

Terence stepped clear of the doorway. Not knowing what else to do, I walked in.

The living room I found myself in was beige and cramped. I stared helplessly about. Nearly every surface was covered with dog beds, dog toys, and dog clothes—on top of knitted potholders stacked on knitted cushions that were in turn stacked on knitted throws.

"Terence, clear a spot for Miss Verity," the woman called over her shoulder while disappearing through a door that led to the back of the house. The dogs scampered after her.

Terence bent slowly to lift an armful of yarn and pointy knitting needles from the sofa. After dropping it on the carpet, he lowered himself into an armchair, then nodded at the sofa to indicate I should sit.

Perched gingerly on its edge, I smiled at him, trying to work up an explanation for my presence that wouldn't shock this elderly couple.

Don't mention the murder case, I thought. *Be discreet.*

Mrs. Stamp tottered back into the room, the dogs prancing around her feet. She held two aluminum cans, one in each hand. "Dr. Pepper?" she asked, brushing aside a well-thumbed copy of *TV Guide* to place the beverage on the coffee table.

"No, thanks. I really don't have time to—"

The *whoosh* of a can being opened was my only answer.

"Thanks," I said weakly, accepting the drink, then taking a fizzy sip. "How refreshing."

Bubbles and *Barney* jumped onto the sofa, one on either side of me, where they balanced expertly on stacks of half-knitted sweaters. They eyed my Dr. Pepper with interest.

Mrs. Stamp opened the second can and gave it to Terence, who accepted it with a quivering hand. After a cautious swallow, he placed it on the table beside him.

Sipping my drink, I wondered how to introduce the topic of Ryker's difficulties. Before I could formulate my first question, my hostess broke in.

"Now," she said, settling herself into a recliner, then pushing a button to activate the chair. As her slippered feet rose in the air, she pinned me with a penetrating gaze. "What kind of trouble has that scamp Ryker Fields gotten himself into this time? The paper says he murdered two women."

I nearly spurt Dr. Pepper out my nose. "Does it?"

"Well, not exactly." She tapped her own, much shinier, nose. "They're playing it close to the vest. But that's the tittle-tattle around the village."

I thumped my can down on the coffee table with a *clunk*. "I don't believe it," I said stoutly. "Ryker would never—"

She gave a flap of her hand. "Don't get your back up, hon. I don't believe it either. I've known Ryker for years—knew his mother, in fact, before..." She hesitated. "Well, no need to go into that. The truth is, I've been waiting for you to come by to cut our lawn."

I would not be able to cut the Stamps' postage-sized grass with my industrial mower. It wouldn't make it up the narrow path without taking out the marigolds lining either side. I'd have to use something else—manicure scissors, maybe.

"I'll take care of it," I said.

"Terence likes to do it." Mrs. Stamp nodded at her husband, who was warily negotiating a second sip of his Dr. Pepper. "We have a nice manual mower in the shed out back." She lowered her voice. "But sometimes it's too much for him."

"I understand."

"So—back to Ryker." She tilted her head expectantly. "What's the latest?"

"To be honest, Mrs. Stamp—"

Another flap of her hand. "Please, hon. Call me Pearl."

I nodded. "Pearl. To be honest, I was hoping to ask you about Ryker. Was he acting strangely the last time you saw him?"

She pursed her lips. "Now that you mention it—he always drops in for a Dr. Pepper after he's finished with our lawn. Last time, he seemed distracted. Didn't even finish it. I thought to myself—" She tapped her nose again. "Financial problems." She flexed non-existent eyebrows. "So I got out a little of my knitting money and offered to pay him."

"Don't you usually pay him?"

She shook her head. "Ryker never takes a penny. He bundles up the recycling for me, too. He refused payment that time as well. Then he left. Terence and I had no idea anything was wrong until we read that story in the paper."

She stared out the window, wrinkled fingers gripping the arms of the recliner. *Bella* jumped onto her lap, and Pearl absently caressed the dog's fur. *Bubbles* and *Barney* were silent, heads tilted as they watched her from their knitted perches. The only sound in the room was the soft fizzing of the opened cans.

Pearl shook her head vigorously before refocusing her gaze on me. "We'll pay *you*, of course, Verity. Don't worry about that."

I smiled, making a mental note not to take her money. "We can talk about it later." I lifted my Dr. Pepper for a sip. "Why do you think Ryker's a scamp?"

"Oh, I meant it in a good way. It's his effect on women. You must have noticed it—being such a good-looking young woman yourself, I mean." She chuckled. "He can't help flirting. Honestly, he even does it with me."

"Did you know he was mentioned in Perry Otis's will? The man who lived in that renovated farmhouse on Tulip Crescent? He left Ryker a valuable painting by Lawren Harris."

Pearl nodded thoughtfully. "I heard about that. But it wasn't just one painting. I heard Perry left Ryker his entire collection."

I recalled the dozens of paintings hanging on the walls at the open house. "Are they all as valuable as *Spirit of the North*?"

"Oh, don't ask me, dear. All I know is that Perry spent a lot of money over the years building that collection. It used to drive his wife to distraction, rest her soul. They never had any children, and he mortgaged their home to buy art in the early days. Once he struck it rich, it only got worse. He wanted to be considered a serious collector. A *supporter of the arts*, if you know what I mean." Pearl rolled her eyes. "It really went to his head, It got so he barely acknowledged Terence and me if we met him in the village. Imagine." She shook her head. "After knowing us for so many years."

"How did he strike it rich?"

"I don't really know. Always assumed it was a business thing."

"Where did he buy his artwork?"

"Most of it right here in the village. At Nigel Hemsworth's shop."

I mulled this over. "If Perry Otis was a serious collector, why did he leave his paintings to Ryker? He's not interested in art. Why not leave those paintings to a museum or something?"

"Well. I'm not one to gossip—"

We both chuckled at this.

"But I think Nigel encouraged it. He knew Ryker was a cousin of Perry's, and there were no other relatives, so he suggested Perry leave the collection to him. I think"—Pearl leaned in, patting her nose—"that Nigel figured Ryker's first move would be to sell the paintings, and he could swoop in and pick up the commission."

"That seems devious."

"Maybe so, but I wouldn't put it past him." She frowned. "Nigel would simply call that good business practice." She glanced at her husband, who had slumped sideways in his chair. His mouth was open, and he was snoring. "Time for Terence's nap."

Pearl walked me to the front door.

"Drop in again, Verity. I hope you'll keep me up to date on your investigation."

"I'm not investigating—"

Another flap of her hand. "Of course you're not." She winked broadly before shutting the door.

CHAPTER ELEVEN

SATURDAY MORNING FOUND me sitting at a pastry-laden table on the sidewalk outside the 5X, helping with Emy's display at the *Go for the Juggler* street performers' festival. As I took up my post under her gaily striped umbrella, I promised myself not to think about Ryker's troubles. Unfortunately, my pledge to take a break from sleuthing didn't last long.

The day started well. Emy insisted I wear a black T-shirt with the logo, *5X Bakery—Where Diets Come to Die,* printed in gold on the front. I added a bright pink button with my own logo, *Coming Up Roses—We Aim to Weed,* in a prominent position.

Although "prominent" on my chest wasn't saying much. I recalled the platinum blonde who snubbed me at Nigel's open house. She would have made an excellent display board. I wondered again if she was the elusive Grace Anderson. The blonde had denied it, but that could have been a lie.

Stop it, I thought. *You're here to help Emy.*

Main Street was closed to traffic for the day so that buskers could perform on the pavement. Gymnasts, jugglers, clowns, and musicians charmed their audiences—especially the children, who watched with rapt attention on their painted faces.

The crowds ebbed and flowed, pressing in around the most popular performers. Normally, that many people milling about would have made me anxious, but I felt calm behind the shelter of the table. And business was brisk, which took my mind off my nerves. Emy always made a special effort for the festival, with one-of-a-kind offerings designed to draw in jaded customers. When she popped out of the bakery and caught me munching on a scone, her eyes twinkled. "Don't eat all the profits," she said before heading back indoors.

I pulled a face behind her back. *Is it my fault she made blueberry-maple scones with almond-coconut butter?* I asked myself. *No*, I replied emphatically. *I'm only human.*

At the other end of our table, Emy's mother, the village's chief librarian, Thérèse Dionne, set up a display of books, then taped a library poster to the nearest antique replica lamppost. Before leaving, she placed a copy of Michael Ondaatje's *In the Skin of a Lion* on the table with a nod to me—a reminder that I had over one hundred pages to read before our next book club meeting.

With a wan smile, I turned my head to watch a surprisingly limber gymnast perform in front of the bakery. My eyes widened as he popped a wireless tennis racquet over his head then squirmed through it down to his feet. I joined the enthusiastic applause.

When the crowd scattered, I spotted the back of Ethan Neuhaus's shaved head on the other side of the street. I wouldn't have predicted that a day watching buskers and street musicians would have appealed to Ethan. Maybe I'd misjudged him. I eyed him curiously.

An older man wearing a beige summer-weight suit, a cigar between his fingers, came up beside Ethan and jabbed his shoulder. I recognized him from his confrontation with Nigel at the open house. It was Isaac Damien.

When Ethan turned and caught sight of Isaac, his habitual scowl deepened. I was too far away to hear their conversation, but it was not friendly. Even from a distance, I saw spit flying. Ethan shoved Isaac's shoulder, forcing him back a step. I stiffened, fearing a fight. Two police officers had passed the bakery on foot fifteen minutes earlier, eating ice cream, but they'd be several blocks away by now. Checking out the cider booth for bylaw infractions, maybe.

Isaac held up both hands in a conciliatory gesture before leaning in to say something else. Ethan stepped back, his face white and drawn. He was no longer scowling.

Isaac turned around to stalk away, shoving the cigar in his mouth. He didn't seem to have many friends in the village. I wondered why he bothered to come back. Aunt Adeline might have an inkling. I made a mental note to ask her.

The shrill wail of bagpipes filled the air.

Isaac melted into the crowd moments before it parted to make room for a band of eight kilted men wearing enormous fur hats. They marched past, pipes skirling.

Behind them came a pickup truck towing an antique steam engine. An overhead banner proclaimed, WILFRED MULLINS FOR MAYOR! Wilf's assistant, the elegant gray-haired Harriet, was behind the wheel of the truck, serenely maneuvering it down the street.

I waved, shouting *"Harriet,"* but she didn't respond.

Human mascots in beaver and moose costumes walked alongside the steam engine, tossing wrapped candies to the children and fridge magnets to the adults.

I grabbed a few of the magnets to read the logos.

WE NEED MORE WILF

WILF'S A NO-BRAINER.

WILF MULLINS—HE DOES THINGS.

I'm not a marketing expert, as Lorne would readily confirm, but these slogans seemed a little off to me. I glanced up to see Wilf leaning out of the steam engine's window, waving at the crowd. Our tiny would-be mayor was a man of the people in rolled-up shirtsleeves, blue suit pants, and a straw panama hat, which he waved enthusiastically.

The rap music blaring from the steam engine was loud enough to drown out even the bagpipes. No wonder Harriet hadn't acknowledged me. She was probably wearing earplugs.

I couldn't quite make out the words, but it sounded suspiciously like a popular tune from an extremely well-known recording artist. *Does Drake know about this?* I wondered. The last three words—*Vote for Wilf*—were in a noticeably different voice from the rest.

Wilf scanned the crowds, waving at anyone he recognized, anyone he didn't recognize, and the odd lamppost.

Verity! he mouthed when he saw me. I waved back.

Then he was gone. The music faded, and the crowd filled back in.

Returning to my post outside the bakery, chanting the catchy rap under my breath, I noticed two well-dressed women conferring over the library books. They each had one open in their hands, but they weren't reading.

One of the women had abundant strawberry-blonde hair, curled and partially pinned up in one of those fake *I-just-rolled-out-of-bed* dos.

"Did you call him?" the other woman asked.

"I tried. He wouldn't talk to me," replied Strawberry Blonde. She lowered her voice to a whisper. I couldn't hear her next sentence.

The intensity of their conversation intrigued me. I strolled to their end of the table, rearranging the baked goods as I went, eyes down.

"Did he tell the police?" the second woman asked.

I leaned in, trying to hear more. It wasn't eavesdropping, not really. If people insist on holding personal conversations in the middle of the street, they have to expect to attract a little interest. I nudged a croissant back into line with latex-gloved fingers, trying to look as if I was too engrossed in my task to be interested in idle gossip.

It hardly mattered, because these two were oblivious. Strawberry Blonde had abandoned all attempts to moderate her tone. She was really worked up.

"I have no idea what he told them. Like I said, he won't talk to me. I'm afraid to call again. What if they're tapping the line?"

"Can they do that on cell phones?"

"I don't know, do I? But I bet they can. What if he tells them about me? What will I say?"

"Why would he?"

"Oh, come on. I mean—murder? That's a scary charge. Who knows what they'll get out of him the next time they question him?"

I was convinced they were talking about Ryker—who, as far as I knew, was the only village resident currently facing a possible murder charge. We've had more than our share of shady customers, though, so I might have been wrong. I edged closer to hear more.

Cheering broke out behind me. I jerked my head around to see Wilf walking our way, flanked by a giant costumed moose holding a boom box blaring the campaign's rap anthem. I suspected we'd be hearing a lot of that anthem over the next month. Unless the copyright lawyers stepped in.

"Verity!" Wilf called over the music, striding up to my table. "How's my favorite client today?" He clasped my hand in both of his then leaned in with a conspiratorial air. "I hope I can count on your support." His grin was infectious as he intoned, "We-need-more-Wilf."

The moose lumbered off. Wilf continued to hold my hand, his head tilted, waiting for my response.

"Of course I'll vote for you, Wilf. Scone?"

He released my hand with a cheerful pat. "Oh, not for me. The campaign trail is laden with calories, I'm afraid. I'd hate to have these pants altered again."

Turning to present his profile, he sucked in his gut while

pressing a hand to his stomach and jutting out his chin. "Looking good, right?"

"You bet, Wilf," I replied.

He winked, then strode off, arms pumping.

I pivoted to face the library display at the end of our table.

The two women were gone.

CHAPTER TWELVE

WHILE WE WERE CLEANING up after the festival, I described the two mystery women to Emy.

"Let me see," she said, pursing her lips in thought while wiping down the folding table with a dishcloth. "Strawberry blonde hair and expensive clothes?"

I nodded. "Actually, her hair was pink."

"It could be Julia Vachon. Her hair changes all the time." Emy paused, her hand resting on the dishcloth, frowning slightly as she stared into the distance. "She even went through a cornrow phase. The last time I saw her, though, she had blue streaks. But that look's a little dated at the moment, so—"

I cleared my throat. "Let's not fixate on the hair. Is Julia a client of Ryker's?"

"Possibly. Lorne says Ryker has a lot of clients. A surprising number are women."

"That's not surprising. Men like to buy riding mowers and do it themselves."

"Not the ones who travel constantly on business. They leave it to their wives. You should focus on Julia. I bet it was her."

I dumped a handful of crumpled paper napkins into the bin. "Because of the hair?"

With a shrug, Emy resumed wiping down the table. "Because her husband's out of town on business." She raised an eyebrow. "A lot."

"What kind of business?"

"An investment company. I don't know the details. Maybe Lorne has an idea."

"I'll ask him."

"It's odd they would discuss Ryker's case in full view of everyone like that," Emy said.

"There was a lot of noise and people milling about, what with the buskers and the parade and everything. Those women didn't even notice me. I think they ducked in off the street thinking they could have a quiet word."

She smirked. "Not realizing they'd be overheard by the village's crack investigator."

"Don't call me that. I'm not a crack anything."

"You are, too. I'm glad you hired a helper for the summer, by the way, because I think you should take on more cases. Keep your hand in. You don't want people forgetting about Hawkes Investigation Agency."

During the winter, Hawkes Investigation had accepted a few minor cases. Lost pets, missing trinkets, and a couple of identity thefts whose victims simply wanted someone else to do the paperwork. But I wasn't committed enough to undertake the training required to open a serious investigation business.

"The only case I'm interested in is Ryker's. Which is completely voluntary. And off the record."

Emy wasn't listening. She was thumbing through contacts on her phone. "Here." She handed it to me, open at *Julia Vachon*.

After reading it, I looked up in surprise. "This is one of Ryker's clients. She phoned me the other day and asked me to drop by. I remember the address."

I copied Julia's other details, including her head-and-shoulders photo, then handed Emy the phone.

Emy arched her eyebrows as she took it from me. "Interesting, don't you think?"

"I certainly do. I'm going over there now to see if she's home." I hesitated. "Oh. I forgot. Lorne took the truck this morning to buy Molly more annuals at the nursery. Can I borrow your car?"

Julia was on her knees in her front yard, weeding a bed of oversized begonias. Pinkish blonde locks tumbled out from under her sweeping straw hat. She wore latex gardening gloves, with rubber knee pads over her stretch capri pants. The professional-grade trowel in her hand was the most expensive make on the market. For someone who relied on a landscaping service to take care of her yard, she was very well-equipped.

She looked up, holding the brim of her hat away from her eyes, as I parked Emy's Fiat in the driveway. When I got out, Julia rose to her feet, stripping off her gloves and dropping them by the flower bed.

Smiling, I extended a hand. "I'm Verity Hawkes. You called me?"

She gave my hand a listless shake, then let it drop. "I did. We're hoping you can take over lawn duties for us."

"From Ryker Fields?"

"That's right."

I turned away from her to study the begonias. "Those are lovely."

"Thanks. The lawn?"

"The short answer is, yes, of course I can. But—" I swiveled to face her. "Could you tell me when you last saw Ryker? And did he seem—different?"

Her face clouded. "Let's go inside."

Shrugging, I followed her up stone stairs to a slate patio, then into the house. A blast of chilly air hit us when we crossed the threshold. I shivered. The air conditioning was turned up to gale force.

Tossing her hat onto a hall table, Julia slipped out of her rubber clogs. "Would you like a drink, Verity?"

I hesitated, hoping to avoid any more Dr. Pepper. "I'm good, thanks."

"Well, I need a vodka and tonic. Come into the back."

I leaned uneasily on the marble island of the Vachons' all-white kitchen as Julia plonked ice cubes into a glass. She followed that with a generous measure of vodka and the barest splash of tonic, then took a long swallow.

"Ahh. That's better." Placing the glass on the island, she turned her attention to me. "Ryker hasn't been here for weeks. Can you fill in for him or not?"

"I don't know what he told you—"

Something flared in her eyes, then was gone. She ran a finger across the marble. "He told me nothing. I know nothing."

I hesitated, eying her warily, then decided to take a leap. Crossing my arms on the counter and leaning over them conspiratorially, I asked, "Did the police talk to you?"

Her eyes widened. "Not yet." Nervously, she picked up her glass to take another long swallow. She replaced it on the island, wiping the condensation off her fingers onto her capri pants before adding casually, "Did you talk to the police?" Without waiting for my reply, she added, "I guess you did, since you and Jeff Katsuro are..." She swallowed hard. "An item."

"How did you know about Jeff?"

"Ryker told me."

"When did you talk to him last?"

She darted a look at me. "Why do you keep asking?"

"No reason. I only thought maybe he told you why he's..." Frantically, I tried to come up with a reason for my question. "Not cutting your grass anymore," I offered.

She frowned. "No. What did you tell the police?"

I hesitated, mulling over the consequences of lying to her. It was worth the chance. I was certain she wouldn't repeat any of it. "I told them nothing. Ryker's a good friend of mine. I'm not going to make trouble for him—or his friends."

She pulled out a leather stool and slumped onto it with a sigh of relief.

"You're friends with him, too, Julia. Very good friends."

She pulled a face. "I'd rather it didn't get out."

"Why not?"

She looked surprised. "Why do you think?"

"Because your husband doesn't know. And you'd like to keep it that way."

"Look," she said. "I can't help Ryker."

"How often do you see him?"

"I don't anymore. Not since he met that...woman in Strathcona." She spit out the word *woman* as if implying something much different.

"The one who's dead?"

She nodded curtly. "She had dangerous friends, obviously."

"Why obviously?"

Julia merely snorted.

"How did you get involved in the first place?"

"My husband's often away on business. I asked Ryker to come in for a drink one afternoon after he cut our lawn. It got to be a regular thing, then—it became more than a drink. We used to meet at that motel on the highway."

"The Sleepy Time?"

"That's the one."

This was a stroke of luck, because I happened to know two residents of that notorious place who would happily tell me anything they knew about Julia and Ryker's trysts.

Actually, I knew three residents, but the rooster was unlikely to divulge anything useful.

Julia straightened on the stool, reaching for her glass. "Ryker was really taken in by that bitch. He said we were over—that he didn't want to mess around anymore."

Another surprise. *Was I right about Ryker wanting to settle down?*

Watching carefully to gauge her reaction, I asked, "Is it possible this conversation took place around the time those women were killed?"

She took another sip of her drink and carefully set the glass on the island before replying. "I don't recall."

"Julia, you have—"

"Hey," she said. "I'm not proud of what I did, but it was only a bit of fun. There's no reason to upset my husband."

"Ryker could go to prison for life," I said coldly. "That won't be much fun."

She shrugged. "Well, that's a shame. But if he got himself involved with someone who caused him grief, how is that my fault?" She drained her glass, then rose to put it into the dishwasher, closing the door with a decisive *click* before turning to face me. "Ryker cut our grass every Tuesday. Is that doable for you?"

At my nod of agreement, she escorted me to the front door.

CHAPTER THIRTEEN

I DROVE my truck into the Sleepy Time Motel's parking lot then immediately slammed on the brakes, hitting them so hard my aunt's Peace medallion hanging from the rearview mirror smacked against the windshield. If it hadn't been for the seatbelt holding me back, I would have, too.

A blur of brown-and-white feathers topped with a red cockscomb darted across the pavement in front of me, followed by a gaunt, middle-aged man with wild hair and a huge nose. His plaid shirt was folded up to the elbows and tucked into saggy-assed blue jeans.

Halting briefly, he waved a gnarled hand. "Verity," he acknowledged before racing after the rooster, who had darted behind the low-slung motel.

"Carson," I replied automatically, even though he couldn't hear me.

Carson Breuer, the handyman who was restoring Rose Cottage, had taken his pop-up tent trailer to Key West for the winter, along with the rooster I'd rescued from one of those shady characters I was always running into. Although Reuben was technically my pet, I'd long since granted owner-ship to Carson, who always carried sunflower seeds in his pocket for his avian friend.

When they returned from Key West, Jeff politely suggested that Carson—whose trailer had been set up in my driveway all the previous summer—might consider seeking new accommodations. Jeff even offered to help with the search.

Not necessary, said Carson, insisting he'd already found "a sweet place" of his own.

Which turned out to be the most notorious motel in Leafy Hollow.

Another middle-aged man, this one lean, muscular, and exasperated, burst around the corner of the motel to run after Carson. My father skidded to a stop in front of my truck. "It's up there," he yelled, pointing to the roof of the motel.

Carson pivoted sharply to look up, shading his eyes with one hand. I did the same. Reuben was strutting along the roof's shallow ridge, puffing up his chest and extending his scrawny neck. I realized he was getting ready to—

Cock-a-doodle-doo.

Frank turned his vivid blue eyes from scrutinizing the roof to scrutinizing me. Then he walked over to my window, which I rolled down.

"Verity," he said.

"Hi, Dad. How're you doing?"

"Git down from there, ya stupid bird," Carson hollered.

With a flutter of brown wings, Reuben sailed off the roof to land a few feet from Carson.

"I'm fine," Frank said. "Nice of you to drop by."

"I thought we should talk. You know, after—"

Carson dove for the rooster, missing it by inches.

Startled, Reuben fluttered briefly in the air before landing again. Then he tilted his head, stepping haltingly on bony legs, searching the gravel for caterpillars.

Carson tiptoed up behind him.

Frank held up a hand to stop me from talking. "I know what you're going to say. And you're right, at the police station the other day I was—"

"I don't want to argue, Dad, but—"

"—completely out of line. Won't happen again. Your personal life is none of my business."

"—I simply can't have you talking to Jeff like that. Wait. What?" I stared at him. "Did you just apologize?"

"Yes," he said with a sheepish shrug. "I'm sorry."

I realized the rest of my rehearsed speech—in which I told him that sure, maybe I didn't know my own mind, but that was no reason for him to muddy the waters with his cockeyed version of parental concern—was now redundant. Too bad. I'd been proud of that speech.

Oh, well. There was every chance I'd get to use it again.

"Gotcha," Carson said, straightening up with Reuben clasped under one arm, his scrawny feet hanging down. The rooster bobbed his head—whether at me, or Carson, or out of chagrin at missing out on the caterpillars, it was impossible to tell.

Carson strode up to my truck, his split and blackened

fingernails stroking Reuben's feathers. "Thanks, neighbor," he said to Frank, as if they were old friends.

Which made sense. Although Frank Thorne had been gone from the village for twenty years, for history buff Carson that was a blink of the eye. His knowledge of Ontario's architectural heritage—and his extremely reasonable rates—had made him the perfect choice to restore Rose Cottage.

"No problem," said my father with a nod, casually twisting his fingers on the sideview mirror of my truck. I recognized the actions of a former smoker uncertain what to do with his hands.

Carson turned his attention to me. "I've been meaning to drop by, Verity. Gonna get a start on repointing the last of the fieldstone."

"That would be great," I said.

Carson mixed the replacement mortar himself. Something about hydraulic lime being better than modern mortar for the cottage's old fieldstone. I didn't really understand it, but fortunately, an occasional puzzled nod was the only input he required from the homeowner.

"You know..." He shifted the squirming rooster to his other arm. "Old workers' cottages like yours often had board-and-batten annexes. We could add one at the back. A replica, like. Be more room inside."

"It's a good idea, Carson, but I could never afford that."

He seemed taken aback by this. "What about that cop you've got living up there? Couldn't he—"

"Whoa, whoa," said my dad. "We're not talking about that, remember?"

"Right, right," Carson muttered. "I forgot."

"That cop's name is Jeff," I pointed out, suppressing a grin.

"Jeff. I knew that. *Jeff.* Nice guy. Well. Gotta get this bird back." Pivoting on one foot, Carson walked to the rear of the parking lot, which faced a shrub-covered ravine. His trailer was set up overlooking the ravine, with a card table, two folding camp chairs, and a beer cooler arranged under its sagging patio shade.

"I thought Carson rented a room," I said, turning to my dad.

Frank shrugged. "He did. But he prefers his trailer."

We watched as Carson tucked Reuben into a makeshift board-and-wire coop, then threw in some seeds before latching the door. Stooping, he disappeared into the trailer.

"Is he okay in there?" I asked.

"Oh, yeah. It's...cozy."

Carson reemerged with a pack of cigarettes in one hand and a beer in the other, then settled himself into a camp chair. After striking a match on its side, he lit a cigarette in his cupped hand, puffed appreciatively a few times, then leaned back to enjoy the sunset.

Frank and I exchanged glances.

"See? He's fine." My dad relinquished the sideview mirror. "Would you like something to eat? Birdie brought me lasagna yesterday." He gestured to his suite, Number 7. It qualified as a "suite," apparently, because it had a mini-fridge and a microwave.

"Who's Birdie?"

He pulled a face. "Birdie Tanner. The new desk clerk.

She's always checking up on my room. *Do I have enough towels, how's the air conditioning*—you know. She seems to have taken a fancy to me."

I grinned. "Like Katia?" Tipsy Jay pub owner Katia Oldani was also taken with Frank. She'd given him so many free meals, refusing to accept payment, that he was embarrassed to set foot in the place. I enjoyed teasing him about it.

"Please don't bring that up," he said.

"Sorry." I smirked, indicating that I wasn't sorry at all. "No to the lasagna, thanks. I have to get home. But I do have something to ask you." Pulling out my phone, I scrolled through my contacts until I found the one I'd copied from Emy. "Do you recognize this woman?" I showed him Julia Vachon's picture.

Frank took the phone from me to peer at the screen before handing it back. "Number 9," he said in a matter-of-fact tone, tilting his head at the motel unit two doors down from his.

"Did she meet Ryker Fields here?"

"Yes."

"Is that why you were at the police station, to tell Jeff about it?"

My dad looked uncomfortable.

"Never mind," I said. "How often did they meet?"

He narrowed one eye. "Are you sure you want to know?"

"Dad. We talked about this. I'm an adult, remember?"

"Yeah. I'm starting to get the idea. They were here a couple of times a week, I think."

"Could one of those times have been the day those women were killed in Strathcona?"

Frank heaved a sigh. "Verity, I wasn't following the guy. I noticed him here a few times, with that woman"—he gestured at my phone—"but I couldn't tell you exactly when. Birdie might know. Although..." He frowned. "Birdie doesn't always write everything down."

I wasn't surprised at that, since this wasn't my first time tracking a suspect to the Sleepy Time Motel. The place was popular with passing road warriors, exhausted vacationers, and prom-night partiers, but most of the year it relied on short-term bookings. Very short term. Apparently, Carson and my dad were able to sleep through just about anything.

On a hunch, I pulled up a photo on my phone of Nigel Hemsworth from his art shop website, then showed it to my dad. "Ever seen this guy?"

He peered at it, brow furrowed. "He looks kinda familiar."

"Then he's been here?"

Frank shook his head. "Not sure. I've seen his face, but I dunno if it was here. You could ask Birdie."

"Is Birdie here now?"

"'Fraid not. Should be back soon, though."

"I'll come back later. Let me know if you need anything in the meantime."

"Really?"

"Nah." I grinned. "I'm just saying that."

He rolled his eyes.

I started the truck and headed home, dreading my solo dinner—frozen pizza, reheated in the microwave. Hopefully there was beer in our fridge.

CHAPTER FOURTEEN

WHEN I OPENED Rose Cottage's front door and walked in, an intoxicating aroma of roasting meat wafted toward me.

"Hi, sweetheart," Jeff called. "I'm in the kitchen."

Yes! I mouthed, thumbs up. Then I did a happy dance in the foyer, Boomer prancing beside me. Jeff, with his consummate cooking skills, would not be reheating pizza.

With Boomer leaping in excitement because, well, meat, I walked through the cottage to the back. It was a short trip. Maybe Carson was right. Maybe I should consider adding a—what did he call it? *A board-and-batten annex.* I made a note to look that up on Google later.

The General watched my progress from his usual spot on the back of the sofa, tail gently swishing. "*Mrack?*"

I stopped to stroke his back. He nuzzled his head against my hand, purring. General Chang had been more affectionate since Wonder Dog's arrival. Either it was Boomer's enthusiastic nature rubbing off on him, or the aging warrior had simply decided to pick up his game in the face of new competition. I don't know why he bothered. The scruffy old one-eyed tom already had Jeff and me wrapped around his paw.

In the kitchen, I leaned against the doorframe to watch Jeff chop onions. He was wearing jeans and a faded black T-shirt, his dark head bent in concentration over the task. His muscular forearms worked the knife as expertly as a cooking-show chef. I marveled at his technique. If I tried to chop onions that fast, I might lose a finger.

Which reminded me of Ethan Neuhaus. *Was it a good idea to hire him?*

I put that out of my mind for now.

"Hi, yourself," I said, rising on tiptoe to kiss Jeff's cheek while steering clear of the knife. "I didn't expect to find you at home. You're working strange hours this week."

"Too many people on vacation. I'm filling in all over the place." He swept the onions off the chopping board and into a waiting pan, where they sizzled and popped. Wiping a drop of sweat off his forehead with the back of his wrist, he gestured to the table with the knife. "Sit down. Dinner's nearly ready. I'm just finishing up the wine reduction."

Casting my mind back over Jeff's patient explanations about other gourmet meals he'd created, I tried to remember what a *wine reduction* was. Something to do with sauces, I recalled. My taste buds tingled in anticipation. "That smells great."

He smiled before turning to the stove to give the pan a stir.

"Nice work on the onions," I added.

"These are shallots."

"I knew that."

Jeff sloshed some wine into the pan. Stirring with one hand, he gestured with the bottle in his other. "Hold out your glass."

I grabbed a wine glass from the table, then accepted a healthy pour of red. "I'm glad you're here," I said. "Because—"

"We need to talk?" Replacing the wine bottle on the counter, he raised an eyebrow.

I noticed there was another, drained, glass by his elbow.

"Something like that." I took a swallow of wine then replaced my glass on the table. My hand trembled slightly.

Jeff slid the saucepan off the heat, wiped his hands on his jeans, and held out his arms. "C'mere."

In one step, I had wrapped my arms around him and lowered my head against his chest. Closing my eyes, I willed the world away. Difficult clients, friends facing murder raps, even puzzling root vegetables—all gone.

Jeff dropped a kiss on my head, then tilted my chin up with his hand. "I'm sorry if I was difficult yesterday."

His black eyes searched mine, triggering a full-body shiver. How could I have said no to this man? *What was I thinking?*

"When I asked you to marry me, I didn't expect you to say no," he continued. "I guess I didn't take it well."

"Sorry," I said dejectedly.

"Don't apologize. I understand." Jeff narrowed one eye. "Unless it was your way of letting me down easy."

"Never," I blurted, tightening my hold on his chest. "I only want to wait a bit."

"That's good." Gingerly, he peeled one of my hands from his back. "But I think I just felt a rib crack." He clasped my hand to his chest, smiling down at me. "I love you."

"Me, too," I said with a fervent sigh. "Love you, I mean." Lowering my head against his chest again, I relaxed into his arms, vowing never to leave that spot.

Until the alarm on the stove started to beep.

"Ooh," I said, taking a step back and giving the oven an interested glance. "Is that the roast?"

Grinning, Jeff pulled on oven mitts, then took a tantalizing tenderloin from the oven. After placing it on a carving board, he slid off the gloves and placed them alongside. "That has to rest for fifteen minutes. Meanwhile—" Picking up the wine bottle, he topped up my glass and refilled his own before gesturing to the table. "Let's talk. For real, I mean."

We sat opposite each other at the vintage melamine table. Jeff slid his chair back to stretch out his long legs, then hooked one arm over the chair back, lifting his wine with his other hand. "So?" he asked, gazing intently at me over the rim of his glass. "How long *are* we waiting?"

I felt a familiar twist of anxiety in my stomach. "Is there a deadline?"

"No, except—with all those lemon cupcakes at Emy's, I'm not certain how much longer I can fit into my old tux."

Jeff smiled in that *just kidding* way I knew so well, but his words had triggered visions of another wedding, in a crowded room at Vancouver city hall. Matthew had not worn a tux, nor I a gown. But I still remembered the scent of the gardenias and tea roses I'd carried. As well as the joy of that day.

And the sorrow that followed.

Pushing my glass away, I sunk my head into my hands. "We're tempting fate."

"Verity, it's not going to happen again. It can't. I mean, what are the odds?"

"I know," I said in a small voice, looking down at the table. "But..."

"I feel guilty too, you know."

I looked up in surprise. Jeff was fiddling with his wine glass, not looking at me. "But Wendy and Matthew will always be a part of our lives." He took another swallow of wine.

Jeff's wife Wendy had died in a hit-and-run accident six years earlier, at the age of 26. I'd been instrumental in determining who was to blame, and Jeff had been grateful. He still carried her picture in his wallet, but he rarely mentioned her.

And I still carried a photo of Matthew, my sweetly goofy husband, in my wallet.

"Grief and joy can coexist," Jeff said, raising his eyes to mine. "I think you know that."

"I do want to marry you," I whispered, close to tears. "More than anything. I hope you know that."

He sipped his wine, watching my face, then put the glass down. "But?"

I heaved a sigh. "But I don't want to walk down the aisle with my stomach in knots, practicing my breathing exercises."

"There doesn't have to be an aisle. If it's the crowd that worries you, we can go to city hall. Just you and me."

"No," I said firmly. "I did that before. This time, I want a bridesmaid and a cake and a band and everything." I hesitated. "Although, maybe I won't wear white."

Jeff snickered. "Sorry. Couldn't help myself."

Leaning over the table, I gave his arm a swat.

"Seriously, though." He wrinkled his brow. "If it's not the wedding, and it's not me, then why—"

"I know it's ridiculous. I know that. But I need to stop thinking about...what could go wrong."

Jeff leaned back in his chair and gave me a long look, fiddling with the stem of his wine glass.

"Please," I said. "Say something."

He smiled softly. "You're right. Something could go wrong. We're taking a leap. But it's worth it. Even if I knew our marriage would absolutely, positively end in disaster, I'd still want to take that step. I love you, Verity. I can't imagine life without you." He dropped his hand from the glass and straightened. "I want to stand up in public and tell the world."

My mouth fell open in amazement. I had never heard such a long speech from Jeff. My heart ached with the desire to jump to my feet, shout, "Yes! Yes!" and leap into his arms.

So why wasn't I?

He studied my face, then smiled again. "Let's talk about something else. How's the investigation going?"

"Wait a minute—are you saying you don't mind me looking into Ryker's case?"

He shrugged. "I was too harsh at the station. Your father has a way of getting under my skin."

"Ha," I said loudly. "Join the crowd." After a twinge of remorse, I reconsidered. "He means well."

"I know. And you were right about Ryker. He could be innocent."

I narrowed one eye. "That's not a ringing endorsement."

"Best I can do for the moment, I'm afraid."

"Then you'll help me?"

Jeff raised a warning hand. "I didn't say that. But I won't discourage you, either. And if I hear anything useful..." He pulled a face. "I guess I'll let you know." He rose to his feet to select a carving knife from his elaborate knife block. "Meanwhile, if the worst happens—and I'm not saying it will—are you able to take on Ryker's clients?"

"All of them? I don't know. I've hired Ethan Neuhaus to help out."

Jeff gave me a lifted eyebrow glance at the mention of Ethan's name, but said nothing.

Morosely, I studied Boomer, who was quivering with anticipation, his gaze fixed on the roast. Every day was an adventure for the little terrier. I wished I could say the same. "To be honest, Jeff, I'm not sure I want to cut lawns forever."

"You could switch to landscaping. Designing gardens, that sort of thing." Pulling over a platter, he laid out slices of tenderloin. "Hire people to do the lawns."

"I guess."

"I take it you'd rather expand your investigation agency?"

"I think...I would."

He shrugged. "At least it's safer than tracking murderers. Or whatever your aunt's been up to all these years."

"Adeline's work always sounded interesting."

Jeff lifted his gaze from the meat to fix it on me. "But dangerous." He transferred the platter to the kitchen table, Boomer a step behind him. While opening the oven to take out the baked potatoes, he pointed to the fridge. "Can you get the salad?"

I opened the fridge door. "When I say goodbye to you every morning, I have no idea if you'll be coming home that night."

He frowned. "You're exaggerating."

I placed the salad bowl on the table. "You can't object to me doing the odd chancy thing when you risk your life every day."

Jeff slid the sauce pan back onto the burner, then flicked it on. "I'm trained for the work I do. And I'm armed. It's not the same."

"I know, but... It's the principle of the thing."

He tilted his head quizzically. "You want me to accept your job change—in principle?"

"Yes. I think I do. At least until it's actually a fact."

He shrugged. "I can do that."

"Pinky swear?"

He smiled, then held out his finger. "Sure."

We linked fingers briefly.

"Now," Jeff said. "Let's have dinner."

Boomer barked in agreement.

With my cell phone alarm vibrating silently under my pillow, I slid out of bed at 2 a.m.—after disentangling myself from

Jeff's arm—then tiptoed to the door in the darkened room. I paused only long enough to pick up the clothing I'd left ready on a chair.

As I reached for the door handle, Jeff stirred and rolled over, leaving a bare arm dangling out.

I hesitated, then tiptoed over to tuck it back under the blanket.

"Hmmfffphh?" he mumbled.

I froze. How could I explain where I was going in the middle of the night? Bending to his ear, I whispered, "Bathroom. Go back to sleep."

"Hmmfffphh." He rolled over in the other direction. This time, his arm narrowly missed General Chang, who had wriggled his way between the pillows and was settling in for a good snooze. The General cracked open his eye, then gave a leisurely feline stretch. It would take a lot more than a roaming arm to roust him from bed in the middle of the night.

Whereas I had an appointment to keep.

CHAPTER FIFTEEN

NIGEL HEMSWORTH SETTLED into a mid-century swivel chair in the antiques showroom of his Main Street shop. If he tilted his head, he could see through the door into his art gallery at the front as well as a sliver of the window with FINE ART AND COLLECTIBLES etched in gold. The art gallery was empty, as usual. He turned his attention to the man sitting opposite.

"What do you expect me to do?"

Isaac Damien blew out a puff of smoke, then leisurely tapped his cigar on an ashtray of blue glass, his gold signet ring glinting under an overhead light. "I expect you to take care of it. Someone has to clean that place out."

Nigel gritted his teeth, fingering the chair's leather arms. "Why do I have to do it?"

"Because you're the only one who *can* do it."

"What about our deal?"

"I told you—it died with Perry. We have to end this."

Nigel's frustration mounted like a trapped creature struggling to escape. He tried to hold it back. Tried to keep his tone friendly. "I don't understand why—"

"You never do," Isaac snapped. "That's how you got us into this mess in the first place." He clamped the cigar back between his teeth. The tip glowed red as he puffed.

Nigel fought back the anger rising in his throat. *Sanctimonious bastard.* "It's not my fault."

Isaac lowered his cigar to glare at him, ignoring the ash dangling from its end. "What? That she's dead?"

"I had nothing to do with that."

Isaac gave a snort. "So you said." He took another pull of the cigar, spewing smoke into the air.

Nigel waved a hand in front of his face, coughing loudly. "Put that thing out. It's bad for the art."

Scowling, Isaac stubbed out his cigar in the ashtray.

"Not there. Take it outside."

Chuckling, Isaac continued to grind the cigar into the blue Murano glass. "What's this thing for, then?"

"You're not supposed to use it. It's from the Stork Club in New York. Early twenties."

Isaac chuckled again. "People still buy this crap?"

Nigel's blood boiled. "It's not cr—"

Isaac rose to his feet, brushing cigar ash from his jacket. "Come on. Who do you think you're talking to?"

Nigel winced as the ash hit the Aubusson. His left eye twitched as Isaac trod over the ash on his way to the door, grinding it into the carpet.

"You have work to do," Isaac said over his shoulder. "I don't want to hear from you until it's over. I'll let myself out."

Nigel waited for the jangle of the bell and the sound of the front door closing. Then he got to his feet to reach for the carpet sweeper.

Once that was done—followed by a quick swipe of the ashtray and a flick of the overhead fan to disperse the lingering cigar smoke—he walked to the front door to snap on the double locks and arm the security system for the night.

After shutting off the showroom lights, he turned to survey his sanctuary. He liked to linger after closing up, with only the soft illumination of streetlamps through the front window to pick out the artwork on the walls. *Nigel and his treasures.* He smiled with satisfaction, his confrontation with Isaac temporarily forgotten.

The shop was divided into three sections. The art gallery made up the first third, and an open doorway led into the antiques showroom that made up the middle, where Isaac and he had been sitting. From there, a door led to a narrow hallway that divided the back third of the building into a locked storeroom on the left and a closed staircase on the right. At the end of the hallway, an exterior door led to parking spaces out back.

The staircase led to Nigel's apartment on the second floor. A thick porterhouse was waiting in the fridge, ready for grilling on the barbecue tethered to a gas line that ran from the kitchen to his balcony. His mouth watered in anticipation.

Then his nose wrinkled briefly as a faint whiff of cigar smoke reached it, puncturing the spell and bringing everything back.

Sanctimonious bastard.

With a shake of his head, he strode through the showrooms to the locked storeroom, where he kept the real treasures—the ones reserved for serious collectors. Too many people objected to items with slightly tricky provenances. Serious collectors didn't care about petty details. What did it matter where something came from, if it was rare and beautiful? And if Nigel added a few dollars to the price to make up for his trouble in procuring it, his clients didn't care about that, either.

He stepped into the dark hallway at the back of the shop, closing the door behind him. A flick of the light switch did nothing. *Damn bulb must be out again.* He glanced up at the ceiling with dislike. He'd have to haul the stepladder out of the storeroom tomorrow.

Well, he didn't need a light. He'd been working in this shop for decades. He could walk the few paces to the staircase in utter darkness, no problem. He even knew exactly how many paces—twenty-two.

He reached the staircase door and placed his hand on its familiar metal doorknob.

Zzzzzzt!

Nigel was lifted off his feet before falling onto the floor's wooden boards with a thud that jarred every one of his bones.

After seemingly endless moments when he couldn't breathe and felt certain his lungs would explode, he finally rasped in a harsh breath. And another.

Then he lay on the floor, collecting his thoughts.

Son of a...

He knew exactly what had happened. With large enough

batteries and a bit of copper wire, you can electrically charge anything metal—like a doorknob.

It was a good trick, he had to admit. Although, in his day, he never would have used that much current.

After a little more deep breathing, and a lot more cursing, Nigel staggered to his feet. He nudged open the wooden door with his foot, then stumbled up the stairs to his apartment, cradling his burned hand.

This wasn't over.

CHAPTER SIXTEEN

LORNE INSISTED we park hundreds of yards from Molly Maxwell's vandalized plants before trudging up the country road to her house. He also insisted we take care not to be seen. We accomplished this by crawling through shrubbery along the side of the road.

"Is this really necessary?" I objected, brushing a scratchy branch out of my face. "There's nobody here to see us."

"Someone could come along and blow the whole operation," Lorne replied over his shoulder.

"Right," I muttered. "And that would be bad because—"

"Keep up, you two," Lorne called.

Emy crashed about in the undergrowth behind me. "Coming," she croaked in a feeble voice.

As team leader, Lorne was wearing a massive backpack. It was far bigger than we needed for the shortbreads and thermos of tea Emy had packed for us—even considering the big bag of crunchy "party mix" I added at the last moment.

That backpack was huge—big enough to hold a dead body. *Where did that horrid thought come from?* I wondered, briefly distracted.

Thwack! A prickly branch took advantage of my moment's inattention to slap me in the face. *Bloody flora.* "Are we there yet?" I called.

"Stop," Lorne replied.

I halted instantly, like a well-trained infantry soldier.

Emy ran into me, sending me thudding into Lorne's backpack. It was like hitting a wall.

"*Oof,*" I said, my face squashed against the canvas backpack.

"*Sorry,*" Emy hissed. "Are we there yet?"

Ducking my head to see around Lorne, I scanned the area. Molly's bungalow loomed ahead of us. The new pink and white begonias I'd planted in her garden glowed in the light of the full moon.

"All clear," Lorne said in clipped tones before stepping onto the lawn and heaving the backpack off his shoulders. He zipped it open.

"Thanks," I said, reaching out a hand. "I could use a cup of tea."

But instead of the thermos, Lorne extracted three metal sticks, painted black, followed by a huge roll of something that looked like nubby brown-and-green-patterned fabric.

He slapped the sticks onto my open palm. "Could you open these for me?"

"Sure." I stared at them.

Lorne was unrolling the fabric on the grass. "Twist them

in the middle and pull them out to their full length," he instructed over his shoulder.

I tried to follow those instructions. "*Ouch.*"

"Mind the sharp end," he added.

"Too late," I muttered through gritted teeth while sucking blood from the cut on my finger. "What's this for, anyway?"

"Camouflage," he replied without looking up.

Emy and I extended all three stakes to their full four-foot length. "Now what?"

"Stick the sharp ends in the ground there, there—and there," Lorne said, pointing.

When we were done, the stakes formed a line opposite Molly's garden. Lorne snapped the unrolled fabric to the first stick, top to bottom, then extended it over the middle stick and drew it to the third, snapping it into place.

He stepped back to assess his handiwork. "Cool, eh?"

Emy and I joined him in admiring the newly erected screen.

"You can't even see it," I marveled. "It fades right into the bushes."

"Camo netting," Lorne said. "Found it online. Same-day delivery, too."

Within moments, we were hunkered down behind the mottled screen. We could see Molly's garden through the netting, but we couldn't be seen from there. I poked a finger through one of the rubber fabric's tiny holes. "This is amazing."

"I know," Lorne said. "The visibility is remarkable."

We crouched in a row, facing Molly's house, and waited.

And waited.

As with all our stakeouts, the initial excitement rapidly segued into uncomfortable tedium. The screen was too short to allow us to stand. Instead, we sat, we crouched, we lay on our elbows, we turned, and we shuffled. No position was comfortable after a while.

"Ow," I complained as somebody shoved an elbow into my back for the umpteenth time. "Watch it. Are we out of tea?"

"I'm afraid so," Emy said, rooting through the backpack. "Shortbreads are gone, too."

"What about the party mix?"

"Lorne polished off the last of it half an hour ago."

"Even those hard little pellets everybody leaves to the end because nobody likes them?" I whined. "Are they gone, too?"

"Afraid so."

"Shhh," Lorne hissed, raising night vision goggles to his eyes. "Look."

Flopping onto my stomach, I turned to take in the scene.

"Awwww," I crooned. "Cute."

A fluffy brown bunny hopped hesitantly across the lawn, stopping occasionally to nibble a few...

"Wait a minute—is that thing eating my begonias?"

"Looks like it," Lorne said from behind the goggles. "But not for long." With his other hand, he pointed to the left.

I followed his finger. Two fat raccoons were waddling across the grass, headed for the rabbit—and the begonias.

The rabbit jerked its head up in alarm, leaves hanging from its mouth.

The raccoons ignored it, heading instead for the flowers.

Once there, they started digging. They worked furiously, their paws a blur, throwing earth up behind them as they uprooted the first plant. Then the next. Those hideous rodents worked their way along the entire row, spewing soil and begonias in their wake.

Behind our camouflage netting, I whimpered. "Look at the mess they're making."

Emy patted my shoulder consolingly. "At least we've identified the vandals."

I sighed. Peering through the netting, I watched the raccoons at work. "It's almost as if there was bonemeal on those plants. Why else would they do that? There aren't any grubs in that soil. I would have noticed."

"Do raccoons like bonemeal?" Emy asked.

"It attracts lots of animals. But I didn't use any in Molly's garden. Aunt Adeline always advised against it. Ryker never uses it either. He told me once that the odor draws wildlife, so to stay away from it."

"Do coyotes like it?" Lorne asked in a noncommittal tone.

I chuckled. "I doubt it. But why do you—*arggh*." My words shriveled in my throat as I pointed a shaking finger. "That's a—coyote," I finally managed.

"Yes." Lorne nodded. "It is."

"*Cripes.* Are we downwind?" I clapped a hand over my mouth, hoping to muffle my carbon dioxide emissions. I read once that can help with pest deterrence. Although, come to think of it, they may have meant mosquitos.

"Coyotes don't attack humans," Emy said.

"I don't know about that. This one looks a little thin," I

countered, lowering my hand and continuing in a whisper. "It might not be particular about the source of its dinner."

The raccoons, too clever to risk a confrontation with the latest arrival, backed away, chattering furiously, fur sticking straight up on their backs.

I figured they were safe. A full-grown male raccoon can easily weigh thirty-five pounds, and their teeth and nails are razor sharp. If I was a coyote, I'd take a pass in favor of a tasty, defenseless bunny.

Sure enough, when the coyote caught sight of little Peter Rabbit, it crouched, tail swishing. With horror, I realized that adorable creature was about to be torn limb from bloody limb right in front of us.

The coyote advanced furtively toward the bunny.

I sucked in a breath. Let nature take its course?

Not while I'm around.

"Stop," I shrieked, jumping out from the bushes, swinging my arms in the air. "*Stop.*"

Too late, I remembered the camouflage netting.

As I burst through it, the stakes yanked out of the ground, and the rubber netting wrapped around me like fingers of doom. The more I tried to fight it off, the tighter it gripped. I staggered forward, stumbled, and fell—wrapped as tightly as Frodo in the lair of the giant spider.

I rolled to a halt, swaddled in the netting—and found myself nose to snout with the astonished predator. I don't know who was more surprised—the coyote, the rabbit, or me.

The coyote lowered its head, fur silently rippling on its neck, to regard me quizzically. I could almost hear it pondering the eternal question: *Is this thing—edible?*

We locked eyes. His were yellow and glowing.

I stopped breathing.

The bunny, no doubt sensing a lucky break, darted off, bounding and zigzagging across the lawn.

The coyote raised its head, tracking the rabbit with its yellow eyes, then trotted after it.

Sucking in a painfully compressed breath, I scrunched my eyes shut, relishing my narrow escape.

"Verity!" Emy's voice rose in alarm as she shook my camouflaged form. "You're not hurt, are you?"

"No," I sniffed, opening my eyes. "But I could have been."

She back-slapped the approximate location of my arm. "Stop scaring me like that. Lorne, we have to get her out of this."

"On it." He rolled me over.

"What are you doing? That won't work," Emy said.

"I need to find the edge of the netting," he said.

"Can't breathe," I said, with my face pressed into the ground.

Lorne heaved me over in the other direction.

I spit grass out of my mouth. "Can we speed this up a bit? My legs have gone to sleep."

"Lorne, you have to cut it," Emy said.

"But then we'll never be able to use it again."

I gave him my most baleful stare.

"Okay, okay." After flicking open his Swiss army knife, Lorne carefully cut the netting into strips.

Before long, I was sitting on the grass, rubbing my arms

and legs to get the circulation back. "Blasted wildlife," I muttered.

By the time I stood up, Lorne and Emy were laughing so hard they had to lean against each other for support.

"I'd forgotten how much fun you were on a stakeout," Emy said, wiping her eyes. "Leaping into action like that."

I regarded her morosely. "I suppose you would have let little Peter Cottontail be eaten in front of our very eyes?"

"Serves him right for all the damage he did," Lorne said.

I scowled at him. "You're a hard man, Lorne Lewins."

Emy doubled over with another snort of laughter.

"Oh, come on," I said. "That's not—"

"Shhh." Lorne grabbed my arm, signaling at the road. The sound of an approaching car grew in volume. "Quick —hide."

We dove into the bushes.

"Ow. Get off me." I swatted an arm away.

By the time the car door opened and a figure stepped out, we were lying shoulder to shoulder under a lilac bush.

Lorne trained his night goggles on the intruder. "Target acquired," he whispered.

"Lorne—it's a full moon. We can see him fine."

He ignored me. "Target on the move."

The intruder approached the house, but since he or she was wearing a black hoodie, we couldn't identify them. Until the newcomer reached the destroyed plants. The figure hesitated, surveying the damage, before tossing back its hood to reveal a tousled thatch of red hair.

"That's a woman," Emy whispered.

I peered at the black-dressed figure, trying to make out her face. *Could this be Grace Anderson?*

As she turned in our direction, moonlight reflected off a can of spray paint in her hand. She strode to the side of the house, vigorously shaking the can, then disappeared around the corner.

I drew in a sharp breath. "She's headed for the gas meter. We have to stop her. That paint might muck up the gauge. You can't be too careful with gas."

Lorne rose, goggles hanging from his neck, and gave a sharp wave. "Move in." He trod silently toward the house, bent over in an impressive semi-military stance.

Emy and I strolled after him, using our normal upright stance. I tugged at her arm. "Move in?" I whispered.

She whispered back, "I blame Gregory Peck."

Before I could reply, an ear-splitting shriek rent the air.

Lorne backed off so rapidly, his hands raised in surrender, that he trod on my toes.

"*Ow,*" I howled, hopping on one foot. "What the—"

I halted mid-sentence.

Before us stood a middle-aged woman, the paint can lying at her feet. Her mouth was wide open and her hands were clasped to her chest. "Who are you?" she asked in a tremulous voice.

Before we could answer, lights came on inside the house, casting rectangles of yellow across the lawn. Then a light over the front door flicked on.

Molly stepped out onto the porch. She held the door open with one hand while the other clutched a flowered robe to her chest. As she squinted at our little group through her Coke-bottle glasses, her mouth dropped open.

"Bridget? Is that you?"

The redhead stepped into the glare of the porch light, hanging her head dejectedly. "Sorry, Mom."

Emy and I exchanged glances. *Awkward*, I mouthed.

We sat around the kitchen table as a thin-lipped Molly filled the electric kettle, slammed it onto the counter, then noisily took mugs from the cupboard.

"Maybe we should leave?" I asked.

Lorne and Emy made for the door.

"No," Molly demanded, pointing a finger at the table. "Sit down. I need witnesses."

We sank into our seats.

"Oh, Mom," Bridget wailed. "You're overreacting."

"Overreacting?" Molly asked, gripping a mug. Her eyebrows rose nearly to the ceiling. "*Overreacting?*"

The temperature in the kitchen rose by several degrees.

"You had no right to damage my property so you could trick me into moving out," Molly continued. "That's what you want, isn't it? For me to sell this old place and move into one of those damned condos?" Wrapping her arms across her sunken chest, she glared at her daughter. "Well?"

"No, it's not—"

With a snort of disgust, Molly turned to the counter to pour hot chocolate mix and steaming water into the mugs, furiously stirring each in turn.

"We worry about you, Mom, out here all by yourself. You're so stubborn—"

"Don't you dare blame this on me," Molly choked out in fury. Her hands shook as she placed the mugs in front of us, then thumped down a platter of tea cakes that rocked as it hit the table.

Nervously, we raised our mugs.

"Well?" she asked, stepping back to cross her arms and glower at Bridget. "Is that all you have to say?"

Bridget morosely studied the hot chocolate in her cup, then set it on the table and pushed it away. "What if you did move? Would that be so bad? This place is a lot of work, especially the garden."

"We cut Molly's lawn and plant flowers for her," I pointed out. "We could do more."

"Yes, but..." Bridget trailed off at another glare from her mother.

"And we identified the vandals," I added.

"Yes. You did," Bridget said, nodding approvingly. "Good detective work, that."

Molly shot her daughter an angry look. "Which means, for the third time, we have to plant the same flowers. Will there be a fourth occasion?"

"No!" Bridget shook her head, eyes wide. "I never touched your plants."

Her mother glared.

"She's right, Molly," I said hastily. "The raccoons were responsible for that."

I had suspicions about what drew those rodents to Molly's garden, but I decided to keep that to myself for now.

"When we replant," I continued, "I'll add pepper spray and ammonia. There won't be a raccoon within a hundred feet of your flowers after that. Although..." I hesitated. "The ammonia might attract the odd cat."

Molly worked her lips. "Thanks, Verity. And thanks for the stakeout, you three. I really appreciate your help." She opened the refrigerator, mumbling, "Especially since my own family is worse than useless."

Bridget winced, looking down at her lap. "That's not fair, Mom," she said in a small voice.

Molly ignored her.

Lorne's flagging attention perked up when Molly pulled out a plastic container and opened it to reveal a dozen sausage rolls. He shifted in his chair in anticipation.

Molly set the container down in front of him. "Help yourself, son. As for you, Bridget—I think you should leave."

"Mom—please. Let me explain."

The atmosphere couldn't get any frostier, so I decided it would do no harm to step in. "I'd actually like to hear that," I said, reaching for a tea cake. "I mean, raccoons can't spray paint, can they? No opposable thumbs."

Lorne smirked over his sausage roll.

Bridget heaved a sigh. "No. That was me."

"Why?" her mother asked, glaring.

"I didn't know it was raccoons destroying your plants. I thought it must be vandals roaming through the neighborhood. It was one more thing you had to deal with, and I thought..." Bridget bit her lip. "I thought, why not add some spray paint? Maybe that way I could convince you this old house was too much trouble."

"How? By scaring me half to death?"

"I never meant to frighten you, Mom," Bridget said, her voice almost a whisper. "But I do worry about you. What if something happened? What if you fell or...took ill suddenly? There's no one nearby to help you." She lowered her head. "I'm sorry. It was a stupid idea, I see that now."

No one spoke. Except for Lorne's chewing, the room was silent. He reached for another sausage roll.

Molly shifted from one foot to the other. "Well... I suppose you meant well."

"I did, yes. And then, when you got that offer on the house—" Bridget spread her arms, shrugging. "It seemed like the perfect opportunity for you to move somewhere safer."

Molly stiffened. "So you wanted my money."

"*No*," Bridget blurted. "How could you think that? Everything's in your name, and it still would be."

Molly folded her arms again. "It's none of your business what I do with my money."

Before hostilities could escalate further, I held up a hesitant finger. "By the way, Molly—I haven't been able to reach Grace Anderson, the woman on that business card you gave me. I get a voice mail message saying, *this mail box is full*."

Molly tapped her foot, regarding her daughter with narrowed eyes. "Don't worry about it, Verity, because I'm never leaving this house."

"*Mom*," Bridget wailed. "That's not—"

Molly pointed a finger. "Don't you tell me what to do. I may be decrepit, but I'm still your mother."

I excused myself. "Bathroom?" I whispered with a tentative gesture toward the hall.

"At the back, Verity," Molly said before resuming her tirade.

Stepping into the hall, I turned in the direction of the bathroom, intending a quick pit stop before dragging Lorne away from the sausage rolls and making our excuses. But my attention was drawn by rows of framed art on the walls. They weren't the usual family photos and out-of-date calendars—although there was one framed picture of Molly and her husband, taken decades earlier when her now-white hair had been bright red.

Most of the pictures on the wall were oil paintings. My recent re-thumbing of *Modern Art for the Time-Challenged* had not been rigorous enough to allow me to identify the artists, but they didn't look like the kind of works you picked up at garage sales. These were beautiful. A business card was tucked into a corner of one dusty frame.

HEMSWORTH'S FINE ART AND COLLECTIBLES
LEAFY HOLLOW, ONTARIO

I nodded, intrigued. That Nigel really got around.

By the time I returned to the kitchen, Emy was tilting sideways in her chair, eyes closed. Molly and Bridget were still talking, although in relatively civil tones.

I caught Lorne's eye, and he shook Emy's arm. "C'mon, babe. Time to go."

As we made our way across the lawn, I paused by the ruined flowers, bending to pick up a handful of soil to sniff.

The unmistakable odor of bonemeal filled my nostrils.

CHAPTER SEVENTEEN

MUCH TOO EARLY THE next morning, I drove my pickup into Ryker's driveway and parked beside his dusty black truck. Someone had swiped their fingers through the *Wash Me* slogan, but the rest of it was still dirty. As I switched off the ignition, the blinds in the front window flickered briefly.

That had to be Ryker, because I knew Emy was detaining Shelby at the bakery, as per our plan. Emy had agreed to text me the next time Shelby came in, so I could dash over and interview Ryker without his sister getting in the way.

It was a good plan, too, except we hadn't counted on a sleepless night stalking plant rustlers.

It was only after I flung one arm out from under the sheets to grapple for my beeping phone, then opened my bleary eyes to read Emy's text, that my sleep-deprived brain realized what time it was. With a groan, I crawled out of bed to splash cold water on my face.

The other side of the bed was already empty—Jeff had let me sleep in when he left for work.

He did leave a note on the pillow, though.

Your turn to make dinner tonight.

I pictured him smirking as he wrote it.

Fine. I might not be as talented a chef as my honey, but I was very clever with a takeout menu and a credit card.

Now, as I watched Ryker's window blinds from my truck, I rehearsed my questions. For instance—why did he refuse to provide an alibi? Was it because of his affair with Julia Vachon?

Ryker had to know I was outside—there was no mistaking my Pepto-Bismol-pink pickup. *Good.* I was tired of beating around the bush. And I meant that literally, given our stakeout of the previous night.

As I walked up the path to Ryker's front door, my running shoes trod over weeds sprouting between the paving stones. Apparently, Shelby's newfound filial devotion did not extend to actual work around the house.

Not that it took long for weeds to sprout at this time of year. Everything grew like blazes in May and June, reaching for sunlight in crowded borders. *Race of the ground covers,* I called it. In Ryker's garden so far, ivy was the clear front runner. Although ajuga was coming on strong.

The weeds gave me pause, though. Ryker was meticulous about his lawn and garden, considering it a showcase for his landscaping services. I'd never known him to ignore it. But then, I'd never known him to neglect his clients, either.

I didn't really know Ryker, though. Sure, we were friendly. But our relationship never progressed much further than a shared meal, a friendly beer at the Tipsy Jay, or a debate about the best organic weed-suppressing practices.

I'd only been in the village a little over a year. Maybe Ryker suffered from episodic depression, and this was the latest bout. But Emy had known him since high school, and she'd never mentioned anything like that. Other than a stint in juvie as a teenager—and that was no secret; everyone in the village knew about it—Ryker had never been in trouble with the law. Even then, Emy insisted he was covering for a girl-friend when he copped to the juvie charges.

Being a murder suspect was depressing—as I well knew— but it couldn't have sparked his current gloom, which started well before the discovery of the two bodies in Strathcona.

However, those women had been dead for some time. If he *did* have something to do with it...

No. Ryker Fields could never kill anybody. The whole thing was ridiculous.

I marched up to his door. I hammered on it, then leaned on the buzzer for good measure.

"Come on, Ryker," I yelled. "I'm not leaving. If you don't answer this door, I'll make some real noise." I kicked the door several times, scuffing the panels with the toe of my running shoe. "Ryker?"

No answer.

"Ryker!"

The door cracked open. Ryker peered out, squinting into the sunlight with a hand over his eyes like a vampire unwill-ingly roused from his coffin. Matted blond hair fell into his eyes, and several days' worth of stubble covered his chin. "What do you want?"

"I want to talk to you."

"No." He gave the door a half-hearted push, but I had my shoulder against it.

"Stop being ridiculous," I said. "Everyone's worried about you." I shoved the door hard.

Caught by surprise, he stumbled back a couple of paces. I stepped over the threshold, then closed the door behind me. "We need to talk."

Ryker turned on bare feet to walk up the three steps that led into the living room of his split-level. A too-small T-shirt stretched over his muscular chest and arms, and wrinkled track pants hung from his hips. I recognized the clothing of someone who hadn't done laundry in a while.

I followed after pausing to glance around. A stack of *Fields Landscaping* baseball caps had fallen off a shelf and lay scattered across the entryway. Several bore dirty shoe prints. Other, equally dirty, prints led up the carpeted stairs to the living room. It looked as if Ryker wasn't letting his cleaning service into the house, either.

When I reached the top of the stairs, I found him flopped on the sofa with his feet on the coffee table. Empty beer bottles clustered on the table, their labels peeled away in strips.

I veered off into the kitchen, where I switched on the electric kettle. "Tea?" I called over my shoulder as I rummaged through the cupboards for tea bags and sugar.

Ryker merely grunted.

"I'll take that as a yes," I said cheerily.

Empty takeout containers were stacked on the kitchen counter. Obviously, Shelby wasn't doing any cooking, either.

I would have thrown them away, but the trash bin was over-flowing.

Once the water had boiled, I carried two mugs of sweet, hot tea into the living room and placed one in front of him. "Drink that."

He regarded the mug forlornly before picking it up to take a sip.

I watched, sipping my own tea, until he drained the mug and placed it on the coffee table.

"Now," I said. "Start at the beginning and tell me what's wrong."

He eyed me suspiciously. "Are you going to tell Jeff?"

"Not if you don't want me to."

"The lawyer said not to talk to anybody."

"I'm not anybody, Ryker. You know you can trust me." When he didn't reply, I added, "Your clients have been calling me. They're concerned. As are your friends."

"Thanks for..." He cleared his throat before resuming. "Taking on my clients."

"No problem. I hope you can take them back soon. But tell me—" I leaned forward. "What's wrong?"

Ryker heaved a sigh, then leaned back, stretching his hands behind his head. The maneuver exposed several inches of well-defined abs. He seemed oblivious.

"What's wrong?" he asked in a monotone. "I'm a murder suspect, for one thing." He lowered his arms then clasped them across his chest.

"Have you been charged?"

"No."

"Then you're simply assisting the police with their enquiries."

Ryker shook his head. "You have no idea—"

"Hang on." I held up a finger. "I have a good idea what it feels like to be a murder suspect."

Sadly, that was true, I thought. On more than one occasion, in fact.

"I don't know why the police pick on me," I continued. "Maybe I just have one of those faces."

A brief grin flashed across his features. "You do get into trouble from time to time, don't you, Verity?"

I smiled back. "Remember the mess I made of Yvonne Skalding's wisteria?"

"She was furious." His lips twitched. "Of course, she's not in a position to care anymore." He chuckled.

Mrs. Skalding had not been a favorite client for either of us. It seemed unkind to make fun of a woman who wasn't alive to defend herself, but if it brought a smile to Ryker's face, I could live with it.

"Whatever's bothering you started before you heard from the police. You're upset about something else. Tell me."

He sighed again. "It'll take some time."

"I'm not in a hurry." I cast a glance over my shoulder at the stairs to the front door. There was no telling how long Emy could delay Shelby. She might return at any moment. But I didn't want to rush Ryker's confession—if that's what it was. "Go ahead. Start at the beginning."

He rubbed a hand across the back of his neck. "Verity, when you first arrived in the village, I had a...bit of a thing for you."

"I noticed, and I was flattered. But—"

"Jeff happened. I get it. No hard feelings."

"I never thought you were the settling-down type, Ryker."

He shrugged. "Time takes its toll on all of us."

I suppressed a smirk at the thought of the handsome, buff, and charming Ryker Fields being affected by the passage of time. He'd still be attracting women in a nursing home.

"Anyway, a while back I met Dakota Wynne. We really hit it off. It was almost as if—as if we'd always known each other. Our relationship was intense." He lifted his eyebrows. "If you know what I mean."

"I get the idea, thanks."

"I thought maybe she was...the one. I was even thinking about—"

"Marriage?" I blurted without thinking.

He looked taken aback. "You look surprised."

"Not at all," I improvised.

"But then—" His face clouded. "She ghosted me. I called. I texted. No reply. Until about two weeks ago."

"What happened about two weeks ago?" Given that Dakota Wynne had been bludgeoned to death in her home around that time, I wasn't sure I wanted to know the answer. I steeled myself. "Go on."

"Dakota phoned me. She said we had to talk. I met her, in Strathcona, at a restaurant. She didn't want to meet at her house. Didn't explain why. The minute I got to the restaurant and saw her, I could tell something was wrong. She wouldn't even order dinner. She had a drink in front of her, and I could tell it wasn't her first." He burbled air through his lips, with his gaze fixed on the far wall, over my head.

"Did she tell you what the problem was?"

Ryker rose to his feet and paced the length of the room. I followed him with my eyes.

"She said she couldn't see me anymore."

"Why?"

"Because..." He hesitated, and his face darkened. "She was my sister."

CHAPTER EIGHTEEN

MY MOUTH DROPPED open as I stared at Ryker. *Had I heard him correctly?*

"Your—sister? How is that possible?"

"My father had more than one family, apparently. Nobody knew."

My mind raced. "She was a half-sister, then. Wait a minute—this is *another* sister?"

"Technically, yes. Which doesn't change the fact that I..." He looked away.

My voice dropped to a whisper, even though we were the only people in the room. "You slept with your sister."

Ryker collapsed onto the sofa with his head in his hands. "Right," he mumbled.

I'm rarely struck speechless. This was one of those times.

My mind churned through possibilities so quickly I felt as if I was on a tilt-a-whirl. My first thought—*what were the chances?*—was almost immediately replaced by a second, more pragmatic, view. Given the sheer number of Ryker's romantic conquests over the years, the odds that he'd accidentally hooked up with his unknown half-sister were actually pretty good.

I decided not to point that out.

But Ryker looked so miserable, I had to think of something. Something else, I meant.

"Look. You didn't know you were related, obviously, and anyway, now she's dead, so—"

At the word *dead*, he groaned and buried his face even further into his hands.

I winced. "Sorry. *Sorry.*" Regarding Ryker hesitantly, I tried to think of something to say that wouldn't dredge up visions of blood-drenched gardening tools.

"Let's not focus on Dakota's tragic death. I only meant that—no one needs to know about..." I raised my eyebrows. "You know."

He peeked out from between splayed fingers, his expression anguished, and groaned again. Then he jerked his head upright. "Wait. You're not going to tell anybody, are you?"

"Of course not."

"Including Jeff?"

"Cross my heart."

"When this comes out, the entire village will ridicule me. Point fingers." He shuddered. "And worse."

"Forget about that for now. Tell me how you learned Dakota was your sister."

"When I met her at the restaurant that day, she said she had been contacted by a woman who claimed to be her half-sister. This woman had been researching her family DNA when she came across the connection."

"Wait—was this Shelby?"

"That's right."

"Did they meet in person?"

"No. In fact, Dakota told her she wasn't interested, and to leave her alone. Shelby agreed, but mentioned that she'd found other family members as well—a cousin and a half-brother who both lived in Leafy Hollow."

"Dakota must have freaked out when she realized who the half-brother was."

He nodded miserably. "That's putting it mildly. When we met at the restaurant, she was...upset."

Vaguely, I wondered if Dakota insisted on a public meeting because she feared Ryker might become violent. I put that out of my mind as absurd.

"Did she show you the DNA report?"

"Yes. Shelby had emailed it to her." He looked vaguely around. "I have a copy of it here somewhere."

"And then Shelby contacted you?"

He nodded. "Dakota warned me she might, so I wasn't surprised."

"Does Shelby know the real nature of your relationship with Dakota?"

"No," he blurted. "God—don't tell her."

"I won't." I hesitated. "But who could have killed Dakota? And that other woman? It's all so unbelievable."

"I know," he said in an anguished tone. "I know."

"What did the police suggest as your possible motive for killing two women in cold blood?"

"They seemed to think I was...jealous. That I flew into a rage, was how they put it. They thought Dakota dumped me and that set me off."

"But she did dump you."

He slumped back with a sigh. "Yeah. But they don't know that."

"Sounds like they were fishing, then. The boyfriend is always the first suspect. You shouldn't take it personally." I tried for an optimistic tone, but Ryker didn't seem convinced.

"Maybe. But what if they find out about...the other?"

"You didn't tell them you were related?"

"Of course not."

"Why?"

Ryker scraped his hands through his hair. "Because of the damned painting," he blurted.

"*Spirit of the North?*"

He nodded. "It's worth a lot of money."

"But Perry left it to you. Why would Dakota be involved?"

"Turns out Perry left it to my father's children. I was an only child, so the lawyer assumed that meant me."

"Then Dakota had a legitimate claim?"

He nodded again.

"Why would Perry write his will like that?"

"It was written a long time ago, when there was a possibility my parents might have more kids." Ryker gave a snort of disgust. "Damn that inheritance. I never wanted it. I don't know why Perry left it to me. What am I going to do with a bunch of paintings?"

"Did Nigel Hemsworth contact you about them?"

"Who?"

"The art dealer in the village. He was a friend of Perry's. I think he wanted Perry to give you the paintings so he could sell them on your behalf and make a killing." Again, I winced. "*Sorry*. Nigel hasn't contacted you?"

Ryker shook his head. "Not that I remember. I suppose he could have."

"Did Shelby mention him?"

"I don't remember. I don't think so."

"Did the police ask you about Nigel?"

"Honestly, Verity, I don't remember a lot of what the police asked me. I couldn't stop thinking about Dakota." He took a deep breath. "They showed me pictures, you know. Of her...body. They said the viciousness of her injuries meant the attack was personal."

"I'm so sorry."

He leaned forward, his nod barely perceptible.

"But wait—didn't Shelby tell them you were related?"

"I made her promise not to tell anybody in the village about Dakota being our sister. For now, anyway."

I studied his face. "You've been giving Shelby money, haven't you?"

He looked miserable. "Well...she is my sister."

What could I say to that? I rose to gather our empty tea mugs and take them into the kitchen. Ryker's miserable gaze followed me, but he remained slumped on the sofa. I put the mugs into the cluttered sink, since there was no room in the dishwasher. After refilling the tea kettle and turning it on, I walked back to the living room.

"Ryker, this is a mess. You have to tell the police. They'll find out anyway. And then Shelby could be in trouble, too, for withholding evidence."

"I can't. It will make everything worse. You know how the police are."

I didn't think his cynicism was warranted, but given Ryker's juvenile record, I suspected he had reason to distrust the authorities.

"Just tell them where you were on the day Dakota was killed. You have to give them a reasonable alibi, even if you were only at home watching TV."

"I can't."

"Why not?"

"Because I wasn't at home watching TV."

Given how stubborn he looked, I took a wild leap. "Ryker, if you were with Julia Vachon that day, you have to tell the police. They can be discreet, you know. When necessary."

"Julia?" He shook his head. "I haven't seen Julia in months. No. I wasn't home that day because I was in Strathcona." He flopped back against the sofa, nervously patting his stomach. "At Dakota's."

I let out a long breath. *This was bad.* I watched his fingers flick up and down.

Pat-pat-pat.

"But you had already split up. Why did you go to see her that day?"

Pat-pat-pat.

"Ryker?"

He lifted his hand to tug it through his hair, almost as if he was trying to pull it out by the roots. "Dakota sent me a text. Asking for money. She said if I didn't give it to her...she'd make our relationship public." He heaved a sigh. "I couldn't understand why she changed her mind. We agreed we wouldn't tell anybody. So I went to see her."

"Did you talk to her?"

"No. She didn't answer the door."

"Was she at home?"

"I don't know. A neighbor told me she hadn't seen her. I slipped a note through the mail slot and left."

"Do the police have this note?"

"They didn't mention it."

I thought this over. "But that's good," I said. "Because that neighbor can confirm you didn't go inside the house."

"No."

"What do you mean, no?"

Leaning forward with a grunt, he shuffled through a pile of newspapers on the coffee table, then pushed one toward me.

I bent over to read it. The story of the double murder spanned the front page.

Residents in the city's east end made a grisly discovery yesterday when a neighbor believed to be on a cruise was found bludgeoned to death...

Quickly scanning the rest, my eyes lighted on this paragraph.

Ms. Wynne's boyfriend, Ryker Fields, a Leafy Hollow landscaper, was questioned by police and released. So far, he has not been charged.

I ignored the rest of the text in favor of a closer look at the photos of the victims. Dakota Wynne was young, blonde, and vivacious. Rosie Parker was middle-aged with narrow eyes, wispy bangs, and scowl lines around her mouth.

I looked up from the paper, tapping it with my finger. "Did this reporter speak to the neighbor?"

Ryker shook his head. "No."

"Why not?"

He leaned over to point at Rosie Parker's photo. "Because that's her."

"She's dead?" I squeaked.

He nodded grimly. "See why I have no alibi? I can't tell the cops any of this."

We locked glances. He looked years older than his normal—with a shock, I realized I had no idea how old he actually was. Emy had known him in high school, but he had been years ahead of her, and even then, he had likely failed more than once, given his stints in juvie. For all I knew, he could be forty. The circles under his eyes made him look even older.

At the sound of a car door slamming, I jerked my head around to look out the front window. I'd been so distracted by Ryker's story, I'd missed hearing a cab drive up outside.

Shelby was back.

"Ryker," I said hastily, with one eye on the door. "Shelby was Dakota's sister, correct?"

"Half-sister. Different mothers."

"Different—" My head felt like it was going to explode. Ryker, Dakota, and Shelby—three siblings, all with the same father, none of them aware of the others' existence.

"Does your father still live in Manitoba? With your mother?"

"Yes. She's stood by him all these years. I don't know why, given what he put her through."

"What does he say about this?"

Ryker snorted. "He denies it. Says DNA is a load of bull."

The front door opened with a gust of air, then slammed shut.

"I'm back," Shelby called.

Ryker leaned in, speaking in clipped tones. "Listen, Verity. My old man got sent up when I was eight years old. Mom moved to Penetanguishene to be near him. That's how I ended up in foster care..." He slumped back with a gesture of disgust. "I wouldn't believe a word he says."

I recognized Penetanguishene as the location of a maximum security prison north of Toronto. Before I could probe further, a woman's voice called, "There you are."

I twisted my head to see Shelby standing in the doorway, her fingers clutching the twine handles of a brown paper shopping bag. I recognized the logo of Bertram's, the village's upscale grocer.

Shelby held up the bag. "I picked up wild mushroom risotto and grilled salmon for dinner. I put it on your tab, Ryker." She gazed at me, unblinking. "Verity."

"Shelby. Nice to see you again. Ryker has been telling me about your amazing reunion."

Limping slightly, she stepped through the doorway, set the bag on the coffee table, then settled into the sofa next to Ryker. "It's amazing, isn't it? I'm still getting my head around it. To find out you have a brother you didn't know about... It's weird."

That's one way of putting it, I thought.

She reached out to squeeze Ryker's hand. "I should say, *we're* still getting our heads around it, aren't we?"

"Sure," he mumbled, pulling his hand free.

"But Ryker's not your only relative, is he? You found a sister, too."

Her eyes widened. "Did he tell you that?"

I nodded.

She shot a quizzical look at Ryker. "I thought we weren't supposed to talk about her."

He looked away.

Shelby shrugged. "Did he tell you she was that woman in Strathcona—the one who was murdered?"

Ryker shot to his feet and paced to the window, where he stared through the slats of the blind with his back to us.

"Yes," I said. "But I won't tell anyone. I did wonder, though... That DNA service you used. How does it work, exactly?"

She crossed her arms demurely. "What do you want to know?"

"Nothing, for myself, but I have a friend who's considering it. She was wondering... Do these companies send you proof?"

"Not the actual chemical results. Just a list of people in their database that you're related to, based on your DNA. Mostly they're distant relatives—third cousins, fourth cousins, and so on. They give you a family tree, with all the names. If you want to track your relatives down in person, though, it's not as easy as it sounds. There's a lot of legwork involved. Most people don't bother."

"You're not most people, obviously." I tossed her a warm smile.

"No, not me. I had to know. I'm fascinated by the whole thing."

"I'd love to see this family tree. So I could tell my friend about it, I mean."

"I'll be happy to show it to you. Once we get it back from the lawyers." Shelby pulled a face. "They're so cautious. But when they're done with it, I'll let you know right away." She brightened. "Then you can tell your friend all about it."

Shelby swiveled her head, giving her half-brother a long look. "It was strange, finding out I had a little sister I'd never met..." She shook her head. "Dakota wouldn't talk to me, you know. I decided not to pressure her. Of course, I hoped she'd reconsider. But I figured we'd have plenty of time." Sighing, she puffed out a breath. "Just goes to show, doesn't it? You never know. And now she's dead."

Ryker's shoulders tensed, so I hastily changed the subject.

"I noticed that you're limping, Shelby. Did you sprain your ankle?"

She waved off my question. "I've been working too hard in the garden. It's nothing."

That was a lie, but I let it go.

She rose, leaning over for the shopping bag. "I'll put this away for now, Ryker. We can heat it up later."

Taking the hint, I also got to my feet. "I should get back to work. Nice to see you, Ryker."

He grunted without looking at either of us. Whatever he was staring at, it must have been fascinating. *Watching the*

164

weeds grow, maybe? I envisioned Sleeping Beauty's castle with mile-high vines choking it. Hopefully it wouldn't come to that here. Especially since the prince was still inside.

Shelby accompanied me to the door. She hesitated, her hand twisting the knob. "Verity, my brother is quite upset." She dropped her voice to a whisper. "I don't know why he told you about Dakota, but I think it's better if we keep it to ourselves for now."

"I won't tell anyone."

"And..." She hesitated, smiling grimly. "I think you should phone before visiting another time."

"Of course." I turned to go, then whirled with a final question. "How is the inheritance hunt going? Any news?"

Her lips thinned. "I don't know what you mean."

"Nigel Hemsworth. Have you talked to him recently?"

"I don't think that's any of your business." Pursing her lips into a pout, she closed the door in my face.

As I walked down the path to climb into my truck, I felt someone watching me. Shelby, no doubt. I didn't turn around to check.

CHAPTER NINETEEN

OUTSIDE NIGEL'S ART SHOP, I paused to inspect the painting of the three cows in the window. It was still unsold. After a glance at the price tag, I could see why. Clearly, I was not as informed on art as I could be. But I was about to remedy that. I pushed open the front door, setting an old-fashioned bell jangling over the doorframe.

The front of the shop was surprisingly spacious, with artwork hanging on stark white walls under overhead spots.

Nigel and his ears were seated behind a broad desk at the side. He looked up with a smile. "Hello. Feel free to look around. If you need any assistance, I'm here to help." He lowered his head discreetly to study the paperwork before him, but I felt his eyes following me as I strolled from one painting to another.

When I paused a little longer at one work—an abstract painting titled *Endless Spring*—Nigel rose from behind the desk then ambled over to stand beside me, hands clasped behind his back.

"It's a lovely piece, isn't it?" he asked. "The use of negative space in the composition is quite striking."

"Lovely." I offered a dry chuckle. "A little out of my price range, I'm afraid."

He nodded thoughtfully. "Verity, isn't it?"

"Yes." I grinned at him. "I'm surprised you remember. We met at the open house the other day."

"I never forget a lovely face." His smile did not reach his eyes. "I have pieces in the back that are more modestly priced, if you'd like to take a look." He motioned to the open doorway in the back wall.

"Lead the way."

The door led, not to the back of the building, but to a room filled with antiques and vintage furniture. As we strolled through, I paused to admire a grandfather clock of gleaming walnut and brass.

Nigel nodded in approval. "A beautiful piece," he said. "Newly acquired. This way, please."

I followed him through a door into a narrow hallway at the back. Nigel inserted a key into the lock of a door on the left, then ushered me in.

This room was also painted white, but the artwork here was leaning in stacks against the walls. Unlike the ostentatious front gallery, this space had a bargain-basement feel. I suspected that was Nigel's intention, and that the bulk of his sales were actually made here, under the guise of "great deals" or "too much inventory."

Noting my interest, he bent over the nearest stack to riffle through it. "These are mostly estate sales," he said. "The families usually demand a quick transaction. I always tell them I could get a better price if they'd be more patient, but..." He shrugged. "Money talks."

"So these are bargains?"

"They're not cheap," he cautioned me. "Although many of these prices are significantly undervalued—correct."

Drawing from the stack a painting of a blue-gray lake under a blue-gray sky, he held it up for my perusal. "This series of prints is particularly popular. The artist is local."

As he hefted the painting, I noticed a bandage on the palm of his right hand. "Did you hurt yourself?"

Nigel glanced quickly at his hand. "Oh, that." He chuckled. "A slight cut. I was a bit overzealous with the box cutter on a new arrival. Such a lot of packing material these days. It's nothing, but I have to be careful. Even a single drop of blood could ruin a painting. Speaking of..." He held the landscape higher. "What do you think?"

"It's lovely."

But not why I'm here, I thought. How could I broach the subject of Ryker and his unfortunate brush with the law?

Nigel turned to replace the print against the wall. "Or these." He shuffled through several others before pulling out another painting and holding it up. "Very evocative."

"Oh," I said, "that reminds me of the Lawren Harris painting at the open house."

Nigel's eyebrows rose slightly as he cast a downward glance at the picture, which happened to be an abstract swirl of vivid colors that bore no resemblance whatsoever to the brown streetscape I'd viewed at Perry Otis's house.

"I meant the...negative space," I improvised, then barreled on before he could reply. "Will you sell that Lawren Harris painting here? I mean, given that Ryker Fields—he inherited it, didn't he?—might be behind bars before long. I suppose that complicates things."

If Nigel was startled by my conversational swerve, he showed no sign. "Ah," he replied with a gracious air, replacing the painting in the stack, "I really couldn't comment on Mr. Fields' situation."

I adopted a disappointed tone. "Really? I heard you were the executor for his cousin's estate."

"Who told you that?"

"I can't recall, exactly. Perhaps someone at the open house? There was quite a crush. A lot of people wanted to see that painting up close. See if it was real, I guess."

His expression became pinched. "Whatever do you mean by that?"

"Oh, you know. That old guy—Perry Otis?—was a recluse. I heard he didn't let anybody see his collection. Wanted to keep it all to himself. That Lawren Harris picture acquired a real air of legend—as if it was not quite real. You must have noticed how many people were talking about it."

"I'm not in the habit of listening in on other people's conversations," he said in a clipped tone.

Like hell, I thought, remembering his intense interest in Shelby Wynne's movements.

"I guess you're more interested in offloading his house. It's quite something, isn't it? Almost like a castle, what with that silo and all. But a little scandal never hurt sales—am I right?" I leaned in, raising my eyebrows. I considered adding a wink to my performance before deciding that might be going too far. "I heard you sold that Lawren Harris painting to Perry originally. What do you think it's worth today?"

Stiff-lipped, Nigel held out a hand to usher me back into the hall. "I really couldn't say." He turned to lock the door, then strode through the hall and into the antiques showroom.

I hurried after him. "But that's your business, isn't it? Valuing paintings, I mean? Shelby—Ryker's sister—told me they intend to get it appraised. I said you'd probably already done that, but she seemed to think you weren't skilled enough to... Well, I suppose I shouldn't repeat that."

We'd reached the front gallery, and Nigel swiveled to face me, his expression dark. "That woman should mind her own business."

Finally. I'd hit a nerve. Which was good, because I was running out of material.

"What did she do?"

"She made ridiculous accusations. That woman has no class whatsoever." He sniffed, absently rubbing his bandaged hand. "I can always tell."

"You mean she's not interested in art?"

"Hah." He snorted. "Not likely."

"How do you know? Shelby may be uneducated about art"—I grimaced as my assessment of the three cows came to mind—"but that doesn't mean she can't learn."

Nigel puffed out a breath. "That woman's interested in nothing but cold, hard cash."

Tilting my head, I tried to look surprised. "That's a bit harsh. What makes you say so? At the open house, she seemed genuinely interested, I thought."

Naturally, I thought nothing of the kind. But Nigel fell for it.

"You are being naive, Verity. And I'll prove it." He stalked to the front desk to retrieve a cell phone from a cubbyhole. After thumbing through it, he handed me the phone. "She sent me that before she'd even hit town."

I read the email.

Mr. Hemsworth,

I'm sure you've heard about Ryker Fields' inheritance, which includes a very good Lawren Harris painting. I'm writing to inform you that, as a sister of Ryker's, I intend to claim a share of this inheritance. I'll be in Leafy Hollow soon to contact you directly for an estimate.

I glanced up at Nigel. He was scowling.

"That's remarkable," I said. "She didn't waste any time."

"What did I tell you?" He gestured for the phone, and I handed it back. "Is there anything else, Verity? Because I have things to do."

I hurried to change the subject. Appealing to his vanity should work.

"I've been told you're an expert on the Group of Seven."

Narrowing one eye, he replied with a drawn-out, "Yes."

"I'd love to learn more about them. They're Canadian icons, after all. I want to do some research. Could you start me off? Since you're such an authority?"

Conflicting emotions flashed across his face. Then, as I knew it would, his love of pontificating overcame his natural suspicion.

"Well. Let's see—"

Adopting an expression of utter fascination, I settled in for the lecture.

"The Group of Seven was formed in the early decades of the twentieth century by artists who wanted to depict the unique character of the rugged Canadian landscape."

"Yes." I nodded vigorously. "Their paintings are beautiful."

"They're more than that. The Group of Seven is integral to the Canadian identity. They broke from the European tradition of the time to present a more nationalistic viewpoint, a new style of painting. They set out to follow '*the bolder course—new trails,*' as A. Y. Jackson once put it."

"He was a member?"

"Of course."

"And Lawren Harris was—"

"Their unofficial leader. Some people refer to him as the Canadian Van Gogh, although I find that a little fanciful." Nigel pulled a notepad towards him. "Why don't I recommend a few books on the subject?" He jotted down a list, tore off a slip of paper, and handed it to me.

I scanned it quickly. No mention of *Modern Art for the Time-Challenged.* "Thanks." I dropped it into my purse. "I'll check these out."

Nigel sat down at the desk, then began to shuffle papers. I imagined he meant to signal our conversation was over, but I was not that easily deterred.

"I guess Shelby and Ryker plan to shop that painting around, do they? Wait until they get the best deal?"

He gave me a sharp look. "Not at all. Shelby wanted it sold immediately. No restraint whatsoever. She even wanted to take it off the wall at the open house so she could take it to someone she claimed to know—" Miming air quotes, he added, "in the art world." He scowled. "I had to explain the legal ramifications to her."

"Uh-huh." I nodded vigorously before adding, "And those are?"

"Perry's will is still under probate, for one thing. Nothing can be sold until the lawyers are satisfied." He impatiently pushed aside a cardboard file.

"But you have the house on the market already."

"Only to gauge interest. A sale can't be finalized yet."

"Nigel, tell me—why do you think Shelby and Ryker are in such a hurry to get rid of that painting? It seems to me it would be best to offer it for sale at a well-publicized auction, so serious collectors could bid on it. It's a Group of Seven— those can't come up for sale often."

"You are correct. However, I happen to have been privy to the actual contents of Perry's will. He wanted that painting to stay here in Leafy Hollow. Not be swept off to get lost among some eccentric collector's hoard, where no one would ever see it." He looked back at the gallery, lost in thought. "Perry always loved painting. He did many of his own oils over the years, but unfortunately..." He shrugged, returning his attention to the paperwork. "None of them were salable."

"The buyer of *Spirit of the North* has to be someone from the village? That seems unrealistic, given its likely value."

He puffed out his chest. "There are serious contenders in Leafy Hollow, Verity. We're not all paupers. I assume you haven't been here long enough to realize that."

Determined not to rise to his bait, I asked the obvious question. "Why didn't Shelby and Ryker know about this stipulation?"

"It wasn't part of the original will. Perry made his wishes known to me quite recently, in a letter. He intended to amend his will to reflect those wishes. Sadly"—Nigel spread his hands with a sorrowful expression—"there wasn't time."

"Where is that letter now?"

"With the lawyers. Now, Verity, I really must—"

"If the painting has to stay in the village, it seems even odder that Shelby should be in such a hurry to sell it."

"As I said, I had to explain a few things to her. However..." He leaned in. "I suspect a close examination of Mr. Fields' finances would reveal things he'd prefer not be widely known."

"How did you—"

Nigel gave me an incongruous wink. "I've heard things."

"Are you suggesting Ryker has debts? That he needs money?"

Nigel gave a half-hearted shrug. "I'm suggesting nothing. I leave all such observations to the police." He glanced at his watch, then looked up at me with a raised eyebrow.

"Sorry," I said. "I'm going."

My knowledge of wills was a little weak. Luckily, I knew someone who could fill in the gaps—mayoral candidate Wilfred Mullins, who also happened to be my lawyer. I strolled a few doors along Main Street to his office.

After stepping into his royal-blue waiting room, I halted in confusion. Instead of the usual Muzak from the overhead speakers, I heard—

Whannnuaaaa.

Eeep, eeep, eeep.

Whannnuaaaa.

I entered, letting the door close behind me, then approached the reception desk, where Harriet was typing furiously. "Why are you playing whale song?" I asked, pointing to the speakers overhead.

Whannnuaaaa.

Whannnuaaaa.

Eeep, eeep, eeep.

No reply. Harriet was wearing earplugs. I tapped on the edge of the desk to get her attention.

"Harriet?"

She glanced up, recognized me, and removed one plug. "Verity. Go right in. Leafy Hollow Councilor Wilfred Mullins is available to village residents at all times."

"Really? Since when?"

Whannnuaaaa.

Whannnuaaaa.

Harriet winced, casting her gaze to the ceiling speakers. "A little bit of that goes a long way."

Before she could insert the earplug again, I said, "Wait. Why the—" I pointed to the speakers.

Harriet raised an eyebrow.

I answered my own question. "Wilf's gone green, hasn't he? For the campaign."

Harriet put the earplug back in and resumed typing.

Whannnuaaaa.

Whannnuaaaa.

Eeep, eeep, eeep.

I pushed open the door to Wilf's inner sanctum, then closed it behind me, shutting out the marine melody. Here, all was quiet—except for the steady *tap, tap, tap* of Wilf's sausage-shaped pen on his desk. He was leaning back in his electric executive chair with the pen in his hand, contemplating the roll-down screen on the opposite wall.

Formerly, the screen had displayed the drawings for Wilf's scheme—now abandoned—to build the *Cameron Wurst Waterpark* near the rendering plant on the village's outskirts. Cameron Wurst, the original backer of the plan, was a sausage maker in Strathcona. Hence the pen.

Today, however, the screen displayed a three-month calendar whose individual days were heavily marked with colored ink. A banner along the top read *Wilfred Mullins for Mayor—Timeline.* Underneath *Timeline,* someone—most likely Harriet—had added in black marker:

Deadlines & Problems

Problems had been crossed out and replaced with *Opportunities* in a cribbed hand that looked like Wilf's.

The last day on the calendar—election day—was marked with a huge red star and the notation, *Victory Party. Rent arena.*

"Wilf?" I said, approaching the desk.

He straightened up, then hit a switch that lowered his chair a notch. "Verity. Nice of you to drop in."

"I know you're busy, but I need a little legal guidance. It won't take long."

"Sit down. I'm always available to my constituents." He rested a thoughtful hand under his chin. "Shoot."

"Well." I slid into a leather armchair. "It's about wills."

Wilf nodded with a smile. "This takes me back."

I knew he was referring to our first meeting in his office, when I asked him about my aunt. Wilf had advised me to have her declared legally dead. I'd long since forgiven him, though.

"What I want to know is—if someone told someone else, before their death, that they meant to change their will, but they didn't get around to it in time, would their comment be considered legally binding?"

Wilf stared at me for a moment.

"That might be problematic," he said slowly. "Can you be more specific?"

"Did Nigel Hemsworth ever talk to you about Perry Otis's will?"

Wilf's eyebrows rose. "He may have. I couldn't repeat that conversation."

"Because Nigel's a client?"

Wilf's reply to this was even slower. "No. He's not. He was...attempting to procure legal advice without actually paying for it, I think."

"So you can tell me."

"No, Verity." Wilf waved an arm. "It would be unseemly. Perhaps even a tad unethical."

"But not illegal," I pointed out.

He gave me an uneasy glance. "This is about Ryker Fields, isn't it?"

"Are you going to tell me or not?"

He leaned back, studying the *Timeline* with a faraway look in his eyes. "Nigel has a convertible, you know. One of the only ones in the village. We wanted to use it for the parade."

"At *Go for the Juggler?*"

"Yes. But Nigel claimed he was going to be out of town that day and needed the convertible himself."

I recalled the pale blue Mercedes I'd seen parked behind Nigel's shop. "But I saw him at the festival. He was haranguing somebody at the *Million Mime March* booth."

"He was?"

"Yes. And it wasn't fair, really. It's not as if they could answer him back."

Pursing his lips, Wilf lounged in his chair, tapping again with the sausage. *Tap, tap, tap.* He straightened.

"You know, Verity, democracy is built on the backs of volunteers."

"Is it?" My brow wrinkled.

"Yes. Civic duty, that's the ticket. And Nigel simply doesn't have any." Dropping the pen, he leaned in. "He told me a woman had contacted him, claiming to be Ryker's long-lost sister, and that she intended to claim a share of the inheritance. The weird thing is that Perry's will apparently stipulated the children of Ryker's father, not just Ryker. I hadn't known that."

I nodded, since I had known that. "But the change to Perry's will?"

"Ah." Wilf gave a knowing nod. "When Nigel spoke to me, it was merely a *what if. What if* Perry had given him specific instructions, in person but not in writing, regarding the inheritance? Would that be legal?"

"What did you tell him?"

"Same as I told you. Problematic."

"It would be hearsay if it got to court, and therefore not admissible, right?"

"Most likely. Unless he could offer corroborating evidence."

"Like a letter."

"Exactly."

"Is that all he told you?"

"Yes. When I mentioned—very diplomatically—that I normally charged for that type of advice, he clammed up."

Rising to my feet, I turned to the door. "Thanks, Wilf. I owe you one."

"Well..." He fingered his chin again in a statesman-like manner. "Perhaps you could hand out a few pamphlets?"

How hard could that be? "Sure," I said enthusiastically.

On my way out, I was mulling over Wilf's revelation about Nigel when Harriet spoke, causing me to double back.

"Verity."

The top of her gray-haired head was peeking out from behind a cardboard box on her desk. The box hadn't been there when I came in.

I craned my neck to see over the top. "Yes?"

"Don't forget your pamphlets." Harriet tapped the box before turning to her computer screen to resume her typing.

My mouth fell open when I peered into the box. It was packed with shiny leaflets. I picked one up.

WE NEED MORE WILF.

A notation on the bottom read, *Printed on recycled paper*. I replaced the pamphlet in the box, then closed the flaps.

I tapped on the desk. "Harriet?"

She removed an earplug.

I pointed to the leaflets. "How many are in there?"

Returning her attention to the keyboard, she said, "The usual. Two thousand."

Whannnuaaaa.

Whannnuaaaa.

Eeep, eeep, eeep.

Picking up the box with a sigh, I closed the door behind me.

CHAPTER TWENTY

I WAS MULLING over my meetings with Nigel and Wilf as I got back in my truck to drive up the Escarpment road to the plateau above. While I was in Nigel's shop, my father had texted, asking me to drop by the motel.

IT'S AN EMERGENCY, his text said.

Which meant—I knew from experience—there was no real rush. I ignored it for the time being. I was hot on the trail of a clue, and I needed to check in with my aunt.

But first... I reached for my phone to text Jeff. While I was talking to Wilf, I realized there was something about my discussion with Ryker that didn't add up. It was probably nothing, but it couldn't hurt to check.

SURE, Jeff replied. I'LL LOOK INTO IT.

Then I headed up the hill to Lilac Lane and my aunt's new home. Hopefully, she could enlighten me on Nigel's reputation. According to Emy's mother, Nigel had been a practical joker in his youth. The man I talked to did not radiate any kind of humor. Of course, he was older now, with his carefree youth—if it had been carefree—decades behind him. But Aunt Adeline would have known Nigel when he was young. I could count on her for the truth. My outspoken aunt never pulled a punch.

I found Adeline and her partner, Gideon Picard, in matching lounge chairs behind their cottage, which neighbored mine on Lilac Lane. There was a pitcher of lemonade on a low wooden table between them, alongside a plate that bore only crumbs. Possibly it had been loaded with Gideon's famous club sandwiches. I turned to him to ask about replacements, then halted.

Something was different. Something was—I gasped —*gone*.

Gideon's gray samurai topknot had been replaced by a buzz cut that rivaled Ethan Neuhaus's prison-break do. His matching gray mustache and goatee were also MIA.

"Gideon—what happened to your hair?"

He raised a wiry hand to pat his skull. "Gone."

"Why?"

"Because," my aunt said casually, "I told him I had no intention of living with an old hippie, and the man-bun had to go."

"What about the beard?"

"Ditto."

"But... But..." Squaring my jaw, I turned to Gideon. "You don't have to do everything she says."

Grinning, he slid a hand over his head. "I kinda like it. Less work."

I had never been entirely clear about the relationship

Adeline and Gideon had shared over the years, and I wasn't about to question it now. I knew they'd both worked for a shadowy sub-government entity known as Control many years earlier. Some people believed Gideon was at one time a double agent. I didn't believe that, or even care, because he'd done everything he could to save my aunt when she had gone missing and the police had insisted she must be dead. Which was the reason I was in Leafy Hollow in the first place.

It was all too complicated for me. I preferred to dwell in the present.

With a gesture at his octagonal, blue-tinted glasses, I asked, "Those are staying, right?"

My aunt sniffed and looked away.

Gideon winked.

"Thirsty?" Adeline asked, picking up the pitcher and pouring me a glass.

"Thanks." I took it from her, then sat on a bench under the shade of a grape arbor whose leaves rustled in the breeze. "I am, a little."

I took a long swallow of the lemonade, then choked.

Adeline jumped up to slap me on the back.

"I'm okay," I croaked, putting the glass on the table. "That lemonade is a little...strong."

"Oh, that's not lemonade," my aunt said. "It's a vodka martini."

Suspiciously, I eyed the lemon slices floating in my glass.

"Well," she added. "It's more like a *lemon-tini*."

"Yes," Gideon said. This time, I noticed a barely percep-tible slur. He'd also not risen to greet me, which was unusual.

"How many have you had?" I asked him.

"Too many," he said with a groan. "She said it was lemonade. I just thought it was...*tart*."

"Honestly, you two," my aunt chided. "One would think you'd never had a drink before." Raising her own glass, she took a healthy swallow, then replaced it on the table. "So. Verity. I'm always happy to see you, but I can tell something's on your mind. What is it?"

I ran a finger down the side of my glass while deciding whether to take another sip. My thirst won out, and I lifted the glass without looking at my aunt. "Is it that obvious?"

"You've come to ask me about Ryker Fields' case, haven't you?"

I put my glass down. "What do you know about it?"

She shrugged. "Nothing, really. It's the talk of the village, so I've heard all about it, but I don't know the truth of the situation. You know how people love to gossip."

"Actually, I wanted to ask you about someone else—Nigel Hemsworth. Did you know him, back in the day?"

"The art dealer, right? The one who's looking after Perry Otis's estate?"

"That's him. Emy heard that his business reputation is questionable. She thinks he might be taking advantage of Ryker."

"What does that have to do with the murder case?"

"Nothing. But it's a coincidence, don't you think?"

Adeline nodded thoughtfully. She put her glass down, then straightened in the chair. "I'll tell you what I know about Nigel, though I'm not sure it will help."

"Please." I took a cautious sip of my drink.

"I knew him in high school. Also after that, but only

sporadically. You know that when I was in my twenties I worked for a group headquartered in Toronto."

I nodded. I'd had run-ins with my aunt's former employer, the mysterious body known as Control. They claimed to be a loosely aligned group of public relations specialists, but their black-ops marketing campaigns had a way of turning deadly. They had put my aunt's life in danger more than once. At one point, they even tried to recruit me.

I had politely rebuffed that attempt.

Well, not all that politely, since I smashed two of their computer monitors in a rage. *Served them right*, I insisted at the time.

What I didn't admit was that their covert operations sounded rather exciting.

"You mean Control," I said.

"Not exactly. Its predecessor. They kept me pretty busy, and I didn't get back to Leafy Hollow for over a decade. When I did, I looked up the old crowd, including Nigel and Perry Otis."

"You knew Perry, too?"

Nodding, Adeline refreshed her drink. Gideon merely groaned when she offered him a refill. After replacing the pitcher on the table, she took a sip, then put down her glass.

I waited impatiently.

"Nigel had changed. I remembered him as a practical joker, always ready with a prank. The teachers were forever trying to rein him in. But when I saw him all those years later, he'd become so serious."

"What kind of pranks?"

"Minor things—jokes, really. Snakes in a drawer. Salt in

the sugar bowls. Hiding alarm clocks set to go off during lectures. Taping air horns under chairs, so when someone sat down—"

"That would be annoying."

"Definitely. But nobody got hurt. Until Nigel went away to university. Apparently, he thought his penchant for practical jokes would make him, if not popular, at least notorious." My aunt sighed, shaking her head. "It did."

"What happened?"

"He oiled a staircase, thinking it would be funny to watch people tumble down it. But one of the students cracked his skull and went into a coma."

"Do you remember the student's name?"

"Sorry, no. I didn't go to university, remember? I only heard about this second-hand. It was distressing for everyone, of course. Nigel was expelled."

"Rightfully so."

"I suppose. But he always insisted it wasn't his fault. He said another student planned the stunt, and he went along with it without realizing the danger. Nigel was never charged. The police said it was a tragic accident stemming from an ill-advised prank."

"What did you think?"

"I wasn't there. I have no opinion. When I asked Nigel years later, he refused to talk about it."

"Who was the other student, the one he claimed put him up to it?"

"I don't know, of course, but the rumor at the time was that Isaac Damien was behind it."

I puffed out a breath, remembering Isaac and Nigel's

confrontation at the open house. "Would that be the Isaac Damien who recently returned to Leafy Hollow?"

"That's the one."

"Where has he been all these years?"

"I heard he went to Europe."

With a start, Gideon sat up. Then he rose to his feet, a little unsteadily, and turned to the back door. "I'm going inside," he muttered to a lilac bush on his way past.

"Have a nice nap," Adeline called after him.

"Now," she said, rising from the lounge chair to perch beside me on the bench. "What's your thinking on Ryker's predicament? Did he do it? What does Jeff say about it?"

"Jeff didn't tell me much. Only that the police believe one of the murdered women, Dakota Wynne, was an intimate friend of Ryker's."

"They can't throw him in jail for that."

I tried to keep my face blank, but Adeline knew me too well.

"What aren't you telling me?"

"I went to see Ryker. He visited Dakota's home around the time she was murdered. He wanted to talk to her because —" I paused, wondering how much to reveal. "Because they'd had an argument. She didn't answer the door, so he left."

"I bet he only told you that because somebody saw him."

"According to Ryker, somebody did see him—talked to him, in fact."

Adeline leaned in. "Who?"

"The other victim."

I could tell my aunt was taken aback, but she did her best

to hide it. "That's circumstantial. A good defense lawyer could poke holes in it. What was the murder weapon?"

"A garden tool of some kind. Jeff didn't want to elaborate."

I must have looked dejected, because Adeline bent closer to study my face.

"Are you and Jeff okay?"

I adopted a jovial tone. "Of course we are."

I must have been convincing, because she settled back against the bench with a slight nod. "If Ryker Fields didn't murder those women—"

"He didn't."

"Then someone else did. Who are our other suspects?"

"Well..."

I delayed my response until I'd mentally ticked off Ryker's potential motives.

First, he feared public exposure of his relationship with his half-sister. Those fears were amplified when Dakota sent him an email demanding money. *She said if I didn't give it to her...she'd make our relationship public.*

Could potential humiliation—or shame—lead to murder?

Second, he could have killed her in a jealous rage, as the police apparently believed. Perhaps another man was involved. Mentally, I put a check mark beside that one. *Find out if Dakota had other boyfriends.*

Third, there was the financial angle. Ryker's inheritance would be reduced if other siblings came forward.

I heaved a sigh. He had plenty of motives. *Was I deluding myself?*

"Verity?" Adeline tilted her head.

Shrugging, I spread my hands. "I'm still working out who else could have done it. But there are possibilities. Ryker's employee Ethan Neuhaus, for one. He's a shady character."

"Shady how?"

"Ethan said it was high-handed of me to take on Ryker's customers without consulting him and that he should have had first pick. Ethan also said Ryker was unfit to continue working. He suggested he was contemplating suicide. And implied that showed a guilty conscience."

"Good heavens. Is that true? About suicide, I mean?"

"Ryker's definitely upset, but I don't think he's *that* upset. The way Ethan explained it, though—it was creepy."

My aunt arched a brow. "But not in a serial-killer kind of way."

"Well, no. But he knew all about Dakota Wynne, and that Ryker had been seeing her, and that if anything happened to her, Ryker would be the obvious suspect. He knew where she lived, too."

"What's his motive?"

"To swoop in and poach Ryker's business for himself?"

"Seems a stretch."

"I have to start somewhere."

"Anyone else?"

"Well... Ryker has one female client who signed on for more than lawn cuts. Julia Vachon."

Frowning, Adeline reached a hand overhead to tweak off a yellowing grape leaf. "I've heard rumors about that." She tossed the dead leaf away.

"I suspected that Julia could provide him with an alibi, but when I asked her about it, she refused to get involved.

When I mentioned Ryker's new girlfriend, Julia seemed pretty jealous. She even bad-mouthed poor dead Dakota."

"Do you think she was jealous enough to wish Ryker harm?"

I shrugged. "Ryker claimed he hadn't seen Julia for months. She was ticked off about something, though, and it could have been that. Or maybe she simply feared their affair would come to light. In any case, she could have decided to kill Dakota and frame Ryker for the crime."

"Why kill the neighbor?"

"Collateral damage. That woman must have surprised Julia in the act."

My aunt made a face. "A little farfetched, I think."

"Then there's Nigel Hemsworth. If Ryker was in prison accused of murder, it would be easier for Nigel to dispose of that Lawren Harris painting at a premium rate—or commission, or whatever he does."

"Maybe," Adeline said thoughtfully.

I counted on my fingers. "That makes three—Ethan, Julia, and Nigel."

"Don't you mean four? Let's not forget Ryker."

"No, it can't—"

"Verity, I applaud your determination to help a friend, but maybe..." She shrugged apologetically.

"You think he's guilty."

"I didn't say that. I'm only saying you can't arrange the evidence to make it come out the way you want. I agree it doesn't seem likely that Ryker did it. That doesn't make it impossible." She regarded me sadly. "I don't want to see you disappointed."

"Why do I have to keep reminding everybody that I'm a big girl? I can handle disappointment." I hesitated, then added, "I haven't had an anxiety attack in ages."

She patted my arm reassuringly. "I hope you can also handle a little sparring practice. Are we still on for tomorrow?"

"Absolutely. I'll meet you at the gym." I rose to my feet. "Got to go. I've been summoned to the Sleepy Time Motel. It's an emergency, supposedly." I arched my eyebrows.

"Ah—say hello to Frank."

"I will, thanks." Smiling, I recalled that my aunt and my father had been sworn enemies for years. I didn't realize how much that had bothered me. Until all that ill will was gone, and I felt the regret of decades lift from my shoulders. It was a good feeling, even now, months after their reconciliation.

Leaving my still-full glass behind, I headed for the truck.

"Oh, I nearly forgot." I wheeled around, then yanked a pamphlet from my pocket. Gesturing with the crumpled paper, I intoned, "We Need More Wilf. He Does Things."

Adeline shot me a withering look.

Smirking, I anchored the leaflet under the lemon-tini pitcher before walking away.

One down.

One thousand, nine hundred, ninety-nine to go.

———

I dropped another two hundred pamphlets at the 5X Bakery, sneaking them onto the counter while Emy made my sandwich and coffee.

Emy twisted her lips when she saw them but handed over my lunch without a mention. There was every chance those leaflets would end up in the trash once I'd left, but my pact with Wilf did not include follow-up visits, so I didn't care.

"Delicious," I said, smiling over my egg salad on brioche.

The jangle of a bell, followed by muffled voices, came through the passage that connected the 5X with Emy's other business, the vegan takeout *Eco Edibles*.

"How's the new student working out?" I reached for my coffee and took a sip. Emy had signed up for the culinary skills internship program at the local college. They sent her a different student each semester. Since Emy started work at 4 a.m., prepping and baking before opening the bakery at 8, the extra help came in handy.

"Terrific," she said. "In fact, Lorne says I should take this afternoon off."

"You should. You must be exhausted after last night. At least I got to sleep in a bit." I gobbled the last of my sandwich, crumpled the wrapper, and finished my coffee in one gulp. "You should take a break."

She puffed out a weary sigh. "Maybe I will. Where are you off to in such a hurry?"

"I have to check in with my dad. Meanwhile, I left Lorne and Ethan to do all the work by themselves. I should get back."

"Say hello to Frank."

"Will do."

Because my father and I were still working out the parameters of our renewed relationship, I found it useful to have a prop—such as a pertinent question, or a casserole—on hand when we spoke. Today it was a brace of T-shirts from Walmart's bargain bin.

"I brought you a couple of shirts," I said, holding up the shopping bag when he opened the door of Suite 7.

"C'mon in. Quick." He grabbed my arm to yank me inside, then stuck his head out to cast a furtive look at the motel office before closing the door.

I halted, my path blocked by teetering piles of clothing. At a quick glance, I identified dress shirts, chino pants, jackets, a puffy parka, and—*were those Speedo swimming trunks?*

"Dad?" My voice quavered. "Where did this stuff come from?"

He spread his hands, looking sheepish. "It's complicated."

Curious, I picked up a pair of red flannel pajamas with an appliquéd moose on the chest. A price tag dangled from the sleeve. I expelled a horrified breath, then shook the PJs in his face.

"You stole them, didn't you?"

CHAPTER TWENTY-ONE

SHELBY TUGGED her baseball cap lower to shade her face, then glanced around. She was alone on the street. Quickly, she mounted the front steps, then pushed open the old door with its pebbled glass window and entered the shabby foyer.

This run-down rooming house on a nondescript street, whose owner didn't bother to check her renters' IDs, was perfect for her needs—a safe place to store the painting when she got it, and a bolt hole to run to if Ryker became suspicious.

She strode through the deserted hall, with its cooking smells and muffled television sounds, to a narrow wooden staircase at the back. Two flights up the creaking steps, she reached the room she'd rented days earlier. She raised a hand to unlock the door. Then whistled when she saw it was already ajar. Just a hair, but enough that she'd spotted it.

What an amateur, she thought, shaking her head. *As if she wouldn't notice something like that.*

It couldn't be the landlady, come to do the weekly cleaning, since Shelby had insisted she'd do it herself. The landlady was happy to agree.

No. This must be—

She lowered her raised hand as a chill slithered down her spine. *What if the intruder was still inside?*

She froze as a stair board creaked behind her.

Then another.

She whirled around, heart thumping, not breathing.

Listening.

But there was nothing to hear, apart from the muffled noises of game shows and sports channels from the floor below. It was only the old house creaking and settling, the stair boards springing back after her passage. She drew in a relieved breath.

There were no sounds from inside her room. Whoever had been there was long gone. But— Shelby straightened her shoulders.

They'd left her a booby trap to deal with.

Fortunately, this had been a favorite trick of her foster brothers. She knew there would be a wire attached to a can on a floating shelf overhead. When the door opened, tripping the wire, the can would tip, splashing its contents on anyone unlucky enough to spring the trap.

She cast her gaze about, looking for something to push open the door and harmlessly trigger the booby trap. A dusty stand against the wall held an ancient black umbrella—the perfect tool to push open the door. She leaned over to pull it from the stand.

As she yanked it free, a faint sound paralyzed her.

Chu-chak, like a gun being cocked.

She froze, her heart racing, not daring to turn.

Then came the sharp crack of a gunshot.

Shelby shied, stumbled, and—frantic for cover—burst through the door. As she dove toward the worn carpet of her room, a blow hit her hard on the head.

With a gasp, she slammed into the floor, then twisted to face the ceiling.

Liquid gushed into her open mouth and covered her face.

Spitting and choking, her head reeling, she scrambled to her hands and knees, eyes closed, frantic to slam the door against the gunman.

But when she forced open one eye, she realized the hall was empty.

Whereas she was kneeling in a puddle of bright red blood. At least, it looked like blood.

After swiping her eyes, Shelby took a closer look.

Then flopped back onto her haunches, feebly wiping red paint from her eyes and mouth. Her hair dripped paint onto the floor. Her clothes were soaked in it. She sniffed her hand. Oil paint. But when she pulled her fingers apart, strands of red connected them. Oil paint—mixed with glue. She groaned.

It would take hours, and gallons of turpentine, to remove it.

Cursing under her breath, she glanced around the red-splattered room. The walls, the floor, the furniture—all of it was splashed with paint.

She slumped back onto the floor, laughing hysterically. *Good thing she'd refused to pay the damage deposit.*

There was no need to check the inside of the umbrella stand for the source of the *chu-chak* sound. She knew what she'd find—a tripwire alarm made with a firecracker, duct tape, wooden matches, and the striking surface from a match-box. It would be rigged so when she pulled out the umbrella, the match would strike, igniting the firecracker, which would flare up, then explode with a sound like a gunshot.

Which, in turn, would scare her into plunging through the door, triggering the first booby trap. The one that was obvious. *The one she should have avoided.*

Her analysis was confirmed by a whiff of sulfur in the air, as well as a tendril of smoke curling up from the umbrella stand.

She'd been an idiot.

Now she'd have to spend the rest of the day cleaning herself up. Then— Scowling, she wiped her hands on a clean patch of carpet.

Part of her, the sensible part, knew she should call it quits.

But a bigger part demanded revenge.

CHAPTER TWENTY-TWO

WHILE I RUMMAGED through the piles of clothing scattered around my father's motel unit, he tried to explain.

"I did not steal them," he huffed. "Thanks for the vote of confidence, by the way."

"Then where did you get them? And why?"

"Birdie keeps bringing me clothes from that liquidation mall on the highway. I asked her to stop, but—" He shrugged helplessly.

"Birdie Tanner, the motel clerk?"

He nodded, shifting a dozen pairs of socks—so thick and woolly they would have been unwearable even in the Arctic —off one of the twin beds.

I sat on the cleared spot, then leaned back on my hands. "Maybe she's sweet on you," I said.

My father did have a way with women. I assumed they found his lean frame, wavy brown hair bleached blond by the sun, and laugh lines crinkling at the corners of his laser-blue eyes irresistible.

It certainly wasn't his wardrobe. He was a little light in the clothing department. In fact, other than the waxed field coat, cowboy boots, and jeans he'd arrived in months earlier, I'd yet to see a meaningful outfit change. My father's unplanned visit was originally meant to be short, which explained his lack of luggage. It didn't explain why he hadn't sent for the rest of his wardrobe from his previous home in Australia once he decided to stay.

I suspected he didn't bother because there was little point in shipping faded shirts, worn underwear, and threadbare jeans halfway around the world. From childhood pictures, I knew my father had once been a clotheshorse. Obviously, those days were behind him. Even with his motel unit jammed to the rafters with brand new sartorial choices, he was still wearing those same old jeans.

Puffing air out his lips, Frank strode to the window to peer out at the parking lot—which was empty except for my truck and Carson's trailer.

"You look jumpy," I said.

"I have to get out of here." He muttered something under his breath before turning to face me. "It's not a good place."

"I know the coffee's bad, but what else is wrong with it?"

"It's not that." He grimaced, not meeting my gaze.

"What is it then?"

"I found something that shouldn't be here." He was staring at the far wall, which was a bit disconcerting.

"Can you be more specific?" I tried to keep my voice free of irritation. After all, I'd been called here on an emergency.

Even allowing for my father's tendency to exaggerate, something must be up.

He heaved a sigh, then walked over to the closet, opened the door, and stepped inside.

I gaped at his disappearing back. "What are you doing?"

He stuck his head out from between his coat and a flannel shirt that originally might have been plaid. "Are you coming?"

"Where? To Narnia?"

"Don't be smart. Look at this." He shoved the clothing on the rod to either side, then pointed to the back wall of the closet. A tarnished medallion was attached to the wall.

Intrigued, I stepped closer.

Frank pushed the medallion to one side. It swept up and over, revealing a hole in the wall between his unit and the next one.

I stared in disbelief. "Is that a—peephole?"

I leaned in to put my eye against the opening. Thankfully, the adjoining motel unit was empty. After replacing the medallion, I grabbed handfuls of hanging clothes, pulling them across to cover it. Then I closed the door.

As an afterthought, I dragged over a chair and placed it in front.

"When did you find this?" I asked. "It isn't...your handiwork, is it?"

He glowered at me, then moved the chair back to its original position. "How the hell did you arrive at that conclusion? I had nothing to do with it."

"We have to report it."

"We can't. If my own daughter thinks I'm responsible, what will the police think?"

I narrowed my eyes. "Dad—that minor criminal record of yours doesn't include anything unsavory, does it?"

"Of course not," he blustered. Then hesitated. "Define *unsavory*."

"Never mind," I grumbled. Overcoming my initial distaste, I opened the closet door and moved the clothes aside to take another look. "How old do you think this is?" I asked, with my face pressed against the peephole. "If it's been here for years, you'll be off the hook. But we still have to report it because—"

A rap on the motel room door caused me to jerk backward. I stumbled. Instinctively, I grabbed the hanging clothes to break my fall. That sudden movement was too much for the ancient clothes rod. With a ripping sound, it detached from one side of the closet.

I stumbled backward, still clutching the clothes. The wire hangers slid off the rod's broken end, one after the other. Within seconds, I was on the floor, covered in clothing, hangers, and decades of lint.

The closet was now empty, the medallion gleaming like the lost gold of the Incas.

The rapping on the door resumed. *Rat-a-tat-tat.*

"Anybody there?" came a woman's voice. "Frank?"

Puffing air through my mouth in a pathetic attempt to shift a woolen scarf that was draped across my face like an overly friendly boa constrictor, I struggled to make myself heard. "*The closet—*"

"Be right there," my father hollered pleasantly, heading

for the door. "Get up," he said, prodding me with the toe of his cowboy boot.

"*The closet*," I hissed, sticking out my foot to keep him from reaching the motel room door. "*Close the door.*"

I had trouble estimating the force required to deter him while weighed down by mounds of clothing and a woolen snake. Not only that, but a dozen cheap wire hangers were digging into my thigh.

Frank went down like a ton of bricks.

"*Oof*," he gasped. "Crikey—whadda you do that for?"

A key rattled in the door lock.

"I'm coming in, Frank," the voice called. "Are you all right? What was that noise?"

With a superhuman effort, I flipped onto my hands and knees to crawl over the mounded clothes to the closet.

The hangers, now a tangled clump of bent wire, dug their hooks into me. Dragging that mess behind me, I made it to the closet door, stretching up one hand to close it. It banged against the end of the broken rod and remained open a crack, but the medallion was hidden.

I collapsed onto the floor with my back against the closet door seconds before the motel room door opened.

A woman's curly brown head poked through the opening. Her red-lipsticked mouth dropped open as she took in the scene.

"Hello," I said wanly while untangling a hanger from my arm.

"Oh, my." She surveyed the room with a hand to her throat. "Am I interrupting anything?" Stepping warily into the room, she kept one hand on the doorknob behind her. In case of a hasty retreat, I assumed.

Frank jumped to his feet with surprising agility, then uttered a curse under his breath and vigorously rubbed one knee. "Birdie, this is my daughter, Verity. She dropped by to..." He looked helplessly at me.

"To organize this wonderful wardrobe that you've been kind enough to provide my father. He really appreciates it." I held up a Christmas-themed sweater with what I hoped was an appreciative look. I gave it a fond pat.

Birdie's face brightened. "How nice to meet you, Verity. Your father's told me so much about you."

"Likewise," I said while surreptitiously shifting a pile of hangers from under my left hip.

"Really?" Her shiny face took on an even brighter gleam.

My father shot me a side-eyed glance that could have melted glass.

Serves you right, I thought, smiling angelically before adding, "Oh, yes. Many times."

"Well. I'll let you get back to it, then. I only dropped by, Frank, to let you know I'm on my way to the market so, if there's anything you need..." Birdie lifted her shoulders suggestively before turning her attention to me. She studied my face intently.

I smiled weakly, hoping the hangers hadn't drawn blood.

"Please don't trouble yourself," Frank said.

"Well," she said again. Birdie seemed to be a woman of few words, and she liked those ones a lot. "Why don't I pick up a few of those maple donuts you're so fond of?"

My father smiled weakly. "If you have to."

I glared at him. "My father's quite appreciative, I'm sure."

Birdie smiled again. "Well. I'm off." She gave us a cheery wave, then furrowed her brow at me—she seemed to zero in on my right eye—before turning to the door.

I sighed in relief, tossing the festive sweater over my shoulder.

At the door, Birdie suddenly turned, lips pursed, then pointed to the broken rod protruding from the closet door. "Is there a problem with the—"

I grabbed the sweater and held it up, blocking her view of the closet. "Just look at the stitching. You don't see this kind of workmanship very often."

"—coffee maker?" Birdie asked.

I swiveled my head. She was studying the bureau with the microwave and coffee maker, not the closet.

"The last tenant complained the coffee wasn't good," Birdie continued.

Frank shook his head repeatedly. "No. It's great." He reached for the door handle.

"Well—" she said, stepping over the threshold.

He tried to close the door.

Birdie slapped a hand against it. "I almost forgot. That previous tenant also claimed they left a laptop behind." She chuckled. "People forget the darnedest things. You haven't... seen anything like that, have you?"

Frank stared at her, his mouth hanging open. "Ah...ah..."

I hastened to step in. "I'm sure Frank would have told you if he'd found a computer in the room." I tried to chuckle, but my throat was too dry from the lint.

"Well." Birdie gave our surroundings a searching glance.

"It's not the first time they've mentioned it. I'm afraid they're insisting on a proper search. Thing is, I'm worried the police might get involved."

I heard my father swallow hard.

"I could do it right now." Birdie shrugged apologetically. "If you're not too busy?"

"Nooo, we're not busy," I said. "Just let us get some of these clothes out of the way first to make it easier for you." I swiveled my eyes to the door while tilting my head at Frank. He took several seconds to catch on, but then positioned himself by the entrance.

"Well—"

"Thanks, Birdie," my dad said, closing the door in her face. We waited, holding our breath, until we heard her heels clicking away.

CHAPTER TWENTY-THREE

I ROSE to my feet with a hanger hooked through the sleeve of my hoodie. While working it out of the fabric, I said, "You have to tell Birdie about the peephole. She'll find it anyway."

"I can't. Not yet."

"Why not?"

He worked his lips while thoughtfully regarding the closet. "Because there's more to it."

"Such as?"

My father gave another furtive glance out the window. Then, after locking the motel room door with a rattle of the chain, he dropped to his knees to slide a silver laptop out from under the bed.

I gaped at it. "Where did that come from?"

"I found it at the back of the closet this morning. Behind a loose section of paneling."

"You stole it."

"No. I told you. I found it."

"That doesn't make it yours. You have to turn it in. Tell Birdie you took another look around after her visit and found it. It's not all bad. There might even be a reward."

He looked dubious, so I added, "Birdie will be so proud."

Frank glowered at me, then placed the laptop on the bed and flipped it open. "I can't turn it in. Look."

Puzzled, I bent to peer at the screen.

He pulled up a video.

"Do we have time for YouTube?" I asked, knowing what even a single kitten video could lead to. We might be there for hours.

Except my father wasn't looking at kittens. Not that kind, anyway.

The video showed the same room I'd been gawking at minutes earlier—the one adjacent to my father's. "Is that live?"

"No. It's a recording."

"Of what?" I asked, not certain I wanted to hear the answer.

"Nothing much. People walking around."

"Then why—"

"There's a bunch of recordings like this on the laptop. Somebody set up a camera that feeds into this computer. If the police see this, they might get the wrong idea. At least, I should watch all the videos to make sure—"

"Of what?" I asked in an icy tone. "Camera angles?"

"Stop that. It's not what you think. I only turned it on to take a look." He hesitated. "See who it belonged to, that is."

To myself, I muttered, *Uh-huh.*

"But then I found these videos," Frank continued. "That

gave me the idea to look for a peephole. And now..." He shrugged, looking worried. "How would I explain it?"

I pointed to the screen. "Are you telling me this thing's been filming activities in your neighboring unit the whole time you've been living here?"

"I think so."

I walked to the closet, flinging open the door for a closer look. Now that the hangers and clothing were all on the floor, it was easy to scan the walls. I checked every corner. Nothing. "Where's the camera, then?"

"It must be next door. It's not here. I've looked everywhere."

"Great." Flopping onto the bed with my hands on my knees, I tilted my head back to stare at the stained ceiling tiles. How I was going to explain this to my upright—and occasionally uptight—law-enforcement boyfriend? I rehearsed a few scenarios.

Jeff, honey—my dad accidentally videotaped other motel room guests, through a peephole, using a stolen laptop. That's not a problem, right?

While Jeff had never been anything less than welcoming to my dad, he was well aware of the more dubious side of Frank's character. I believed my father was telling the truth about his closet discovery, if only because who would make up a story like that? I wasn't quite as confident about Jeff's response to it.

"Okay," I said. "Here's what we'll do. I'll call Lorne and tell him we have a slight computer problem and ask him to drop by to take a look. He's great with computers. He'll know how to find that camera."

Looking dubious, Frank thumbed his ear. "Do we have to tell Lorne?"

"I trust him. We've been through a lot together."

"But he'll bring Emy, won't he?"

"Of course he will. They're a package deal. Anyway, I wouldn't keep this from my best friend. She'd never forgive me." I felt a smirk twitch my lips and fought to suppress it. It was a losing battle. "You know, when you think about it, it's actually pretty funny."

"Very funny. Not as funny as your face, though."

"What's that supposed to mean?"

He jerked his head at the mirror by the front door. Puzzled, I ambled over for a look.

Oh. No wonder Birdie stared at me. Two green smudges bracketed my right eye. I rubbed at them with no discernible results. "That medallion's made of copper, isn't it?" I asked with a sigh. "Why didn't you tell me?"

"How was I supposed to know you were going to plant your mug right on it?"

"Well, excuse me. I'm new to surveillance work."

Which wasn't exactly true, I thought.

Pulling my cell phone from my bag, I tapped out a rapid text.

I need the team at Sleepy Time Motel.

Then I added a bat-signal emoji.

B right there, Emy replied.

What about Ethan? Lorne texted.

Tell him to knock off for today. We'll start early tomorrow.

Check. On our way.

Once the team had arrived, I pushed aside the coffee maker to make room on the bureau for the laptop. With my father pacing in the background, I explained the problem to Lorne and Emy. We contemplated the computer.

"The easiest thing would be to wipe the hard drive," Lorne said.

My dad swiveled to face him. "We can't do that," he blurted.

"Why not?"

"Because," I broke in, "Frank has to return this thing." I glared at my father, who rolled his eyes. "Preferably with the contents intact."

"Do you want to delete the videos, then?" Lorne asked.

"No. We can't do that either. They could be...evidence."

"Of what?"

"Who knows? But we have to be able to prove Frank knew nothing about it. If the camera switches on while the police are checking the laptop..." I shrugged. "It won't look good."

My father raised his hands in a *Hello!* type gesture.

"Then what?" Lorne asked.

"Can we disable the camera?"

Nodding, he pulled over a chair. "We should be able to do that from here." He tapped a few keys, frowned, then tapped a few more. Lorne slumped back, puffing out a breath. "Problem."

"What?"

"See this icon?"

I leaned over his shoulder to peer at the screen.

"That's the camera," he said. "It shows up as a device linked to this computer. But when I try to eject it, it pops right back."

"How can we get rid of it, then?"

"We have to find the actual camera. Otherwise, it will keep on loading videos."

I bit my lip, hoping the pain would distract me from the unease twisting my gut. *What were we getting into?* "That sounds complicated."

Lorne shook his head. "It's not. Basically, we just need to turn it off."

"Does it have an on-off switch? Or a plug we can pull?"

He mulled this over, studying the screen. "Probably not." He tapped a few more keys. "I assume it's transmitting wirelessly. The camera will have a power source, but I won't know what it is until I see it. If all else fails, we can take a hammer to it." Pushing his chair back, he stood. "So—where is the camera?"

"We don't know. Except that it's not here. It must be next door."

"We'll have to search that room."

"I don't see how, unless you happen to have one of those picklock thingies."

"I've been meaning to get one of those," Lorne muttered, then brightened. "There are plenty for sale online. Should I order one?"

"We don't have time for that." My unease mounting, I turned to my father. "Maybe you could persuade Birdie you need to see that room for some reason. You could—"

"No," he said loudly. "Forget it."

"There's a simpler way," Lorne said. "The bathroom windows on these units face the ravine at the back. No one will see me if I go in that way."

This was getting worse and worse. I bit my lip. "Okay, but make it quick."

Lorne went out the door, then darted around the end of the motel to the back. Emy and I huddled around the laptop screen, which still showed an empty room. My father continued to pace.

Within minutes, Lorne texted us.

I'M IN.

I clicked on the full-screen option to make the video larger. "Where is he?"

"He must still be in the bathroom," Emy said. She sucked in a quick breath. "Oh, no. Look—someone's coming in." She pointed to the screen, where the unit's front door was opening.

A middle-aged man wearing a blue suit and aviator sunglasses stepped into the unit, then closed the door. He turned, facing the camera, displaying a pair of enormous ears.

"I don't believe it." I pointed at the screen. "That's Nigel Hemsworth."

Emy stared at the laptop, her mouth slack. "What's he doing here?"

Nigel had a rectangular object under his arm, about two feet by three feet, wrapped in brown paper. He propped it up on the sofa, then turned to a wall mirror to straighten his tie.

Frank stopped pacing to stare at the screen over my shoulder. "That guy looks familiar."

"I showed you his picture," I said. "He's the village art dealer who's trying to muscle in on Ryker's inheritance."

"Yeah, but—" my dad said. "Something else." His brow furrowed. "Wait—does he own a Mercedes convertible?"

"As a matter of fact, he does."

"That's where I've seen him. He brings it into the garage for oil changes every other week." Frank whistled. "He puts a *lot* of miles on it."

"We have to get Lorne out of there," Emy said, texting frantically on her phone.

I paused her hand. "Stop. You can't send a text. It'll chime on Lorne's phone when it's delivered. Nigel will hear it."

"What should we do?" she whispered, watching the screen.

Meanwhile, in the neighboring unit, Nigel strolled to the window, hands clasped behind his back.

"Is he...humming?" Emy asked.

I pricked up my ears to hear the unmistakable strains of comic opera. "When was the last time you heard somebody hum Gilbert and Sullivan's *Three Little Maids*?"

Behind us, my father shrugged. "I'm not into folk duos."

Emy and I slowly swiveled our eyes to him, then each other.

"What?" he asked.

At a sudden *rat-a-tat-tat*, I jerked my head around in alarm. How could we explain this to Birdie? Without using the word *unsavory*, that is. Or *unseemly*. Or—

"It's coming from next door," Emy said, shaking my shoulder and pointing to the laptop.

213

We watched as Nigel opened the door. A voluptuous woman with platinum hair, blood-red nails, and an enormous handbag stepped through.

Emy and I exchanged shocked glances. "It's Dragon Lady from the open house," she whispered.

On the screen, Nigel said, "You're early," shutting the door behind her.

"I made surprisingly good time on the highway." Her voice was low and sultry. "That commuter lane is fantastic."

"Don't you need two people for that?"

She gave him an odd look. "I'm driving a Ferrari."

Behind me, my dad whispered, "Nice." I didn't know if he meant the woman or the sports car. I suspected the latter.

On the screen in front of us, Nigel was holding out a hand. "Before we get down to business—may I take your wrap?"

Dragon Lady slipped out of her silk shawl, letting it drop luxuriously to the floor. Nigel grabbed it before it could hit the carpet. *Good idea*, I thought, eying the mysterious stains on the carpeting in my father's unit.

After setting her handbag on the bed, she lowered herself gracefully. Casually, she slipped off her four-inch heels. "Shall we get on with it?"

Emy leaned in to peer at the handbag. "Wow. That's something."

"I know," I said.

"That's enough," my father said briskly, reaching for the laptop. "Turn that thing off."

"It's just getting good," I countered, hunching over the keyboard.

He tried to grab it. "No daughter of mine..." He puffed. "Is going to watch...*that.*"

"Yes, I am." I wrested the keyboard back. "I'm a grown woman, Dad. Don't be ridiculous. Don't you want to know who planted that camera and left this laptop in your closet?"

"Stop arguing," Emy said. "Lorne may need our help."

We resumed our scrutiny of the screen. "Where is Lorne?" I asked. "Did he get out of there before—"

Emy's eyes widened, then she pointed to a section of the screen. I followed her finger.

Two large running shoes stuck out from between the twin beds. If Dragon Lady stood up and turned around, she couldn't help but see Lorne lying on the floor.

Slowly, the shoes drew back.

"We need a distraction," I muttered.

On the screen, Nigel returned from hanging Dragon Lady's shawl in the closet. "Now then," he said. "What were we doing?"

"You were getting me a drink," she purred.

As we huddled over the laptop, Frank whispered urgently, "Lorne can't stay there."

"Verity, what are we going to do?" Emy asked.

"Technically," my father continued, "it's breaking and entering. He could be charged."

"Not helping," I said tersely.

In the adjoining room, "G and T?" Nigel asked.

Dragon Lady leaned forward, smiling seductively. "How did you know?"

He grinned. "I'll get the gin."

At the sound of the mini-fridge opening, Lorne's tousled hair slowly appeared above the bed.

"Don't do that," Emy and I blurted in unison, like horror-moviegoers when a young woman descends the steps of an ancient cellar even though dozens of characters have already gone down there and none have come back.

I realized my teeth were chattering and clamped my jaw.

The door of the mini-fridge closed.

Lorne ducked down.

"We've got to get him out of there," Emy said.

"I know."

Next door, Nigel was apologetic. "Sorry," he said with a shrug. "All out of ice, I'm afraid."

Dragon Lady raised an impeccable eyebrow.

"I'll get some from the front desk," Nigel said, jerking his thumb at the door.

"Good idea," she said.

"That's our cue," I said, jumping up and heading for the door. On the way, I grabbed a baseball cap from the nearest clothing stack and jammed it on my head. After plucking an ice bucket off the bureau, I halted with my fingers on the doorknob. "Tell me when Nigel's gone."

Emy held up a hand, still staring at the laptop screen. "Wait."

My father was watching the screen over Emy's shoulder. "The cops might throw in a burglary charge, too."

"Dad," I said, my lips set in a grim line. "Stop it."

"Now," Emy blurted. "He's out."

I counted to five, to give Nigel time to reach the office,

then opened our motel room door. Within seconds, I was knocking on the unit beside ours.

"Room service," I called cheerily.

Of course, there had never been room service at the Sleepy Time. At least, not the kind that delivered nachos and beer. I was counting on Dragon Lady not to know that. While I waited, I swiveled my head to see if Nigel was coming back. I caught sight of a low-slung cherry-red sports car parked in front of the office. An honest-to-goodness Ferrari. That was an unusual sight in Leafy Hollow. Up to now, the most exotic vehicle had been Wilf Mullins' refurbished Hummer.

The motel unit's door opened.

"Ice?" I asked, holding up the bucket while lowering my head so the cap's visor would cover my eyes.

With a slight frown, she reached out to take it.

I held it away from her. "Sorry, I have to bring it in myself."

"That's not necessary." She grabbed the bucket's rim.

I held on to it, resisting her grasp.

We struggled over it.

"I have to place it in the room myself," I said, finally wresting it away. "Motel regulations."

She stepped back with a look of surprise. "Motel what?"

"Regulations," I said briskly, brushing past her and into the unit.

"Wait. Where are you—"

"Uh-huh. Just as I thought." After placing the ice bucket on the bureau, I picked up an unused glass, then tore off its paper wrapping. "This wrapping is not regulation. I'll have to replace all your glasses."

"That's really not necessary."

"Ma'am," I intoned. "It's a matter of hygiene."

In my peripheral vision, I saw Lorne creep into the bathroom behind her.

Dragon Lady fixed me with a penetrating gaze. "Why are you here?"

"I told you, ma'am. I'm here to—"

"Deliver an empty ice bucket?"

Silence. I felt my eyes widen under her steady gaze.

Then, "Is it empty?" I squeaked. "I must have—"

"I know who you are, Verity. We've met, remember?" She waved red-lacquered fingers. "You have to get out of here before my associate returns. You could ruin everything."

Associate? Intrigued, I took a leap, leveling a penetrating gaze of my own. "You mean your *client*, don't you? Don't think I don't know what's going on here. Because I do. Know. What."

Her smile broadened. "I doubt that. Now—leave. And preferably not out the bathroom window like your friend."

CHAPTER TWENTY-FOUR

UH-OH. *Cover blown.*

Peeling off the baseball cap, I twisted it in my hands. "Were we that obvious?"

"Amateur-ville," Dragon Lady replied. "Why do you think I sent Nigel out for ice? To give your friend time to get out of here. Also—you might want to take that price tag off your baseball cap."

She strode to the door. "Now move."

"No."

Looking surprised, she pivoted neatly on her bare feet. "What do you mean, no?"

"Not until you tell me what you're really doing here. And where you've hidden the camera."

Her lips twitched in amusement. It clashed with the cold look in her eyes. "I spent months setting this up. If you ruin it—"

I raised a hand in protest. "I'm not leaving until you explain it to me. Nigel Hemsworth is a friend of mine."

"I doubt that." This time, her smile was genuine. "Not only because I've never seen you with him, but because that man doesn't have any friends. Not real ones, anyway."

I bristled. "How would you know—"

"I'll level with you, I promise. Later—*after* you get out of here." She opened the door then gestured to the parking lot. "Now."

I hesitated, still twisting the cap.

"Otherwise," she said calmly, "I'll show Nigel the hidden camera and tell him I discovered you've been spying on him. It will be my word against yours—and I'm betting you've already made a pest of yourself, whereas I am a valued acquaintance." She tapped a lacquered fingernail on the door and raised an eyebrow. "Your choice."

Stymied, I headed for the exit.

"Take that ice bucket with you," she said, pointing to the bureau.

Sullenly, I pivoted to pick it up before sweeping out of the room. On the sill, I paused to deliver what I hoped was a chilling *coup de grâce*.

"You better not be lying," I hissed. "Or else."

She merely rolled her eyes before slamming the door.

Back in my dad's motel room, Frank, Emy, and a disheveled Lorne were glued to the laptop screen. Lorne was absently rubbing his elbow.

"Are you all right?" I asked.

"Caught it on the window frame," he replied. "Just a scrape."

I'd seen *The Expendables*, so I knew in guy-speak that could be anything from a scratch to an amputation. I decided to ignore his injury in favor of joining the viewing party.

Emy glanced over her shoulder. "What was she talking about? The sound was muffled when you moved out of range. Did she say, *You could ruin everything?*"

I nodded. "She promised to explain it later."

"Good work standing up to her," Lorne said in an unusually sarcastic tone.

"What was I supposed to do?" I huffed. "I was busy saving your rear. While these two"—I jerked a thumb at the rest of the team—"were squirreled away in here hoping to make X-rated videos."

"That's not true," my father countered sternly.

Emy merely smirked.

"Whatever. I'm only trying to say she had me dead to rights and it seemed wise to comply. We can always blow her cover later if she doesn't come through with an explanation."

"Do you think that's a disguise?"

"Maybe. She's definitely not used to wearing those heels." I pointed to the screen. Dragon Lady was seated on the bed, massaging her insteps and grimacing.

The motel room door opened, followed by a cheery, "I'm back."

The blonde slipped her feet back into her shoes and stood. "I was beginning to worry you weren't coming back," she purred, walking over to take the filled ice bucket from

Nigel. "Oh, dear," she said, catching sight of his bandage. "You've hurt your hand." She extended her lower lip in a sympathetic pout. "Let me see that."

"It's nothing." He held out his hand.

"It looks painful." After clucking over it for a moment, she strolled to the bureau and reached for the gin bottle to pour the drinks. "Maybe this will help."

She handed him a glass, then raised her own in a mock salute. "Santé."

"Santé," Nigel intoned, raising his glass. He downed his drink with a grimace before plonking it back on the bureau. Dragon Lady's back had been toward him while she prepared it, but we saw her clearly. Thus, we knew his drink held a double portion of gin, while hers was mostly tonic water.

"Shall we get down to business?" Nigel asked.

"Certainly." She downed her drink, set the empty glass on the bureau, then reclined languidly on the bed. "Let's see it, then."

Behind us, my father groaned. "Turn that thing off."

"It's not what you're thinking, Dad."

"How do you know what I'm thinking?"

"Look." I pointed to the screen.

Nigel drew a pen knife from his pocket to snip the string of the rectangular object on the sofa. With a swish of brown paper, he unwrapped it, then held it up with a flourish.

Given the heavy wooden frame, it was obviously a painting. But Nigel's back was to us, so we couldn't see the picture.

"Oh my gosh," I whispered. "Could that be the Lawren Harris?"

"Shh," Emy whispered, poking me with her elbow.

Dragon Lady cupped her chin in her hand, studying the painting.

"Isn't it magnificent?" Nigel asked.

"Even better than I imagined." She beckoned with one hand. "Bring it over here into the natural light so I can take a closer look."

He walked past her to place the painting on the bed. This time, it faced the camera.

I'd seen it before. It was an abstract work, done in browns and blacks, somber and foreboding. It had been in Nigel's storeroom when he tried to sell me the landscape print. It had been leaning against the far wall, alone. Already selected, I assumed, for its turn in the spotlight.

"It's a genuine deal?" she asked.

Nigel looked hurt. "Genuine? Of course it's genuine."

"I meant, how do I know the owner is willing to sell it at the price we agreed? Can I speak to him?"

"You'll have to take my word for it. The owner wishes to remain anonymous." He sniffed. "As you know. If the terms of our agreement are no longer satisfactory..." Nigel made a show of re-wrapping the painting with a great deal of rustling paper.

The blonde straightened up on the bed, then swung her legs over the side. "Keep your shirt on. I'm fine with our terms."

Nigel tied the last of the string, then tossed her a lecherous grin. "I was actually hoping to take my shirt...off."

I thought that was a brave proposition for old Nigel, but it was probably the gin talking.

"Some other time. I have an appointment I can't miss." Dragon Lady ambled over to caress the painting's frame.

"Very well," said Nigel, looking disappointed. "Cash first, though."

"Of course." She opened her enormous purse, pulled out a leather wallet, then counted out bills onto the quilted bedspread. "There," she said. "Fifty grand. As agreed."

Nigel swept the currency into a single stack, straightened its edges, and tucked it into the inside pocket of his suit jacket. "If you're interested in anything else, give me a call." He tilted his head at the door. "Can I walk you out?"

She glanced around. "I had a late night, and I'm exhausted. It's not like me to have a nap in the afternoon, but I think I'll make an exception today."

"No problem," he said. "I'll let the front desk know you'll be here for a while." He leaned in. The lecherous look was back. "Sure you wouldn't like a little company?"

"I'm sure." She sauntered to the door, opened it, then ushered him out with an obviously fake smile. Once he was gone, she leaned back against the door with her hands behind her.

Outside, a car started up. Dragon Lady waited until it drove away, the engine noise growing fainter. Then she pushed off from the door to flash a grim look in the direction of the camera. "Come on over. And bring the laptop." She perched on the bed, slipping off her shoes.

I turned to the team. "Let's go."

The blonde stood aside as we piled into her room. Then she shut the door and walked over to the bureau. "Drink, anyone?"

Frank raised his arm. I pulled it down—with a bit of a struggle.

"No, thanks," I said. "We only want to know what's going on here."

"Would you believe a simple business transaction?"

"No."

"All right. Sit down." She dropped ice cubes into a glass, then followed it up with a splash of gin. No tonic this time.

Lorne, Emy, and Frank perched on the beds. I remained standing, with my arms crossed. The blonde raised an eyebrow at me but said nothing.

She plopped into an armchair with her drink, then reached up with her other hand to tug a platinum wig off her head and toss it onto the nearest bed. Underneath, her hair was a short brunette bob.

"Blast. That thing is itchy." Scratching her scalp with one finger, she fixed me with an expectant air. "What do you want to know?"

Before I could answer, Frank blurted out, "Are you a cop?"

She paused, lowered her fingernail, then burst into laughter. "Good heavens, no. Was I that incompetent?"

"Hey," I broke in. "Our cops are not incompetent."

"Really? As far as I can tell, Nigel Hemsworth's scams have been going on for years. That sounds like incompetent to me." She took a long swallow of her drink.

"What scams?"

She pointed to the wrapped painting on the sofa. "That was stolen three years ago from a collector in Montreal."

"You're a private detective," I guessed, unfurling my arms. "Did the painting's owner hire you?"

"I'm an insurance investigator. The company that insured that painting had to pay out a lot of money when it was stolen. They want their money back."

"Are you going to report Nigel to the police?"

"It doesn't work that way."

"What do you mean? If he stole—"

She waved her glass. "I have no idea who stole that painting. Nor do I care. The company I work for wants it returned to the collector, and fifty thousand is a small price to pay."

While Lorne and Emy were tracking our conversation with rapt attention, my father had been nervously eying the door. I ignored his hint.

"What's it really worth?" I asked her.

"Ten times that."

"And the insurer paid the full sum?"

"Correct."

"What happens now?"

"I turn the painting over, then collect my percentage."

I pressed my lips together. This was a fascinating story. But while I wanted to hear more about art theft and fraud and all the tales this woman could tell, a crime had been committed, and it should be reported to the police.

I was torn. It must have shown on my face.

Dragon Lady downed her drink, then lowered the empty glass. "I know what you're thinking, but I assure you the police are rarely interested in art fraud. A wealthy collector gets ripped off—who cares? They have more serious crimes to deal with."

"But—"

"Look at it from their point of view. They charge Hemsworth with possessing stolen goods—not a serious charge, by the way. He says he didn't know they were stolen. Lawyers get involved. Expensive legal wrangling results. The case takes years to get in front of a judge. And in the end, the whole thing is likely to be thrown out on a technicality—or dismissed for lack of evidence."

Rising to her feet, she padded over to the bureau to set the glass down. She picked up the gin bottle, gave it a long look, then replaced it on the bureau with a sigh and turned to face us.

"And that's only if the police actually haul ass to investigate it properly in the first place. Meanwhile"—she held up her hands—"that painting's locked up in evidence and the insurers are out the claim money."

She paused, looking at each of us in turn before continuing. "Or, we do it my way."

I unfurled my arms. "Which is?"

"My sources tell me when a special painting is being shopped around, no questions asked. I pretend to be a wealthy collector with no scruples about the origin of my acquisitions. That flushes out somebody like Hemsworth, who offers me that special painting under the table. No provenance. In *this* scenario, the original collector gets his artwork back, Nigel gets his cash, the insurer gets their refund—everybody's happy."

"It's still a crime."

She smiled. "Verity. Don't be naive."

By this point, my father was so anxious to get out of there he was almost bouncing on the bed. I turned to the team. "Can I have a few minutes alone with this woman?"

They filed out the door.

"Leave the laptop," said the former blonde.

Lorne, who had tucked it under one arm, complied, looking sheepish.

Once the door was closed, she turned to face me. "What do you want?"

"Look," I said. "Maybe your way is better. To be honest, I don't care about a stolen painting. But a good friend of mine is about to be charged with a crime he didn't commit, and I think Nigel Hemsworth knows something about it. It's only a hunch, but I can't ignore it." I took a deep breath. "So —I will promise not to go to the police about your sting operation, if you'll find out what Nigel knows—and then tell me."

She gave me a long look. I could see she was intrigued. Picking up the wrapped painting from the sofa, she walked over to the door with it. "What kind of crime?" she asked, propping the painting against the wall.

"Murder."

Her eyebrows arched. "That's a little out of my league."

"I doubt that. I'm willing to bet there's a criminal justice background somewhere in your CV. Maybe you're working for an insurance company now, but—"

"Actually," she broke in, "I'm a freelancer."

"Whatever. It wasn't always about the money, was it? Doesn't it gall you that the bad guys simply walk away after one of your jobs? I mean, you recover the goods, yes, but what about the perps?"

Her lips twitched at my use of *perps*, but I suspected I'd hit a nerve. She stared a long while at the wrapped painting.

I held my breath.

Then she pulled over the armchair and sat, draping her arms over the sides and crossing her legs. "I'll doubtless regret this, but—give me the details."

After I filled her in on Ryker's predicament, she shook her head. "I admire your determination, but this friend of yours is probably guilty."

"He's not. He can't be. Those were brutal, horrible murders. One of those women he didn't even know. And the other one he really liked."

"You only know that because he said so."

"I know it looks bad. But you don't have to believe he's innocent to help me. Don't you think it's suspicious that Nigel is involved with the sale of an inheritance that Ryker has no interest in?"

"I hate to keep harping on about this, but you only know your friend is indifferent to his inheritance because he told you so."

"I know that. But there are other coincidences. His half-sister showing up, asking about the painting. The mysterious addition to his cousin's will that stipulates *Spirit of the North* has to stay in Leafy Hollow. And now—because of you—we know Nigel's a fraud artist. He has to be up to something."

She tapped her fingers on the arm of the chair. "Maybe so, but there's nothing to indicate that it's murder." She regarded the painting by the door for a moment before adding, "I agree it looks suspicious, but I'm not sure how I can help you."

"You can set up another meeting with Nigel. Tell him you're interested in the Lawren Harris painting."

"That one's not stolen."

"As far as we know." I raised my eyebrows.

She shook her head. "It's never been on my radar."

"It's never been on anybody's radar—because it's been locked away in Perry Otis's collection for decades. Hardly anybody's seen it. That's suspicious, don't you think?"

"Not really. Obsessed collectors are often eccentric. Besides, it was displayed at the open house. Everybody saw it then."

"Only people from the village. There were no art experts in the crowd—no one who might recognize it as having been stolen years ago."

With her lips pursed, she rose to retrieve her handbag from the bed. After rummaging around, she pulled out a pair of leather driving moccasins and slipped them on. Then she tossed the red-soled pumps, the platinum wig, and the laptop into her bag and lifted it onto her shoulder.

"Wait. That laptop is—"

"Mine. Yes. Thanks for that, by the way. I've been wondering how to get it out of your father's room. I'll come back later for the camera."

"Did you record any other transactions on it?"

She strolled over to the closet to retrieve her silk wrap, then flung it around her shoulders. "Of course. I find it keeps everybody honest." At the expression on my face, she smiled. "Don't worry. I'll call off Birdie."

"Thanks. So—are you going to help me?"

She shrugged. "I'll talk to Nigel. Then I'll ask around to see what I can find out. Call it professional curiosity."

"You can call it whatever you like, but I'm calling it a really big favor for which I will be forever grateful."

She handed me a business card. "Don't thank me yet. There may be nothing I can do for your friend."

I scanned the card. It read simply,

CAYENNE COLE

Followed by a phone number.

Cayenne hoisted the painting under her arm, then opened the motel room door and stepped through.

"Wait," I said, looking up from her card. "That Ferrari outside? Is it really yours?"

She grinned, gave me a wink, and closed the door.

CHAPTER TWENTY-FIVE

NIGEL HAD BARELY SQUIRRELED AWAY his takings in the strongbox in the basement of his shop when Cayenne contacted him again.

"You know, Nigel," she purred on the phone. "Our transaction went so fluidly it left me with quite an appetite."

"Really?" He pitched his voice low to cover a sudden quaver. "We'll have to do something about that." Tucking a finger under his shirt collar, he pulled it away from his neck.

"Silly man." She chuckled smoothly. "I meant an appetite for more art. In particular, that spectacular Group of Seven. Despite your denials, I've heard that you might be persuaded to sell it." She paused. "For the right price."

"Where did you hear that?"

"Is it true?"

"Maybe," he replied, thinking fast. *No reason to scare her off*. Of course, he couldn't let her have *Spirit of the North*, but Cayenne Cole was a solid buyer. He could always use one of those. Especially given her other attributes. He tugged at his collar again. "There are a few difficulties, but you never know. Difficulties can be overcome."

"Good to hear. Meanwhile, can I take a closer look at it?"

"I don't see why not." He smiled to himself, picturing her curves. "It's at the farmhouse. Are you still in the village?"

"I am, as it happens."

"Meet me there in fifteen minutes."

He gave her the address before hanging up. Hopefully he'd have time to set out a few drinks before she arrived.

Once at the house, he left the front door slightly ajar.

In the kitchen, he double-checked that the latch on the counter window was closed. *Can't be too careful,* he thought, chuckling.

Then he got down two crystal glasses, tossed ice cubes into a makeshift bucket—after removing a potted plant—and retrieved the vodka he'd stashed in the freezer after the open house. The booze had already been charged to Perry's estate. No reason to waste it.

Now—where best to place the beverages?

He walked through the great room, assessing the furniture placement, all the while thinking about the way Cayenne filled out that silk dress. And her long legs in those killer heels. *Wait*—he paused—*what about the other paintings?* The ones on the second floor? Wouldn't she want to see those, too?

He smirked. *She certainly would*—especially the small Rembrandt in Perry's opulent bedroom. And if the drinks happened to be close by, well—

He tucked the vodka bottle under one arm, picked up the glasses, then bounded up the stairs, whistling.

Whapp.

A blow struck the side of his head.

Nigel stumbled backward, shrieking in pain, then tumbled to the bottom of the stairs. The vodka bottle and crystal glasses flew out of his hands, smashing against the wall.

For several seconds, he lay there, bewildered. Groggily, he rose to his feet. The side of his head was on fire. He raised a hand to his ear, then winced in pain and pulled his hand away. Numbly, he stared at it. It was covered in blood. Stunned, he looked around. There was blood everywhere, mingling with the vodka dripping down the stairs.

He raised his eyes, then gasped.

A knife hung in the stairwell, attached to the ceiling with a wire.

Nigel stared dumbly at it.

Slowly, he pulled his cell phone from his pocket and jabbed 9-1-1.

Rrring-rrring-rrring.

Holding the phone to his good ear, he closed his eyes. Blood dripped down his neck.

Please answer, he thought.

Rrring-rrring-rrring.

Please.

A voice crackled in his ear. "This is—"

"Someone tried to murder me," Nigel wailed.

"Calm down, please, sir. Tell me what happened."

"My ear," he roared. "There's blood everywhere."

"Do you need medical attention?"

"Of course I need damned medical attention," he screamed. "Are you an idiot?"

"Calm down, please, sir. I'm sending an ambulance to your location. Are you alone in the house? Is there an intruder?"

"Yes. I mean—no, I'm alone."

"Are you able to answer the door?"

"Of course I can answer the damned door. What's keeping them?"

"They'll be there shortly, sir. Do you know who assaulted you?"

Nigel hesitated. Now that help was on the way, he was less panicky. He looked up at the kitchen knife hanging from a wire above the staircase, its blade dripping with blood. Glancing down at the baseboard, he saw a much tinier wire—the one he must have triggered when he bounded up the stairs.

He sucked in a breath through clenched teeth. *This is what happens when you don't keep your mind in the game.*

"Sir? Do you know who assaulted you? Are they still in the house?"

After taking a deep breath, he spoke calmly into the phone. "Whoever set it up is gone. It was a booby trap."

"A what, sir?"

"A booby trap. A knife rigged to swoop down on anyone who went up the staircase and tripped the wire." Feeling weak, he studied the blood sprayed on the stairwell's white wall. *His blood.* Willing himself to speak calmly, he added, "It was an accident."

"Please wait in the house, sir."

Nigel grunted a reply. Then, after dropping his cell phone on the hall table, he leaned toward the mirror and removed his hand from his ear.

The pain was excruciating. He bent over, vomiting violently onto the floor. Then he straightened up and stared in the mirror, his eyes wide and his stomach churning.

Half his ear had been ripped away.

And it could easily have been worse. He could have been killed. If he'd strayed a few inches off center as he ran up the stairs... A chill gripped his spine.

Followed by rage.

Somebody's dead, he vowed.

Shakily, he made a brief inspection of the staircase.

On the bottom step lay a bloodied lump of flesh.

Nigel keeled over in a dead faint. He did not hear the *whirr-whirr-whirr* of the police siren. Or the ambulance.

On the other side of Tulip Crescent, a red Ferrari slowed slightly as it came abreast of the flashing lights. Then it sped off, headed for the highway.

CHAPTER TWENTY-SIX

I WAS at the bakery the next morning, raising a still-warm butternut scone to my lips while vowing to forget about the crooked art world, when Emy filled me in on the shocking events of the previous evening.

"You can't be serious." Dropping the uneaten pastry on my plate, I stared at her in astonishment. "Nigel lost half his ear? How could that happen?"

"It was the weirdest thing. A knife fell from the ceiling."

I tried to take this in. "I don't understand. Why would there be a knife on the ceiling? Was it attached in some way?"

"Supposedly."

I narrowed my eyes. "Are you sure this really happened?"

"Nigel's shop is closed today. He's in his apartment recovering from 'a traumatic injury,' according to a note on the door."

I snorted. "He could have made the whole thing up. How did you hear about it?"

"One of the emergency room nurses likes to pick up freshly baked scones after her night shift. She said the police brought in half an ear, packed on ice. A plastic surgeon sewed it back on. While they were working on Nigel, she overheard the police talking. They said his ear had been sliced off by a knife that fell from the ceiling."

"That can't be right." Shaking my head, I picked up the scone. "Nigel must have made that up. He either had an accident and doesn't want to admit it, or somebody used that knife on him deliberately." I gave an involuntary shudder. "The more I learn about Nigel Hemsworth, the more he gives me the creeps."

Holding the scone in one hand, I dipped a knife into the butter dish. It was gilding the lily, but I'd had a tough week.

Immediately, I dialed back that assessment. *Tough, yes, but not as tough as Nigel and his ear.* Then I giggled. Which probably meant I was a horrible human being. How could anybody laugh at a thing like that? After buttering my scone, I took a healthy bite, chewed thoughtfully, and decided I could live with it.

"I agree with you," Emy was saying, "but that's what she heard."

"Where did this happen?" I reached for my coffee.

"At Perry Otis's place. Nigel must have been checking up on it."

"Could a workman have taped a knife to the ceiling, intending to use it, and then forgotten about it?"

"Maybe. I've never seen anyone do that though, have you?"

"No. It would be too dangerous," I said solemnly. "Somebody could lose an ear."

At Emy's horrified expression, I clapped a hand to my mouth to hide my giggles. "Sorry," I said, lowering my hand in embarrassment. "It's not funny."

"No," she agreed, stifling a giggle of her own. "Not at all."

We exchanged stern looks.

"Well, it's a lawsuit waiting to happen, that's for sure," I said. "Do they know who's responsible?"

"The nurse said Nigel insisted to the police that it was an accident."

"Did this nurse say anything else?"

"Just that the police didn't seem to believe him. They thought it was done on purpose."

"Then why would Nigel call it an accident?"

"I don't know." She leaned in. "But there's a rumor going around that it was the work of a disgruntled client. Someone that Nigel ripped off."

"Really? Are art buyers that violent?" I recalled the genteel crowd of well-heeled patrons at the open house. "It's hard to believe. It's not like Nigel's selling drugs at *Fine Art and Collectibles*. Although—" I narrowed my eyes, thinking it over. "Nah. That's unlikely. You know what I think?"

I polished off the last of my scone and coffee.

"What?" Emy asked impatiently.

"Well, think about it. We saw Nigel in action, selling a stolen painting to Cayenne Cole. That can't be the first time. He's a crook. It's not surprising he got his fingers burned." I reconsidered. "I mean—his ears clipped."

"Stop it," Emy said, stifling a chuckle.

The bell jangled over the front door.

I turned to see Shelby Wynne standing in the entrance, giving me a long look. She maintained her grip on the door handle, almost as if she was reconsidering her choice of eatery, given the unsavory characters it obviously attracted.

"Shelby," I called. "How are you?"

"Fine," she mumbled, letting the door go, then approaching the counter. "Turkey-brie sandwich. To go."

As the door swung shut behind her, I did a double take. She was wearing leggings, a T-shirt whose sleeves hung over the back of her hands, and a scarf tied under her chin so tightly no hair was visible. It would have been odd, except her face showed signs of a vicious sunburn. *She probably wants to avoid any more skin damage,* I thought.

As Emy prepared her order, Shelby shifted uncomfortably from one foot to the other.

"Is your foot any better?" I asked.

"What are you talking about?"

"Your gardening injury," I said, pointing. "Or was it your ankle?"

"I'm fine," she blurted.

"How's Ryker?"

From the expression on her face, I fully expected to have *none of your business* thrown back in mine. Instead, she managed a smile. Then, over her shoulder, she said, "He's fine. It's a long journey."

"It's a—what?"

"Grief. It's a long journey."

Behind the counter, Emy froze.

I knew what she was thinking—that I was still traveling that road myself and might take offense. But I wasn't about to let some woman who wasn't smart enough to come in out of the sun ruin my day with her pop psychology.

So I ignored Shelby. "Emy, can I have a lemon cupcake to go?"

She smiled, sliding the pastry into a paper bag. "For Jeff?"

"Yeah. You know how he loves them."

"What about my turkey-brie?" Shelby snapped.

"Almost done," Emy replied pleasantly, returning to the sandwich. "Shelby, how long are you staying with Ryker?"

"What do you mean? Why shouldn't I stay with my brother?"

"Well, sure, but when you were here the other day, you mentioned finding a place of your own. I suggested that rooming house on Clarence Avenue as a stopgap." After wrapping the sandwich, she handed it to Shelby. "Any luck?"

Shelby pulled a bill from the pocket of her hoodie then dropped it on the counter. "Keep the change. No, that place was full up." She swiveled, heading for the exit.

"See you later," I called as the door swung shut with another jangle of the bell. "Give my best to your brother."

When I turned back to the counter, Emy was shaking her head. "That's some sunburn. Poor girl."

"I noticed. She didn't have that when I saw her the other day at Ryker's. Thanks, by the way, for delaying her that morning."

"It was fine. We had a nice chat."

"What about?"

"This and that. Nothing interesting. Although, come to think of it—" Emy snapped her fingers. "We talked about Perry Otis's farmhouse and how beautiful it was. Shelby mentioned that the second floor of the main house is also stunning. Something about an Italian marble bathroom."

I mulled this over. "I never saw the second floor. Did you?"

"No. There was a red velvet rope strung across the staircase. Like the one in front of the Lawren Harris painting. Nobody was supposed to go up there. There was even a sign, *No Admittance.*"

"You're right," I said, recalling the scene. "So when did Shelby see that fancy bathroom?"

Emy shrugged. "Maybe Nigel gave her a special viewing, since she's one of Perry's heirs."

"When would he have done that?"

We locked glances.

"Last night," we said in unison.

Emy puffed out a breath. "Are you thinking what I'm thinking?"

Reluctantly, I shook my head. "It doesn't make sense. It's far more likely Shelby toured the second floor during the open house. She was checking every room, which is why Nigel kept such a close eye on her. I wouldn't be surprised if she simply ducked under that rope and scooted upstairs when no one was looking."

Emy nodded. "I'm sure you're right. It was a dumb idea."

"Not at all," I insisted. "Because it tells us something else. The booby trap—if that's what it was—couldn't have been there during the open house, or Shelby would have triggered it when she went upstairs."

Which begged another question. Who had become so incensed with Nigel in the past three days that they'd slice off his ear?

CHAPTER TWENTY-SEVEN

AS I SAT in my truck, waiting for Ethan Neuhaus to show up at the next job on our afternoon list, I revisited an earlier problem.

Who was Grace Anderson? And why did she want Molly Maxwell's house?

Common sense told me Molly's home was in a prime location on a coveted lot and that realtors often made cold calls. But common sense could be wrong.

Which was why I needed to speak to Ethan.

His beat-up Camaro pulled up with the roar of an untamed muffler, and Ethan emerged. After waving briefly, he went around to the back of my truck. I followed.

"You still want me to do this place on my own?" Ethan asked, opening the truck's back door then easing the lawn-mower down the ramp.

"Is that a problem?"

"Not at all. I'll text Lorne when I'm done, and he can

pick up the mower." Ethan bent to switch on the motor. It roared into life.

Crossing my arms, I stood in front of the machine.

Ethan shut off the engine. Straightening, he gave me an irritated look. "Are you getting out of the way, or what?"

"In a minute. There's something I'd like to check first."

Pivoting, I walked over to his Camaro and opened the trunk.

Ethan gave a start, then darted toward me. "What are you doing?"

I hoisted a half-empty bag of bonemeal from the floor of the trunk and held it up. "What's this?"

He scowled. "What does it look like? Bonemeal."

"I don't use it. I think I told you that."

"That's from...last season."

I lifted my eyebrows.

"Ryker still uses it."

"No, he doesn't. In fact, I stopped using bonemeal on his recommendation. It attracts too many animals." I dropped the bag by my feet with a thud. "Care to explain?"

"I don't know what you mean," he said sullenly.

"Let me make it clearer, then. Why did you top-dress Molly Maxwell's flower borders with bonemeal?"

"I didn't."

I scuffed the bag at my feet.

"I told you, that stuff is left over from last season."

"It's a fresh bag, Ethan. It hasn't been sitting in the trunk of your car all winter."

He uttered a curse under his breath and looked away, his lips moving silently.

I took a step toward him with my hands up. "I'm not angry. I just want the truth. In some ways, you did Molly a favor. Maybe now she'll take her children's concerns more seriously."

"Yeah," he said, looking down at his feet. "Silver lining, eh?"

"Maybe. But that's not the reason you did it. I want to know why."

He continued to look down, pressing his lips together.

A breeze lifted a strand of my hair. I brushed it off my face.

Finally, he looked up. "It was a mistake."

"Were you trying to ruin my business?"

"No," he blurted. "I only wanted to keep Ryker's clients from jumping ship."

"So you could keep them for yourself?"

He lifted his chin. "Maybe."

I studied Ethan's sullen face, his aging Camaro, his battered hands. The chances he could procure enough funds to buy or lease the equipment needed to run a lawn service company were not good. Not to mention the business smarts I was pretty sure he didn't have. Ethan was a hard worker, yet job after job had fallen through for him. There had to be a reason. Recalling his tussle with Isaac Damien at the *Go for the Juggler* festival, I suspected it had something to do with the company he kept. I took a deep breath.

"I don't believe you. There must be some other reason. Did you destroy those plants for fun?"

"No," he blurted. Grimacing, he ran a hand over his shorn skull. "I need this job," he muttered, not looking at me.

"I'm not firing you, Ethan. I only want to know what happened."

He puffed out a breath, his hand still clamped on his head.

I took a leap. "Did Isaac Damien put you up to it?"

He dropped his hand and turned a wide-eyed look on me. "Who told you that?"

"I'll take that as a yes. So you did it for money."

He frowned. "Not exactly. Isaac...knows things. I had no choice."

"What things?"

He shook his head. "Can't tell you."

"But why Molly's flowers? It's so petty. Was it a joke?"

"He wanted to scare her into selling."

"By ruining her garden?"

"Yeah. It didn't work. The old girl's too tough. She's not the scare-easy type."

"Is that why Isaac argued with you at the festival?"

Ethan nodded morosely. "He said I screwed it up, and he wanted me to do more. When I showed up the second time, somebody had already spray-painted the house. Lucky break, I thought. I figured I'd scatter the bonemeal, get out of there, and tell Isaac I did the paint, too." He scowled. "I didn't know you lot were gonna get involved." He hesitated, fixing me with an intense stare. "Are you gonna turn me in?"

"Depends."

"On what?"

"On whether you tell me the rest. For instance—who's Grace Anderson?"

Chuckling grimly, Ethan plunged a hand into the pocket

of his jeans to pull out a creased and filthy business card. He handed it to me.

Grace Anderson, I read.

I waved the card at him. "What does this mean?"

"It means she doesn't exist. Damien had those cards printed up. It's a fake name. He said the old lady—"

"Molly."

"—yeah, Molly. He said she'd recognize his name. She knew Isaac from years ago, supposedly. He had me drop one of those cards at her house, with a letter promising a really good deal if she sold."

"Why does he want her house so badly? Isaac's not a developer."

"He doesn't want the house. He wants something that's inside the house."

"What?"

"I dunno."

"Didn't you ask?"

He gave a snort of disgust.

"All right. Never mind." I turned to walk back to the truck.

"Hey," he said. "You promised not to fire me if I told you the truth."

Pursing my lips, I studied him for a long moment. "I promised not to turn you in. It's not quite the same thing."

"Figures." He issued another snort. "I knew you'd cut me loose sooner or later."

"Why would I?"

He shrugged. "I'm not one of those clean-cut guys who grins like an idiot and says please and thank you all the time."

I had to smile at his depiction of Lorne. "Listen, Ethan. Lorne is nearly through his business studies. He doesn't want to mow lawns forever. I'll need help even after Ryker returns to work."

If he does, I thought, and immediately felt disloyal.

"You wouldn't wanna hire me," Ethan said flatly. "Not after this."

"Don't be so hard on yourself." I studied his sullen face while he shuffled from foot to foot. Ethan was a good worker. He showed up on time, and he did the job. Being diplomatic with customers was not his strong suit, but that was my responsibility anyway.

"You're hired. For now. But I'll be keeping an eye on you. Any more sabotage and I'll report you."

He nodded, looking relieved. "What are you going to do about Isaac?"

"I haven't decided yet. Although he does owe me for twelve flats of flowers and the time it took to plant them."

"You can't tell him I told you."

"I wasn't planning on it. But—why not?"

"I can't be on the wrong side of Isaac Damien."

"I wouldn't worry about it. I have a feeling he'll be heading back to Europe before long." I paused, thinking it over. *Or somewhere much less hospitable.*

My aunt and I only had the gym for an hour, so we got right to work. Adeline was an old friend of Leafy Hollow's high school principal. I suspected he had a crush on her and that's why he let us use the smaller of the school's two gyms once a week for free. Behind the gym's closed metal doors, we heard students shuffling back and forth in the halls, laughing, calling to each other, and slamming lockers shut.

I practiced a few stretches in my shorts and T-shirt before our warmup. Adeline insisted on jumping jacks, sit-ups, pushups, and planks at every session, despite my protests of overkill.

Then we squared off on mats laid on the basketball court, our stances neutral, our feet bare. I tensed my knees.

On the wall above us, a clock ticked over loudly in its wire cage. Then a bell blared throughout the building, and the noise in the halls gradually faded.

We sparred diligently for fifteen minutes, until a sheen of sweat stood out on our faces.

"You know," I said, confidently parrying another blow from my aunt. "I've been thinking I don't really need any more Krav Maga training."

Thwump.

I hit the mat, victim of a sneaky leg sweep.

After executing a backward roll, I jumped lightly to my feet to resume my stance. "You're going to be sorry for that," I promised.

Adeline merely smiled. "Pay attention, then."

I got her back with a hip throw.

"Nice work," she said, before staggering to her feet. She bent over, breathing heavily.

"Are you okay?" I stepped nearer. And walked right into an elbow strike. *When would I ever learn?*

"You know what?" I asked while lying on the floor, contemplating the ceiling's cracked acoustic tiles.

"What?" Adeline called from six feet away. She was too shrewd to come within striking distance of my foot.

"Nigel Hemsworth sells stolen paintings." I paused. "Well, one, anyway."

"You're kidding."

"No, it's true."

"Break," she called, then padded over on bare feet, extending a hand to help me up. "You better explain that."

I told her what the team had witnessed at the Sleepy Time Motel. Adeline listened with rapt attention.

"Should we report it to the police?" I asked.

"You promised Cayenne you wouldn't."

"I know. But I haven't heard back from her. Maybe she never had any intention of helping me. It could have been a decoy to get me off her back. The longer I wait before reporting that sale, the more questions the police will ask me."

"As well as Frank," she pointed out.

"There's that," I said. "What should I do?"

She shrugged. "I tend to agree with her."

"Really? Won't I get in trouble if this comes out?"

"How? You only had her word for it that the painting was stolen."

"Why would she lie?"

"Who knows? I'm sure she can fabricate a good story, though. Anyway, since the painting's been returned, who's going to file a complaint?"

Behind me, a metal door cranked open. I turned to see Gideon's newly shorn head peeking in.

"You almost done?" he asked.

"C'mon in and sit down." Adeline waved a hand. "We won't be long."

The door closed behind him. As he headed for the narrow rows of bleachers, I returned my attention to Adeline. "Remember telling me about Isaac Damien? How he's been in Europe for years?"

She nodded. "What about him?"

"I think I've found another link between him and Nigel Hemsworth." I told her about Ethan's confession and the dusty business card from *Hemsworth's Art and Collectibles* I saw in Molly's house.

When I was done, Adeline frowned. "That's a tenuous connection." She rubbed a hand over her mouth, looking serious. "Verity, when I suggested earlier that you might be indulging in wishful thinking, this is the kind of thing I meant. Whatever unethical dealings those two are involved in, it's a far cry from murder. And it has nothing to do with Ryker."

"Yes, but—"

I froze.

It was no more than a whisper, but I knew the sound of bare feet treading on vinyl when I heard it. Dropping to my knees, I swiveled to execute a flawless single-leg takedown.

Thwack.

Gideon hit the mat with a thud. He lay on his back, not moving.

We bent over his spread-eagled body.

"Problems?" Adeline asked.

"I'm fine," he wheezed. "Just getting my breath back."

Adeline and I shared a glance, then repaired to the bleachers, where we hung towels around our necks. Wiping our faces, we regarded my fallen adversary.

"You've got to stop setting him up like that. I never fall for it." I narrowed my eyes, evaluating Gideon's prone form. "Should we call for help?"

"He'll be all right. It takes a little longer to spring back at his age."

"He shouldn't be doing this," I said accusingly. I did not know Gideon's exact age, but I suspected he was too old for combat training.

"Try telling him that."

"You shouldn't either, come to that."

She sniffed. "Don't be ridiculous. I'm not even seventy yet. Prime of life."

Wisely, I decided not to contest this assertion, and only nodded in agreement. However, I was unable to ignore her next statement.

"Control's been in touch."

I gaped at her. Alarm bells went off in my head at the mere mention of the mysterious black-ops marketing group known as Control. They once forced me into a dangerous mission by implying my aunt's life lay in the balance—which, unfortunately, it did. After that ended successfully, they promised never to contact me again. And Adeline vowed she'd retired for good.

"Why did they contact you? To top up your pension plan?" I asked hopefully.

"Not exactly."

"Then what?"

"There's been a bit of bother. An offensive that—"

I held up a hand to stop her. "Let me guess. One of their idiotic global publicity campaigns has gone wrong and they need you to fix the damage."

"Something like that."

I noted that she ignored my description of their endeavors as *idiotic*. Good judgment on her part, I thought.

"Is it dangerous?"

"Well," she said in an elaborately drawn-out way intended to make light of it.

It didn't fool me for a minute.

"It might be a teensy bit—"

"Oh, come on," I blustered. "You promised to retire. You crossed your heart and everything. Was that a lie?"

"I am retired, Verity. I didn't lie to you. But sometimes—" She shrugged. "One has to get back in the ring."

"No. One doesn't," I said in a level tone. "You owe that lunatic group nothing. You did their bidding for years. It's time to lay off the plucky stuff."

Her eyebrows rose. "Plucky?"

"You know what I mean."

"There is a slight problem," she said in a small voice. "My usual partner is..." She bit her lips as she watched Gideon. "Not up to it."

Gideon had rolled to a crouching position on the mat. Even from our seats in the bleachers, I could tell he was breathing heavily. When he saw us looking at him, he gave a desultory wave and a forced grin.

"Still catching your breath?" Adeline called.

He nodded gamely with one hand on his knee. "I'm fine."

She lowered her voice. "See? I'd be putting him in danger."

"Him? What about you?"

Ignoring my question, she stared into the distance, obviously thinking something over. "If I take on another case, I'll have to go it alone. There's no one else I trust."

I didn't like the look in her eye—that steely glint of Hawkes determination I'd seen too often over the years. It had been a constant worry for my mother, and now it was getting to be a pain in the neck for me, too.

"You have to refuse," I said. "It's not hard. Repeat after me. *No. I can't do that. I can't leave my niece alone on the eve of her wedding.* Say it."

At the mention of a wedding, she jerked her gaze back to mine. Her expression softened. "Wedding? Then you are going to—"

I raised a hand. "I didn't mean that, exactly. It's a possibility. In the future. Not right now—"

She heaved a sigh. "I don't know what you're waiting for. The entire village is baffled. They talk about you at the farmers' market, you know."

I was startled for a moment until I saw the glint in her eyes. "They do not. Stop joking."

She sighed again. "Well, I can't tell you what to do."

I narrowed my own eyes. Telling her niece what to do was one of my aunt's favorite pastimes. Although she usually framed her advice with, *It's only a suggestion, but—*

"Okay, I'll bite. What do you think I should do?" I meant

to get her advice on Jeff and my response to his proposal. I wasn't prepared for her reply.

"Do you want to be a landscaper forever?"

I reared back. "It was good enough for you," I countered.

"After nearly a lifetime of doing something else, sure. I loved it. It's a great way to spend the summer. Keeps the muscles toned."

"But?"

"But what about the other six months in the year? Are you going to stay home and make sushi?"

"Jeff loves sushi. It's comfort food for him."

"He makes wonderful sushi himself. Frankly, all of his food prep is superior to—"

"Hey. Could we leave my cooking out of this, please?"

"Sorry. I only meant—"

"I know what you meant."

Her criticism was particularly galling, given that my aunt's idea of home cooking included slugs and caterpillars roasted over a fire on one of our survival camping trips. She wouldn't know a wine reduction if it fell on her.

Gideon rose to his feet, then ambled over to sit on the bleachers a few rows away. "Good workout, Verity," he intoned. "You're really coming along."

Adeline smiled. "Coming along? She cleaned your clock. And it took her, what?" She raised her wrist for a glance at her watch. "Three seconds?"

"Don't change the subject," I said.

"I'm not." Adeline raised her voice. "Gideon, I've decided to take on the new case."

He nodded. "Thought you would. That means I—"

"And," she said before he could volunteer to accompany her, "I'll have a new partner."

Gideon and I regarded her with surprise.

"Who?" we asked in unison.

My aunt got to her feet, tugged her T-shirt down over her bicycle shorts, and smiled. "Verity."

Then she heaved her gym bag over one shoulder and headed for the door.

I watched her go with my mouth agape. By the time I recovered my voice, she had disappeared. I turned to Gideon. "Did she just say—"

"Yes. She did." He rose to follow Adeline.

"Well." I clapped both hands to my waist. "I'm not doing it."

He tossed me a grin over his shoulder as he reached the door.

"I'm not doing it," I called after him. Then, in a louder voice, "Not. Doing. It."

My words rang off the gym's metal bleachers and polished floors. There was no one around to hear them.

CHAPTER TWENTY-EIGHT

"YOUR AUNT'S NOT SERIOUS, SURELY?" Emy looked worried as she poured fresh hot water into my tea mug at the 5X. "About recruiting you for Control, I mean?"

"She seemed serious to me."

"Is that scary holographic thingy still in your basement?"

"Yes, but... It's supposed to be inoperative."

In the past, the basement's rows of monitors had switched on without warning to display the gray-faced marionettes that relayed Control's orders. It was never clear who pulled their electronic strings. But once, they threatened to blow up Rose Cottage, frightening me half to death.

"Hmmm." Emy handed me the mug over the counter. "Fortunately, you don't have to join Control."

I paused, the mug halfway to my lips, meeting her eyes.

"Oh, no," she said. "You're tempted."

"It might be interesting."

"Did you tell Jeff?"

"Not yet. Not until I make up my mind."

"You better do that fast."

"Why?"

She lifted her chin at the front door. "Because he's here now."

A second later, the bell jangled. I turned to see Jeff walk in. I could watch him do that all day.

"Hi, sweetheart," he said, smiling broadly.

I offered my cheek for a quick kiss.

He nodded. "Emy."

"Lemon cupcake?" she asked with a smile.

"Not today. Coffee, black."

She filled a mug from the carafe.

"Thanks." Jeff took a swallow before lowering the mug and clearing his throat.

"You've got news," I said. "Tell me."

"It's confidential." He regarded Emy, a smile playing on his lips. "But I suppose you know all about it."

"If you mean Ryker's case," I placed a hand on his arm. "Yes, she does. Now—what's the news?"

"I checked into Mr. Fields' prison term, like you asked." Jeff took another sip, watching me over the rim of his mug.

"And?" I asked, nearly jumping out of my skin in anticipation.

"Is this Ryker's father we're talking about?" Emy asked.

I nodded rapidly without taking my gaze from Jeff's face.

"He was in Penetanguishene for nine years," Jeff said.

"How old is Ryker now?"

"Thirty-eight."

I did a quick sum in my head. "Ryker told me his father

went to prison when he was eight years old. That means his father got out of prison when Ryker was seventeen—twenty-one years ago."

"Correct. But why did you—"

"How old was Dakota when she died?"

"Twenty-two."

My heart sank.

Emy—also good at math—puffed out a breath. "Oh," she said in a small voice.

Jeff searched our faces. "Why are their ages significant?"

"I couldn't tell you before. I promised Ryker."

He placed the mug on the counter, his expression locked in blank-detective-look mode. "Go on."

"Dakota believed that Ryker was her half-brother. Same father, different mother. But if Dakota was twenty-two, then Ryker's dad can't possibly be her father. He was in prison when she was conceived."

Emy's eyes widened. "Dakota and Ryker weren't siblings."

"No."

Jeff grimaced. "You should have told me about this."

I scrunched up my face in remorse. "Sorry. But I'm telling you now."

"Does this help Ryker's case?" Emy asked.

Miserably, I pushed my mug away, shaking my head. "If we can do the math, then Ryker could, too. He may have decided Dakota lied to him all along. Especially when she demanded money."

Jeff grimaced. "Which would have made him angry enough to—"

"Don't," I blurted.

"What about Dakota's DNA test?" Emy asked.

"Shelby must have forged it somehow," I said.

"Why would Shelby lie about Dakota being their sister? It's so mean."

Jeff cleared his throat. We turned to face him.

"There's more. When I was checking on Mr. Fields' prison sentence, I talked to the detectives on the Strathcona case. Turns out Shelby has a criminal conviction for fraud."

Emy and I exchanged shocked glances. "Wow," we said in unison.

In hindsight, I shouldn't have been surprised. I knew Shelby wasn't truthful. I just didn't suspect her lies extended to actual crimes. Although, when I thought it over, it made sense. The entire Fields clan appeared to have a turbulent relationship with the law.

"What happened to her?"

"Six months in jail."

"That's a lot for a first offense."

"Shelby was offered probation in exchange for information, but she refused to cooperate. The investigators knew she had an accomplice, but she wouldn't name him."

"We have to tell Ryker about this," Emy said. "He deserves to know what his half-sister's been up to."

Jeff was adamant. "No. You two have to back off."

"But—"

"No, Emy. Let the police handle it."

I watched them argue with growing unease. Then I clapped a hand to my forehead. *How could I be so dumb?*

"What is it?" Emy asked with a look of alarm.

I shook my head. A casual comment of Shelby's had floated to the top of my mind. *It was so strange, finding out I had a little sister I'd never met...*

"Little sister" implied Shelby was older than Dakota. A cold feeling grew in the pit of my stomach as I realized Shelby couldn't be Ryker's sister, either.

And worse—that casual remark of hers might have tipped Ryker off.

Before I could open my mouth to explain, Jeff's cell phone rang. He raised it to his ear.

"Yes?" He frowned as he listened. "I see." His expression was grim as he clicked off the call. "No one's seen Ryker for hours. His truck is no longer at his house."

I recalled the last time I'd seen that truck. It had a flat tire. *You'd have to be oblivious to drive it like that*, I thought. *Or furious.*

"There's an APB out for the vehicle," Jeff added. "Meanwhile—have either of you seen Shelby?"

"Not since this morning," Emy said. "She came in for a sandwich." She caught my eye, looking uneasy. "Do you think she's in danger?"

I returned her glance, biting my lip. I didn't believe Ryker would harm Shelby, despite her lies about Dakota. *Or did I?*

"I don't know," I said miserably. "It's...possible. Jeff—about those DNA tests—"

But he was already headed for the exit, his lips tight.

I started after him—then halted as a *BOOM* echoed off the walls.

Emy grabbed the counter with both hands as a tremor

shook the floor of the bakery, rattling the china. "What was that?" she squealed.

We rushed to the front door. Jeff had already flung it open. Once outside, we stood on the sidewalk, mouths slack.

Smoke was billowing from the back of Nigel Hemsworth's building. Flames licked up the side walls of his apartment on the second floor.

"Stay back," Jeff shouted, rushing to the scene.

Right, I thought. *As if.*

We raced after him and around the corner to the back of Nigel's shop. Sirens wailed as a firetruck roared past.

Emy and I joined the gathering crowd at the back of the building. Greasy black smoke swirled through the air, making us cough. I squinted, trying to make out the back wall through the murk. I knew Nigel had a balcony on the second floor, but I couldn't see it.

Firefighters unspooled hoses, then trained them on the building. The whoosh of water hitting the walls competed with shouts from patrol officers to "Move back!" Cars halted on the street behind us, blocking the road as drivers jumped out to take videos.

Within minutes the smoke subsided, revealing the extent of the damage. The back wall was completely destroyed. All that remained of Nigel's balcony was a pile of bricks. The crowd sucked in a collective breath, then let it out slowly. We exchanged shocked glances.

Emy leaned toward me. "Do you think Nigel's underneath those bricks?" she whispered, looking squeamish.

"I hope not." Craning my neck to see over the crowd, I

scanned the parking lot for his blue convertible. "His car's not here."

"Oh. That's a good sign." Emy tapped my shoulder. "I can't stay. I have to get back to the bakery." She dug a set of car keys out of her pocket, then handed them to me.

"What's this for?" I asked.

"Lorne has the truck, right?"

I nodded.

"I know you, Verity. Whatever you're doing, you'll need wheels." With a flap of her hand, she raced off. I dropped the keys into my pocket.

The fire was out, and emergency crews were assessing the charred and smoking bricks from a distance, pointing and conferring. It would take hours to clear the site.

I turned to walk away. The explosion must have been an accident. Unless...

What if it was a decoy? I wondered. Nigel had been furious at Shelby's ham-fisted attempts to claim the Lawren Harris painting. An explosion like this would create a diversion that would distract the police and leave him free to deal with Shelby.

I shook my head. *That was a crazy idea. Who would blow up their own apartment?* With growing unease, I realized how desperate my theory sounded. Maybe Adeline was right. Maybe I had focused on Nigel as the killer simply because I wanted to clear Ryker.

But where *was* Ryker? Why would a man too depressed to leave his house suddenly bolt?

One thing was certain. Shelby had made enemies in

Leafy Hollow. It was possible Nigel finally snapped and went after her, but it was equally possible Ryker had, too.

She could be in danger. *Or was that just my paranoia speaking?* I rocked on my feet, wondering what to do. I hated Shelby for tricking Ryker, but I didn't want her harmed.

Jeff was instructing uniformed officers to move the crowd back. On his way past, he stopped to speak to me. "We're expanding the perimeter so the crews have more room to work. You might as well go home."

"Do they know what caused it?"

"Natural gas explosion, they think. Nigel had a gas barbecue on the balcony."

"An accident, then?"

Jeff thinned his lips, watching the scene. "Probably," he said slowly. "They won't be able to determine that for a while."

"Did they find his body?"

He shook his head. "Engineers have to shore up the wall before the crews can do a thorough search."

"Nigel could be fine."

"He's not answering his phone."

"His car is gone," I said, pointing to the empty parking space behind the building. "He could be at Perry Otis's farmhouse, cataloguing the artwork for sale. Shelby could be there, too." I hesitated. "And Ryker. Do you want me to check?"

"No. We'll send a squad car. I appreciate that you're trying to help, but stay out of it, Verity. I'll see you at home."

A few minutes later, as I revved up the engine of Emy's

Fiat, I considered my next move. I could join Lorne and Ethan at work. They'd appreciate the help.

Or I could drive to Perry's farmhouse.

Stay out of it, Verity.

I tried to come up with a third alternative, then brightened.

What about looking for Shelby somewhere else? Just because she wasn't at Ryker's didn't mean she was at the farmhouse. I headed for Clarence Avenue, on the other side of the village.

It was easy to find the rooming house Emy had recommended to Shelby. Three-story brick, peeling paint on the trim, weeds in the front yard—and a hand-lettered sign propped up in the front window.

Rooms to Let

After peering unsuccessfully through the front door's pebbled glass window, I pushed the door open, stepping into a fog of cooking odors and stale cigarette smoke, seasoned with a whiff of lemon-oil furniture polish.

A hand-lettered sign on the first unit read, Office. I rapped on the door.

Footsteps sounded, then the door opened to reveal a middle-aged woman, her wispy hair tied back in a ponytail.

"If you're looking for a room, we're full up. Come back next week. I might have something then." She went to close the door.

I slapped a hand on it. "I'm not looking for a room. I'm

looking for a person." I described Shelby. "She may have come here in the last week or so."

"What do you want her for?" The landlady's expression was guarded, but not unfriendly.

I decided to embellish my story.

"I only want a friendly chat, but she's hard to track down. Someone mentioned they saw her here." I tried to look hard-bitten, whatever that meant. "That bitch owes me money."

The landlady shrugged. "I'm not surprised." Pursing her lips, she studied my face, obviously mulling it over.

"I won't cause any trouble," I added hastily.

She broke into a grin. "Ha. I can tell that."

Inwardly, I sighed. My attempt at hard-bitten hadn't worked. File that for future reference.

"Listen," she said. "I'd like to get my hands on her, too. I never should have let her rent a room without a damage deposit. She talked me into it. I should have known better." Rolling her eyes, she added, "You wouldn't believe what she did up there."

"What?"

"I'll show ya." Snatching a key from a hook on the wall beside her door, she stalked down the hall. "Follow me."

The vinyl-floored hall led to a staircase at the back of the house. After two flights of creaky wooden steps, the landlady pushed open a door. "Take a look."

I edged past her to enter the room, then gasped. The floor, the walls, the sagging bed, the worn floral armchair—everything was splashed with red.

"Is that...blood?"

"I wish," said the landlady. "Her blood, preferably." She

shook her head. "It's paint. *Oil* paint. I didn't think you could buy that anymore. Not only that, but my handyman says it's been mixed with glue. Glue! What kind of idiot does that?"

She surveyed the damage. "We can repaint the walls, but we can't get this stuff off the floor. Or the furniture. She tracked it into the bathroom, too, and the tub. If you see that woman"—she shook a furious finger at me—"you tell her she owes me money."

"Mind if I look around a bit?"

"Be my guest. Let yourself out. No reason to lock this room now." She stalked off.

I opened the three drawers of the worn bureau. They were empty. The bathroom held a few essentials—soap, shampoo, a comb, and a rusty razor in a corner that looked as if it had been there for years. Two red-stained towels hung over the edge of the tub. If Shelby had rented this room, she certainly hadn't been using it.

Outside, as I climbed back into the Fiat, I thought it over. Why would Shelby throw paint around? What was she trying to accomplish? It was pointless.

It was far more likely someone else did it.

Possibly as a warning.

I recalled Shelby's appearance in the bakery. Her reddened skin must have been from scrubbing paint off her face, not sun bathing. And her limp? Not from weeding, that was certain.

With a start, I remembered Nigel's reputation for practical jokes. His obvious hatred of Shelby. And his severed ear, which could have been the work of a practical joker.

Turning the key in the ignition, I realized with a sinking feeling it might already be too late.

I pulled away from the curb, headed for the Escarpment road.

Only one place left to look...

CHAPTER TWENTY-NINE

I DROVE up Perry's driveway and over the crest of the hill. Sunlight glinted off the Silo's white tower. The trees lining the driveway swayed in the breeze. In the distance, a row of dark green spruce trees framed a field of brilliant yellow canola. Through the Fiat's open window, I heard birds chirping.

It was an idyllic scene that would have soothed my troubled nerves, if it hadn't been for the two vehicles parked by the front door—Nigel's blue convertible and Ryker's pickup truck, its flat tire nearly worn through.

I pulled the Fiat in beside them, then turned off the engine to call 9-1-1. An understandably harried dispatcher answered. I tried to explain.

"I'm calling to report the possible presence of a man police would like to—"

"Is this an emergency?"

"No. Not an emergency. I think Ryker Fields might be at

a farmhouse on Tulip Crescent—"

"This line is reserved for emergencies. Call the police station if you have something to report." *Click.*

After trying to leave a message on Jeff's cell phone—*this mail box is full*—I got out of the car, then leaned against it, watching the front door. Jeff had promised to send a squad car. All I had to do was wait.

After a few minutes of inactivity, I decided there was no harm in strolling around the side of the house to look in the windows. When I reached the Silo, I peered through a window. The center of the room was lit by sunlight coming through the skylight, but the edges—where the paintings were hung—were in shadows. All the spotlights were out.

Then I saw Shelby.

She was huddled against a far wall, her knees clasped to her chest, her head lowered. I tapped on the window.

She looked up, bleary-eyed.

I gasped at the blood on her face.

When she saw me, she shied back at first, looking frightened. Her eyes widened.

It's me—Verity, I mouthed.

She rose, resting a hand on the wall to steady herself. Her lips moved. Ever so faintly, through the walls of the Silo, I heard her muffled cry, *"Help me."*

Glancing frantically about, I realized there was no exit door in the Silo. By design, no doubt, in order to protect the paintings from intruders.

I'm coming, I mouthed at Shelby through the glass. Then I raced around the house to the front door.

When I saw it was ajar, I paused. But only for a moment. Backup would arrive soon. Meanwhile, Shelby needed help.

I trotted through the foyer, my steps slapping against the tiles, then through the great room. Ignoring the eight-foot suede sofas and granite coffee tables, I swerved to the left, heading for the Silo.

Shelby appeared in the doorway in front of me, looking terrified. Blood was dripping onto her face and shoulder from a scalp wound, and she was cradling one arm.

"Verity," she wailed, staggering toward me. "Thank God you're here."

I rushed forward. "What happened?"

"He's here," she wailed. "Nigel. He came after us."

"Us?"

"Ryker's in the next room. He tried to protect me. Oh, Verity... It was awful."

"Is Ryker hurt?"

She burst into tears. After smearing blood, tears, and snot across her face with the back of her hand, she jerked her chin at the Silo.

I darted though the door.

Ryker was sprawled on the floor a few feet away. I hurried forward, then halted. There was something about—

Thwump.

Every muscle in my body relaxed as the room went black. I didn't even feel the floor when it rushed up to meet me.

Pain. In my head.

I groaned.

Hurts.

I opened my eyes.

Shelby stood before me, wiping blood off her face with a towel. She was grinning. Now that the blood was gone, I saw the streaks of paint in her hair.

"You hit me," I said groggily.

Somehow I couldn't do anything other than state the obvious. Deep inside, my inner Aunt Adeline shook her head in disbelief. *You fell for that?*

Still grinning, Shelby kicked a broken lamp out of the way, then walked out of the room.

I tried to stand, battling the fog that swirled through my brain. But my wrists were bound behind me, and my unsteady feet couldn't get purchase on the tiled floor. After a few minutes of pointless floundering, I slumped back down, hitting the floor with a thud.

I lay there, breathing heavily.

Just for a minute. I have to clear my head.

My gaze fell on a roll of black duct tape a few yards away. Clenching my teeth against growing nausea, I groaned. *Why does it always have to be duct tape?*

Ignoring the overwhelming urge to close my eyes and pass out, I searched my surroundings for a box cutter or scissors to free my wrists—regretting that knives never fall from the ceiling when you really need them.

I looked over at Ryker. His hands and feet were bound, and tape covered his mouth. His eyes were closed. I couldn't tell if he was alive or dead.

Shelby came back through the door, rolling a hand cart in

front of her. "You're wasting your time, Verity. Don't bother looking for your phone, either. Or the keys to that stupid little car. I have them both."

Leaving the cart by Ryker's body, she bent to check the tape on my wrists.

Feebly, I tried to trip her with an outstretched foot. Chuckling, she nimbly avoided me, then reached for the roll of duct tape, tore off a strip with her teeth, and wrapped my ankles.

"Help," I screamed. "Help."

My voice echoed off the walls.

"The only reason I haven't taped your mouth is that no one can hear you," Shelby said. "But I will if you don't shut up."

I shut up.

Shelby flopped Ryker onto the cart, hoisting first one end, then the other.

"What have you done to him?" I slurred.

She ignored me. Grunting, she pushed the cart toward the great room, stopping once to wipe sweat from her eyes. "Bastard," she muttered. "How much does he weigh?"

I assumed it was a rhetorical question.

Shelby and the cart disappeared into the great room. Moments later, I heard a door slam.

Desperately, I glanced about. Through the haze clouding my vision, I saw *Spirit of the North* hanging in its usual spot. Nigel hadn't taken it after all.

But where was Nigel?

Shelby reappeared, pushing the cart in front of her. "You're next, Verity."

"The painting," I said, hoping to delay her. "Nigel won't let you take it."

She gave me a sad look. "Oh, I'm afraid poor Nigel had to give it up."

"To you?"

"Yep. Don't worry, though." She winked. "He's not going to miss it."

I struggled to understand. "His car..."

"Isn't it nice? I always wanted a convertible. I took the keys off his bureau when I broke in to set up my little surprise. As well as the keys to this farmhouse." She paused, gazing thoughtfully at the painting. "Too bad I'll have to ditch the car. It's too conspicuous."

I scrunched my eyes shut as tightly as I could, then opened them again with a shake of my head. The fog was beginning to clear.

"How did you do it?"

She shrugged. "Easy. I nicked the gas line to the barbecue on Nigel's balcony. Because it was outdoors, he didn't notice the smell of escaping gas. And when he lit that thing —boom!"

"So he's dead?"

"I dunno." She grinned. "What do you think?"

"How did you know he'd use the barbecue today?"

She laughed. "That was brilliant. I paid the organic butcher to deliver a box of ridiculously expensive steaks to his apartment with an anonymous get-well note. Nigel couldn't resist. I knew he'd have that thing up and running in no time. Which gave me the opportunity to come up here to claim my painting."

She hoisted a rusted metal can in one hand. "I do need to get on with it."

With a lurch in my stomach, I read the can's peeling label.

TURPENTINE

Underneath, there was a large FLAMMABLE warning, complete with skull and crossbones.

Noticing my gaze, Shelby shook the can and sighed. "You're right. Gasoline would be better, but this is all I could find. It was in the garage. But first—"

She put down the can, then bent over to grab my feet. "Let's go," she said, dragging me in the direction of the cart.

I squirmed and tried to sit up, to prevent her.

Shelby heaved a sigh, dropped my legs, and kicked me in the stomach.

"*Ow.*"

"You can't stop me, Verity. I'd allow you to get up and walk, but you're not trustworthy." Bending over, she grabbed the neck of my shirt and hauled my top half onto the cart. Then the bottom half. My attempts to stiffen my body only made it easier for her.

"I know you're not Ryker's sister," I said as the cart's wheels squeaked across the floor. "So does Ryker. And so do the police."

She paused long enough to scowl. "Ryker never would have figured it out if Dakota hadn't been stupid enough to tell him her age. I warned her not to."

I gasped. "Your fraud charge. The one you went to prison for. Dakota was the accomplice you refused to name."

Shelby slumped against the nearest wall, breathing heavily. "You're heavier than you look." Chuckling, she added, "I should have taken Ryker up on his weightlifting tips."

"Your accomplice," I repeated. "It wasn't another man. It was Dakota, wasn't it?"

She shot me a vicious look. "What if it was? She's dead."

"Did you kill her?"

Pursing her lips, she looked beyond me, her gaze fixed on the Silo gallery.

Thinking about her prize, I imagined.

"You don't get it. I went to jail rather than turn Dakota in. She owed me." Wiping a line of sweat from her forehead, Shelby stood to grab the cart's handle again.

We moved forward. *Squeak, squeak, squeak.*

"We worked together for years," she continued. "Small stuff, mostly. Then I read about these new DNA tests online and saw an opportunity."

Grunting, she maneuvered the cart into the front hall.

As we rounded the corner, my overhanging feet banged against the wall.

"Watch it," I said.

"Shut up," she said.

My vision was growing hazy again. I fought to stay conscious. "But why Ryker?"

"Dakota sold her grandmother's stuff to an antiques dealer from Leafy Hollow, one piece at a time." She chuckled. "Nigel Hemsworth, it was. And he couldn't stop himself from bragging. Poor old Nigel." She chuckled again. "One day, they got to talking about estate sales. He mentioned that some guy in the village had inherited this really valuable painting and that he—Nigel—was going to profit from it. It didn't take us long to find out who the guy was."

Leaving me on the far side of the great room, near the foyer, Shelby walked off, returning with the can of turpentine. She set it on the cart.

I eyed it warily.

"Dakota was supposed to charm Ryker. She was good at that. But this time, it backfired."

"She fell for him," I said, my voice flat.

"It was sickening," she hissed. "I would have done anything for her. What did she need Ryker for?"

"You were jealous."

"Shut up." She wheeled me into the foyer. *Squeak, squeak, squeak.* "I told Dakota that if she didn't explain the situation to him, I would."

"You mean, tell him he was her half-brother?"

She shrugged. "It's worked before."

"Didn't Ryker ask for proof?"

"Nope. Nobody ever does. It looks official, the way we present it. Most of them simply pay us to go away and not tell anyone."

She crouched at my feet to swipe my legs off the cart. "But in Ryker's case it was different, because he'd shown Dakota the will. When she told me about it, I realized immediately what it meant. Instead of keeping it hidden, we needed everyone to know they were related, so she could claim a share of his inheritance."

"The lawyers would have figured it out."

"By then we'd have the painting."

"What went wrong?"

She flopped my top half onto the floor, thumping me onto my shoulder, which throbbed in protest.

"Dakota carried out the first part—telling Ryker," Shelby said. "Then she refused to make it public. I told her she didn't have to ask Ryker to *give* her money—it would be hers by rights. I told her she had to do it. That everything would change between us if she didn't. But she wouldn't listen." Shelby scowled. "I can still hear her. Ryker was *distressed*. She couldn't *bear* it. *Poor* Ryker."

With a muttered curse, she kicked the turpentine can across the foyer. I held my breath, watching as it bounced off the wall and clattered to the floor. The cap stayed on. I sucked in a grateful breath.

Shelby stared at the can, pain contorting her face. "We were so good, the two of us. Why wasn't I enough for her? But she wouldn't listen." Her voice dropped to a whisper. "Why wouldn't she listen?"

With a grim face, she unlocked the door of a walk-in closet off the foyer. I hadn't noticed it during the open house. Perry must have used it to store paintings, since there were several propped against one wall, leaving plenty of room for the hand cart.

Ryker was propped against the other wall. He wasn't moving.

CHAPTER THIRTY

I CONSIDERED ROLLING AWAY from Shelby before she could drag me through the door and stuff me into that closet. But my stomach was still cramping from her kick. I decided to bide my time.

"How did you convince Dakota to go through with it?" I asked.

She shrugged. "I didn't have to. I used Dakota's phone to send Ryker an email from her, demanding money. But she found the email...and we fought over it."

"You killed her."

"I didn't mean to. I...lost control." Her eyes widened. "It was an accident."

"What about the neighbor, Rosie Parker? Was that an accident, too?"

Shelby looked surprised. "Oh, I had no choice. That meddling gossip would have turned me in. I did the neighborhood a favor, really."

With a series of grunts and muttered oaths, Shelby dragged me inside the closet by my feet. Then she slammed the door. I heard a key turn and the lock thud.

The faint light coming under the door was enough to make out a light switch on the wall. Struggling to my feet, I flicked it on with my chin, then turned to Ryker, praying he was still alive. "Ryker?"

He opened his eyes wide, then flexed his eyebrows at me.

I issued a sigh of relief. "I thought you were dead."

"*Rrrhhmrmphh,*" he said.

After dropping to my knees and inching forward, I lowered my face to his. Once I had a good grip with my teeth, I ripped the duct tape off his mouth.

"Thanks." He gulped in several deep breaths. "I've been such an idiot, Verity. She's not my sister."

"I know."

"How could I have been so stupid?"

Should I answer that? I wondered. Opting to take the high road, I countered with, "You're not stupid. Although, following Shelby here was not the wisest course."

He managed a crooked grin. "Look who's talking."

"Touché." I struggled against the tape. "We have to get out of here. Shelby has a can of turpentine, and I don't think she's planning to use it to lift stains out of the carpet."

"How can we? The door's locked, and our hands are bound."

Rising to my unsteady feet, I backed up to the wall, slid down it until I was on the floor, then butt-hopped over to the door. "If we coordinate our movements, we can kick it in." I hesitated. "Or out, in this case. Anyway, something's bound to give."

I hoped it wouldn't be my knees.

A rap on the door caused me to jerk back.

"Everything okay in there?" Shelby called. "Are you two comfortable?"

"We're fine, you bitch," I yelled. "Let us out."

"I'm so glad," she replied in a pleasant tone. "I only wanted to tell you it's going to get a little warm in here." Even through the closed door, I heard her chuckles.

Then her footsteps, walking away.

"Come on, Ryker," I said, lining up my feet. "We're running out of time."

Shelby Wynne's triumph was almost complete as she placed the turpentine can by the front door.

It had all gone according to plan. Too easy, really.

Then, with a scowl, she patted the remaining patch of paint in her hair. *You made him pay, though, didn't you?* She grinned at the memory.

Fingering the match box in her pocket, she reviewed her next moves.

First, she'd stow the painting in the Mercedes. Police and emergency services were dealing with the explosion in Leafy Hollow. She had time to take the whole thing, frame and all. No need to slice out the canvas with a box cutter.

Then she'd return to splash around the turpentine and toss a lit match from the doorway.

It would be days—weeks even—before anyone realized *Spirit of the North* wasn't among the ashes. By that time, she and the painting would be thousands of miles away.

It didn't have to be this way, she thought, her mouth turning up in a pout. Dakota could have been by her side to enjoy their victory. A spasm of pain gripped her chest. It subsided almost as rapidly. With determination, she pivoted on one foot then marched into the Silo.

The painting came away easily. A slight yank upward, and it was off the wall. She hoisted it in front of her, admiring the brush strokes, feeling a surge of joy. *At last.*

Before she could turn away, she froze at the sound of a soft *click* in the wall where the painting had hung.

It was the last sound she ever heard.

We had finally started to make progress on the closet door. "A few more kicks and it'll give," I promised Ryker. "Now, heave!"

But as we raised our bound feet to slam on the solid wood, the whole house shook. A *BOOM* hit us like a blow. We rolled back onto the floor and lay there, limbs tangled.

Cripes. Not again. I desperately wanted to cradle my throbbing head in my hands, but of course they were still tied behind me.

"What was that?" Ryker asked.

Sniffing the air, I blurted, "Is that smoke?"

We exchanged panicked glances, then resumed our

attack on the door with increased fury. The frame around the lock cracked and then splintered.

One more kick and the door flew open.

We tumbled out.

I expected to see flames, but there were none. Above our heads, smoke swirled into an industrial-strength ceiling fan.

On the other side of the foyer, Shelby's turpentine can had fallen over. Thankfully, it was still unopened. That old cap must have rusted in place.

Ryker hopped on bound feet in the direction of the exit, his hands still taped behind him. "We have to get out of here."

"I agree, but...where's Shelby? Did she take the painting?"

"Forget about Shelby." He hopped twice more, then switched to shuffling. I'd seen ancient tortoises with more vroom.

I watched him impatiently. At the rate he was moving, we'd still be here in a week's time. "No, wait. We have to cut this tape off first."

Hoping to find a knife, I hopped into the great room. And halted.

"Wow," I said, then cleared my throat against the dust swirling through the air. "Look at this."

Ryker hopped over. It took quite a while.

"Shit," he said, shaking his head.

Most of the paintings had fallen off the walls. The few still hanging were lopsided. Shards of broken window glass lay in clumps on the floor. A flower vase had smashed on a coffee table, strewing petals everywhere. Water dripped off the suede sofas.

"Why would Shelby blow this place up?" Ryker asked.

"I don't know."

He glanced around, looking worried. "Speaking of Shelby —where is she?"

My curiosity got the better of me. Yes, we should have made for the exit. But I rationalized it this way—if Shelby was still in the farmhouse, we'd be easy pickings whether we were outside or inside, so long as our limbs were tied together. *Might as well take a look.*

I hopped to the entrance of the Silo.

For endless moments I stared, mouth slack, unable to take in what I was seeing.

"Oh, my God," I said in a small voice. "Ryker. Get over here."

He shuffled over, then gasped at the scene in front of us. We exchanged horrified glances.

On the floor of the Silo, Shelby lay on her back, not moving. Only the bottom half of her body was visible. The rest of her was underneath *Spirit of the North*.

At least, I assume that's what lay on top of her, given that her outstretched fingers were still gripping bits of its carved wooden frame. The painting itself was completely destroyed, shredded into countless fragments by thousands of nails that also littered the floor.

Painting, nails, and Shelby were soaked in blood.

"Oh, no," I said, as the room swirled around me. "I'm going to be sick."

After several minutes slumped against the nearest wall, I eventually struggled back to my feet. Then I hopped into the great room, wiping my mouth on the shoulder of my shirt.

Ryker shuffled after me. "Where are you going?"

"To the kitchen. We have to get this tape off."

In the massive kitchen, we stared with longing at a magnetic knife strip on the wall. A paring knife at one end looked like a good bet. Leaning on the counter, I tried to knock it loose with my nose.

"No, don't," Ryker said. "You'll cut yourself when it falls off. Use one of those." He jerked his chin at a ceramic holder full of wooden spoons.

I grabbed a spoon between my teeth, returned to the knife rack, and in one fell swoop knocked off two paring knives, a chef's knife, a bread slicer, and something that might have been a lemon zester. Hard to tell without Jeff's input.

"Good thing you used the spoon," Ryker said, evaluating my haul. "You could have lost an ear."

"Lost an ear," I gasped. *"Lost...an ear."*

I doubled over, gripped by hysterical laughter. I couldn't stop. I had to lean against the counter to stop myself from toppling over. I tried to catch my breath. I tried to stop guffawing. But I couldn't do it. Whether it was the tension of facing imminent death or the horrific scene in the Silo that triggered my meltdown, I was out of control.

My howls of laughter echoed off the walls.

Eventually, I sank to the floor with my back against the

cupboard, still tittering. After a concluding series of hiccups, I wiped my face against my shoulder.

Ryker regarded me skeptically. "Are you done?"

"Sorry," I said, inching my way up the cupboard to stand upright.

"Don't mention it. Now, could we—" He jerked his head at the paring knives.

"Yes." I bent over, using my nose to move one to the counter's edge. "Grab the handle."

While Ryker held the knife steady behind his back, I slid the tape on my wrists over the blade. After three passes, the tape gave way. Sighing in relief, I rubbed my wrists. Then I cut the tape on Ryker's wrists.

While he grabbed the other paring knife to work on his ankles, I flopped to the floor to free my own feet. Once that was done, I wobbled my way to the sink, hanging on to the counters as I went, and splashed water on my face.

Resting my hands on the sink, I looked out the window, admiring the field of yellow canola swaying in the breeze against the row of trees in the distance. Two turkey vultures soared overhead on their massive wings, silhouetted against fluffy clouds. It was such a peaceful setting. No one would ever guess that inside Perry Otis's farmhouse was a scene so brutal—

Cripes. We still hadn't called 9-1-1.

I reached for my phone, then remembered Shelby had it. Along with the keys to Emy's Fiat.

"Is there anything to eat?" Ryker asked, depositing his knife on the countertop.

"How can you even think about food?"

"I haven't eaten since yesterday," he whined, looking sheepish. At least, I think he was sheepish. It was hard to tell, what with the red stripe across the bottom half of his face from the duct tape, the dried blood on his head, and a swollen eye that was developing into a first-class shiner. Now that the tape was off his legs, I noticed he was limping.

"Give me your phone." I held out a hand.

"Can't. Shelby took it."

We turned our faces toward the door that led to the great room and from there into the Silo. We exchanged glances.

I shook my head. "I'm not going in there to look for our phones. You'll have to do it."

With a grimace, Ryker turned to the door, moving slowly. Again.

"No, wait—we can't," I blurted. "It's a crime scene. There must be a phone in here somewhere."

"A land line?"

"Maybe." Helplessly, I glanced around. My gaze fell on the massive stainless-steel refrigerator on the far wall. I recalled my tour of the kitchen, when Emy had said, *The appliances are all hooked up to the Internet...*

"We don't need a phone." After shambling across the room, I pressed my finger to the fridge door. A screen sprang to life.

"Call 9-1-1," I said loudly.

"*Calling...*" said a metallic voice.

After I'd relayed our situation, I opened a set of French doors, then staggered onto the patio, where I sank into the nearest chaise. I pressed a palm to my forehead to shield my eyes from the sun. My head was throbbing viciously and my stomach was queasy.

Ryker followed, standing in the doorway. "I think you just set off the burglar alarm."

Twisting my neck, I stared at him with my mouth open.

"Right. Doesn't matter." He slumped into the chaise beside me. For a long moment, we both stared at the canola.

"While we're waiting," he said. "Do you think there's any food?"

The sun was too bright anyway, and my sunglasses were in my purse, which I assumed was with Shelby in the... *Never mind*. Groaning, I rose to my feet.

"Let's check the freezer. There's bound to be canapés left over from the open house. Nigel wasn't the type to throw food away. Besides, I need an ice pack."

We were slumped on stainless steel stools at the kitchen island—Ryker devouring a plate of defrosted lobster crostini, and me holding a bag of ice to my head—when the wail of multiple sirens announced the arrival of emergency crews.

The first thing the police did was arrest Ryker.

They ignored my protests.

"Never mind, Verity," he said, holding out his wrists for the handcuffs. "We'll sort it out at the station."

Three ambulance attendants—after determining there was nothing they could do for Shelby—hovered over me. "You might have a concussion," said one briskly, while another checked my blood pressure. "We need to get you to hospital."

The third offered moral support. "Let me know if you

feel faint," she said. "Do you want to put your head between your knees?"

Since that would have meant loosening my grip on the ice pack, I declined. "I'm fine. Really."

Then Jeff burst through the door looking worried—his usual reaction to finding me at a crime scene.

"I'm okay," I called. "Honestly. Don't worry."

Leaning over with a hand on my shoulder, he peered at the lump on my head. Sighing, I inhaled the familiar scent of coffee, strong mints, and Old Spice.

"It doesn't look like you're okay. Are you taking her in?" he asked the attendants.

All three nodded. "She should be checked for concussion."

"I'm not going anywhere except the police station," I said, sliding off the stool. "We have to spring Ryker."

Jeff overrode my decision. "If you insist on doing things like this, I insist on proper medical attention. Otherwise—" He didn't actually shake a finger at me, but he came close.

At the hospital, I breezed through the vision test and CT scan—all of it old hat, since this wasn't my first concussion scare—then insisted on going to the station.

Jeff insisted we go home. "You can give your statement to an officer there," he said.

Then his phone rang.

After a brief conversation, he slid the phone back into his pocket. "They want to see you at the station, Verity. Something's...come up." He looked puzzled.

CHAPTER THIRTY-ONE

AS SOON AS we entered the police station lobby, Cayenne Cole strolled over to us, smiling languidly.

I was taken aback. "What are you doing here?"

After giving Jeff a leisurely head-to-toes appraisal, Cayenne turned her attention to me. "I came to back up your story."

"My story? It's not a story. It's the— Hang on. How did you know I was here?"

"Adeline called me."

I was incredulous. "My aunt called you?"

"Great woman. Such an inspiration."

"You know my aunt?"

"You're repeating yourself, Verity. Of course I know Adeline."

I stared, uncomprehending. "She's never mentioned you."

"I'm hurt."

From the twist in her lip, I could tell she was anything but.

"When I didn't hear back from you, I thought you'd decided not to help me," I said.

"You doubted my word?"

"Well, my friend Emy did refer to you as Dragon Lady after we met at the open house."

Cayenne beamed. "Dragon Lady. I like that. Now, who's calling the shots here?" She gave Jeff an appreciative glance. "Is it you?"

I stepped between them.

A beefy, mustachioed man came charging toward us, hand outstretched. After introducing himself as the officer in charge, he ushered us into a conference room.

A dozen people were crowded inside. Some were local cops, but not all. Narrowing my eyes at the badge on a nearby chest, I read the words INTERPOL LIAISON.

Someone pulled out a chair halfway down the table. I sat.

With Jeff standing behind me, I recounted my visit to the farmhouse, followed by what I'd learned about Nigel Hemsworth. After reflecting, I decided to leave my father out of it. Birdie still didn't know about that hole in the closet.

Pens scribbled in notebooks, lips pursed, and eyes narrowed. The door opened, and a young constable walked in with two trays of coffee. He handed them around.

Jeff paused my arm when I motioned for one. "No caffeine for you," he said. "Not for forty-eight hours."

So he *was* listening at the hospital. Sighing, I withdrew my hand.

"Thank you, Verity, for walking us through it," said the

mustachioed officer. "That must have been a difficult ordeal for you."

Jeff squeezed my shoulders. He knew better than anyone what it cost me to appear so calm. My stomach was churning. I wouldn't be able to stay in that room much longer. Not with everyone's eyes on me. But there was one question I really wanted answered.

"Why would anyone destroy *Spirit of the North*?"

"I think I can explain that," came a voice from the back of the room.

Cayenne, who had been perched on a table, got to her feet. All eyes swerved to her as she stepped forward.

"Ms. Cole," said the officer in charge. "Thank you for agreeing to come in today and clear up a few things for us."

"Happy to be of assistance," she said. "As for Verity's question, it's complicated. I believe the answer lies with Nigel Hemsworth's original backers. The silent partners who bankrolled his business—Perry Otis and Isaac Damien."

"We know they were friends," I said. "How is that significant?"

"Ah. That's the interesting part. In his youth, Perry Otis loved to paint."

"Yes. But Nigel told me Perry's work wasn't any good."

Cayenne chuckled. "He was right." She paused, wrinkling her nose. "Although, some of the frames are exquisite. Solid wood, hand-carved. They're worth a few bucks."

"Then what—"

"It's his other work that was valuable."

"What other work?"

"The paintings in the Silo."

"They weren't painted by Perry. They're all by famous artists, people like..." My jaw dropped, along with the penny. "They're forgeries, aren't they?"

She nodded. "Perry's garage is full of old painting equipment. Easels, palettes, oil paint tubes—most of it decades old. I had a look in there yesterday."

One of the local cops frowned. "Did you have a warrant?"

Cayenne tapped a finger on her chin. "Hmm. Let me think."

"Never mind that," I broke in impatiently. "How did you figure it out?"

"We have you to thank for that, Verity," Cayenne said.

All eyes swiveled to me. Jeff squeezed my shoulders. I crossed an arm across my chest to clasp his hand.

Cayenne continued. "Your insistence that Ryker was innocent—and that Nigel was up to something—convinced me to take another look at that painting I bought from him at the motel. It seemed...off somehow. So I asked Nigel to let me take a closer look at the Lawren Harris."

"And? What did you think of it?"

All eyes swiveled back to Cayenne, who preened a bit under the attention.

"Nothing, because when I drove past the farmhouse that night, there were two police cars and an ambulance outside, lights flashing. I kept going. I thought maybe Nigel was being arrested." A smile played about her mouth. "I heard about his ear later. But I still had the other painting, the one I bought from him at the motel. I took it to an expert for a complete forensic rundown. The report came back this morning."

She pulled a manila envelope out of her bag and held it aloft. "It's a fake."

Cayenne placed the envelope on the table. The Interpol Liaison reached for it, then slid out a sheaf of papers. She leaned toward the man on her left, and they leafed through the report, heads together.

"But that picture was stolen," I said.

Cayenne smiled. "It was."

"Oh. I get it. The owners forgot to mention it was a forgery when they filed the insurance claim."

"They're claiming they had no idea it was a fake."

"Can you prove otherwise?"

"Probably not. To be fair, they could be telling the truth. Not many collectors can spot a counterfeit. They simply took the dealer's word for it that the provenance they'd been shown was genuine. They are extremely embarrassed. They have paid back the insurance claim—plus interest and expenses—and asked the insurer to keep quiet about it."

"Which I assume is also in the insurer's best interests."

"You assume correctly."

The Interpol Liaison pointed out something in the papers to her companion. He nodded in agreement.

"But maybe that Lawren Harris was the exception," I said. "Maybe it was genuine."

Cayenne shook her head. "Not a chance. I've done a lot of digging, and there's no record anywhere of that painting. The Group of Seven has been exhaustively documented. The chances that a work like that would have escaped cataloguing—" She shook her head. "Not possible." She frowned. "Plus—did you see it?"

"Yes," I said slowly, not willing to commit myself.

"It was hideous."

I let out a breath. "It certainly was."

Smiling, she glanced around the room. "I'm sure the authorities will allow experts to examine the fragments and perform the standard tests, but I'm confident it was a forgery. Now—" She smiled benignly at the onlookers. "Are we done?"

"Thank you for coming in, Ms. Cole," the officer said, rising to his feet. "We'll be in touch."

"We need to leave, too," Jeff said. "Verity has to rest." The three of us headed for the exit.

No one watched us go. As mingled voices rose around the conference table, Jeff firmly closed the door on them.

"What about Ryker?" I asked.

"He's back home, after a brief visit to the urgent care center. He'll be fine. There are questions to answer, naturally, but he's no longer a murder suspect." Jeff paused. "He's very grateful to you, Verity."

I smiled. "I'm sure he'll send flowers."

While Jeff went outside to bring the car around, I cornered Cayenne in the lobby.

"Why would Perry Otis forge the work of such a famous artist?" I asked. "It was certain to be discovered."

She shrugged. "I'm sure he regretted it many times over the years. But half a century ago, no one could have predicted Lawren Harris paintings would one day sell for millions of dollars. And once everyone knew Perry owned that painting, he couldn't destroy it."

"What did he intend to do with it?"

"He may have meant to give it to Isaac Damien to sell in Europe, like his other forged works. Perry must have sold quite a few to pay for that renovation."

"Wait a minute—what about Molly Maxwell?"

"Who?"

"My landscaping client. Isaac Damien tried to scare her into selling her home, because..." I hesitated, not wanting to implicate Ethan. "I think he was after something in her house."

"I take it this woman is elderly?"

"Yes."

"Well, think about it. If she sold her home, she'd move somewhere smaller, which wouldn't hold all her belongings. She'd have to give away or sell many of them."

"Such as her paintings," I said.

"Correct."

"Molly's husband must have bought one of Perry's forged paintings from Nigel years ago. And Nigel and Isaac hoped to buy it back before anyone noticed it was a forgery."

Cayenne nodded. "Probably."

"Why didn't they sell the Lawren Harris forgery in Europe?"

"They would have, if Shelby Wynne hadn't arrived in the village to screw everything up. They couldn't let her have it. Better to destroy it."

I nodded. "Nigel saw a way to get rid of the painting and Shelby at the same time. But how was he planning to explain the explosion in the Silo?"

Cayenne shrugged. "He could have said it was an anti-burglary device that malfunctioned. He could have claimed Perry set it up, and he knew nothing about it."

"Which means—if Nigel were still alive, he'd be submitting a substantial insurance claim on behalf of Perry's estate right about now."

We shared a smirk.

Although, I did feel a twinge of guilt about it. I mean, the poor man was dead.

As Jeff walked through the front doors and came toward us, Cayenne placed a hand on my arm. "Verity, no one would have suspected anything if you hadn't decided to investigate. I could use someone like you. If you're ever looking for a career change—" She fished a card out of her purse and handed it to me. "Call me."

With a wink at Jeff, she walked out.

TWO WEEKS LATER...

I could have sworn I'd seen a jeweler's box in Jeff's sock drawer. But that morning, when I went back to check—it was gone. My stomach twisted as I studied the empty cubbyhole. Nothing but lint.

Was I too late?

I closed the drawer with a sigh.

Back in the living room, I took stock.

I was wearing Jeff's favorite black dress.

Chinese takeout was warming in the oven.

General Chang was perched on the back of the sofa, tail gently swishing. An adorable kitty necktie lay beside him, which was as close as he would allow. Suggestions that he might actually *wear* the necktie had been met with disdain.

Boomer was on standby, tail quivering. Unlike the General, he was perfectly happy to dress up like an idiot.

And four dozen white candles were positioned throughout the room.

I waited, alternately puffing air out my cheeks and pacing. Sometimes both at once. Boomer watched me nervously. Eventually, he settled onto the floor, still watching me. For the umpteenth time, I checked that the lighter had enough fluid, then wondered why I hadn't bought two.

At the sound of Jeff's pickup in the driveway, I snatched up the lighter and raced around to each of the candles in turn.

Then I took up my post by the wall, facing the door.

The door opened, and Jeff walked in. He turned to close it. "That was quite a shift. I'll be glad when vacations are over. You know, they're still talking about you at..." With one hand on the handle, he paused, his gaze sweeping the room to take in the candles, the pets, and me. "...The station."

Boomer lifted a paw.

"What's all this?" Jeff asked, with a wary half-grin.

"Boomer—*now*," I said, pulling one end of a ribbon attached to a rolled length of fabric hanging on the wall. Boomer tugged on the other end.

The fabric unrolled down the wall, revealing huge red letters.

Will You Marry Me?

Jeff stared at the sign, but said nothing.

I held my breath.

Boomer—his red cape trailing on the floor, and a Cupid's arrow quivering on his head—whimpered.

Jeff swiveled his dark eyes to meet mine.

My heart skipped a beat.

He broke into a grin. "You bet I will."

I fell into his arms. As Jeff picked me up and twirled me around the room, the candles blurred until we were enveloped in a cocoon of white.

Jeff stopped twirling, without releasing his hold on me. I slid down till my feet were on the floor.

"Verity," he said softly.

I will never forget the look on his face.

Then he kissed me.

After a while, he drew back, looking offended. "Weren't you supposed to get down on one knee?"

I giggled. "Not in this dress. No ring, either, I'm afraid."

With a soft smile, he reached into his pocket to slip out a jeweler's box.

I must have looked astonished, because he added, "I knew you'd come around," before flicking the box open. "Give me your finger."

Jeff slipped a ruby-and-diamond ring on my hand.

I held it up, admiring the stones' sparkle in the glow of the nearest candles. "I love it. Thank you." Then I winced.

"What's wrong?"

"It's only...I can't wear a ring like this when I'm cutting lawns."

He held up the open box. "Check the bottom."

After shooting him a puzzled look, I tugged out the velvet-lined base. A platinum chain was tucked underneath. I drew it out, trailing it from my fingers.

"You can wear the ring around your neck when you're at

work," he said. "Good idea?"

Tears welled in my eyes. "It's brilliant. And so are you." I fell into his arms again.

Eventually, Jeff pulled back to glance around, brow furrowed.

Forty-eight candles produce quite a glow. Normally, even one candle would give my safety-conscious soon-to-be-husband cause for concern.

"This is a fire hazard," he said, looking alarmed.

"Don't worry." I patted his chest. "I disconnected all the smoke alarms."

I was jerked awake by a strange sound. For a second, I couldn't tell where I was. Then I turned my head to face my familiar bedroom window, where glimmers of light behind the shutters meant dawn was breaking. Blinking in the semi-darkness, I identified the noise.

It was the sound of a key rattling in a lock, and it was coming from the kitchen. But who had a key to Rose Cottage's back door?

Oh. Right.

Swearing under my breath, I swung my legs over the side of the bed, then reached for my robe. The back door opened, sending a current of air through the house. Then it closed.

By the time I'd shut the bedroom door on the soundly sleeping Jeff and crept through the living room and into the kitchen, the basement stairs had started to creak.

Tightening the belt of my robe, I followed, pausing at the

top of the worn wooden staircase.

Voices came from below.

I descended the steps, then flicked on the overhead light.

Adeline jerked her head around. "Did I wake you?"

"Oh, no. I always do a perimeter check in the middle of the night."

A sleepy-eyed Boomer trotted down the stairs behind me, perhaps realizing he'd fallen down on the job. When he saw Adeline, he darted over for an ear rub.

"Good work on the burglar alert, mutt," I grumbled. Then, to my aunt, "How come you still have a key? We talked about this."

"There's no time for that now. Where's Jeff?"

"He's sleeping."

"We have to be quiet, then."

"Verity Hawkes?" A mechanical voice boomed through the basement. A row of dusty electronic monitors on the far wall sprang to life, each displaying an identical, grinning puppet head. "Nice to see you again," the heads chimed in unison.

"Shut up," I hissed. "You'll wake Jeff."

I narrowed my eyes, regretting my decision not to rip Control's irritating artificial-intelligence unit out of the basement. *Whatever made me think I could trust them?*

"You promised never to contact me again," I said accusingly.

"It wasn't an actual promise, was it, boys?" The heads swiveled back and forth as if they were looking at each other. "Wasn't it more of a suggestion?" They chattered amongst themselves, swirling in and out of focus.

Adeline stepped forward. "Stop fooling around."

The faces snapped to attention—as much as faces can. Red berets with stiff maple leaves materialized on their heads.

"Adeline," they snapped, the maple leaves flapping over their foreheads in a synchronized salute. "Welcome back."

"Count me out of this," I said. "You're all nuts."

Before I could reach the stairs, Adeline yanked me back by my arm. "Control needs our help." She assumed a mournful expression—which I almost fell for.

Almost. "Forget it." Shaking my arm free, I whirled to face the door.

"I'll do it without you if I have to."

That halted me in my tracks. I expelled an exasperated breath before turning to face her. "You said you were retired."

"I am, but our country needs us."

"There is no *us*. I told you that at the gym."

Adeline shrugged sadly.

The electronic faces expanded until they were only eyes, peering curiously at me. "Verity does not seem ready for this."

"She's ready," Adeline said.

"I'm not, though." I held up my hands in a gesture of defeat. "Look how Shelby got the jump on me. I never saw it coming. Isn't that proof I'm not fit for...whatever this is?"

"Analytical abilities are every bit as important as physical combat skills," Adeline said. "More so, even."

The faces nodded. "She has a point."

Ignoring Control, I said, "You're never going to let this go, are you?"

My aunt adopted a pained expression. "Not until you agree to help me."

The electronic eyes continued to peer at me.

What was it I'd said to Jeff? *Adeline's work always sounded interesting.* I puffed out another breath, thinking it over.

"Okay," I said reluctantly. "But the minute you're in any real danger, we abandon the mission. Promise me."

"Absolutely." She crossed her heart.

"Don't do that," I said.

The monitors clicked off one by one. I heaved a sigh. "When do we start?"

On the kitchen landing above us, Jeff cleared his throat.

I jerked my head around. He was standing on the landing, in pajama bottoms and bare feet, looking down at us.

"Did you hear all that?" I asked.

He nodded. "When were you going to tell me?"

"The minute I got back upstairs." At his raised eyebrows, I added, "Honestly."

Jeff turned on his heels. "I'm going back to bed." Halting, he added over his shoulder, "Does this mean the wedding's off?"

I bounded up the staircase to plant a quick kiss on his cheek. "Definitely not. You can't get out of it that easily." I reached up, wrapping my arms around his neck for a real kiss.

"I'll be on my way," my aunt said, brushing past us.

Jeff lifted his head long enough to nod—without taking his eyes from mine. "Lock up when you leave, Adeline." Then his arms tightened around me.

We didn't even notice the back door closing.

ALSO BY RICKIE BLAIR

When not hunched over her computer talking to people who exist only in her head, Rickie spends her time taming an unruly half-acre garden and an irrepressible Jack Chi. She also shares her southern Ontario home with two rescue cats and an overactive Netflix account.

Contact Rickie at rickieblair.com or on Facebook at www.facebook.com/AuthorRickieBlair/

Made in the USA
Monee, IL
28 April 2020

The Strike Wings: Special Anti-Shipping Squadrons 1942-45

ISBN 0 11 7722687 7

CORRECTIONS

Page 4, line 19	*for* Arnold *read* Armed
Pages 126 and 127	Captions for the photographs have been omitted in error. Please find below self-adhesive captions to be positioned as required.

May 1995

London: HMSO

(*Left*): Wing Commander David O.F. Lumsden. (*Right*): Flying Officer E.H. 'Tommy' Thomas.

A Beaufighter TFX of 404 Squadron at Davidstow Moor, painted with the black and white stripes of the Allied Expeditionary Force. The rocket rails are set at slightly different angles to give a spread of hits.

pp126

A Narvik class destroyer. This is *Z-37*, similar to *Z-32*.

6 June 1944. The attack on the German destroyers near Belle Ile, taken from the tail of a Beaufighter into the sun. (*Bottom*): 9 June 1944. *Z-32* aground off the Ile de Batz, under attack by Beaufighters with bombs and rockets.

pp127